AGENDA FOR SECESSION

"It is for us, the lawmakers, to propose. It is for you, the people of Texas, to decide, in accordance with law. At 9:25 P.M., those who favor Texas' remaining in a Union that submits to the Russian yoke—if any such there be—will step outside into the night and show a light. A match, a flashlight, even the glow of a cigarette will be tabulated instantly, such is the resolution of TexCom Satellite 23 LBJ. I say again, anyone who wishes to remain a citizen of the craven, misguided, gutless United States will step outside and, in his loneliness, show his feeble beam."

He paused several seconds, then resumed.

"At 9:35, those in favor of a proud, independent Republic of Texas, ready to fight anybody and everybody who would deny us the honor we will die to preserve, will step proudly out into the velvety blackness of the Texas night and light the lamp of freedom."

Also by Daniel da Cruz
Published by Ballantine Books:

THE GROTTO OF THE FORMIGANS

THE AYES OF TEXAS

TEXAS

DANIEL DA CRUZ

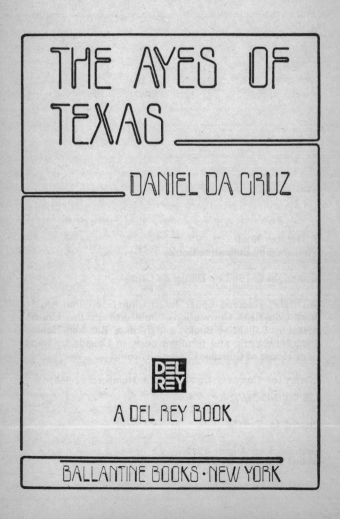

DEL REY

A DEL REY BOOK

BALLANTINE BOOKS · NEW YORK

A Del Rey Book
Published by Ballantine Books

Library of Congress Catalog Card Number: 81-66656

ISBN 0-345-29602-8

Printed in Canada

First Edition: August 1982
Second Printing: December 1982

Cover art by Ralph Brillhart

2 MAY 1998

"Name?"

"Gwillam Forte."

"Spell it."

Gwillam Forte spelled it.

"Age?"

"Fourteen."

"Race?"

"White."

"Address?"

"Liberty Towers."

The desk sergeant's pen paused in midair. He looked down sternly at the young man. "Get smart with me, boy, and I'll boot your ass all the way down to the drunk tank—*Address?*"

The arresting officer coughed discreetly. "That's where he lives, Sarge. I checked."

"The Liberty Towers is a whorehouse."

"Right. The kid here helps out at the bar in the Kit Kat across the street. He works from ten at night to five in the morning—same working hours as the Liberty. Charley Miller—he owns them both, you know—lets him sleep on the pool table downstairs."

"What about his family?"

The arresting officer shook his head.

"How long's he been at the Liberty?"

"How long, kid?" The officer hadn't bothered to ask earlier.

"Since November," Forte replied.

Six months. Desk Sergeant Pyle put down his pen. He

1

asked other questions, but those answers too were not reassuring, and he didn't write them down. The boy had been brought in for assault with a deadly weapon— a barroom stool—on a Kit Kat customer who propositioned him. The customer was in the emergency room with multiple contusions and scalp wounds. As a minor, Forte would appear before Judge Landrum of Juvenile Court. Landrum was a hanging judge. The sexual provocation was bad enough; he would like even less the Kit Kat's violation of the child labor laws, and that young Forte worked at night behind a bar and slept in a cathouse by day, and had been doing so for months in Sergeant Pyle's precinct without him knowing about it. Suddenly, his chances of making the next lieutenant's list began to look thin. There was one ray of hope, though: the kid was big for his age. And Pyle hadn't yet written down the particulars of the charge. Maybe he could work something out.

"Know what the penalty is for assault and battery, young fellow?"

Forte shook his head.

"Three to five years," Pyle said, looking sharply at the arresting officer, who was about to correct him. Considering the circumstances, even an adult would probably get off with a warning or a suspended sentence. Forte, however, wouldn't get even that. Under common law, he was a child, presumed incapable of committing a crime. In fact, Judge Landrum would probably pat the kid on the back for putting a pervert in the hospital. But it wouldn't do to tell the kid that.

Forte licked his lips, but said nothing.

"Yes, some judges would give you three," Pyle went on, his tone grave, "but others would give you five. Depends on the *mens rea*."

"Huh?"

"That's lawyers' talk for criminal intent."

Forte's eyes were tired and uncomprehending. He didn't understand a word the man was saying.

"Three to five years," Sergeant Pyle mused. "That's

a long stretch for a young man. The best years of your life." He paused for that to sink in. "But there may be another way to handle this. You're a big lad. You could easily pass for seventeen, even eighteen. With the war on, nobody gets nosy about age any more. And think how much better it would be for you to serve your country—come out with a wad of cash and a string of medals instead of a prison record. You'll see the world, make friends, find adventure, save your money to start off business when the war's over."

Gwillam Forte just looked at him.

"Well, what do you say?"

"Say?"

"About joining up. As a matter of fact, one of the Navy recruiters is a friend of mine. Chief Armstrong. If I put in a word for you, maybe—just maybe—he might be able to get you in."

"I don't know."

The boy was bewildered. He knew there was a war on, but it didn't mean anything to him. Soldiers and sailors came in the Kit Kat all the time—there were a lot of bases around Atlanta—and they drank and boasted and cussed a lot and had a lot of fights. He guessed it was all right. He had just never thought about it.

"I haven't got all night, young fellow," the sergeant said, picking up his pen. "Make up your mind—the Navy or five years in the state prison."

"All right," the boy said quickly, afraid the big man would change his mind.

Sergeant Pyle smiled. "You've made a wise decision, lad. Now, here's how we're going to handle this. You're already on the book. I can't do anything about that. But I'm going to write down the charge as vagrancy. Later this morning, when you appear before the judge, you tell him you just got into town last night, on your way to join the U.S. Navy. Got that?"

"Yes, sir."

"And if he asks your age, tell him eighteen. Now, how old are you?"

"Fourteen."

"Eighteen. You're eighteen years old. Now, how old are you?"

"Eighteen, sir."

"Good. He'll dismiss the charge—I'll see to it. Then I'll introduce you to Chief Armstrong. . . ."

Everything went as Sergeant Pyle predicted, and at midafternoon that same day, Gwillam Forte was sworn in as an apprentice seaman in the United States Navy. On 3 May 1943, he joined the draft headed for boot camp in Norfolk, Virginia.

2 MAY 1945

HE USED TO LIE IN HIS HOSPITAL BED AT NIGHT, SLEEP-less from pain, and try to remember what it was like to have two hands and two feet. Like everything else about his earlier years, though, the memories were elusive, probably because so few were fair.

The mean, blustering voice of his father—that was his first recollection. His whiskey-hoarse cursing seemed to crowd out all other early recollections. It was followed, as often as not, by a cuff on the side of the head when Gwillam became old enough to hold down a newspaper route and came up short when the old man wanted to "borrow" two dollars for his Saturday-night toot. Not that his mother, with the succession of "old school friends"—all male—who kept her company for half an hour or so those nights his father passed out on the living room sofa, was all that much better. Still, when it came to that, neither was Gwillam himself, he had to admit. He peddled pens and perfumes pilfered from neighborhood drugstores to finance the movies he sneaked off to see when he should have been at school, where he squeaked by from one grade to the next only because his teachers found him too quarrelsome to tolerate another year. His only talent was playing the trumpet, which he did inexpertly in the school band. But if he didn't play well, he played loud and fast. It was talent enough, he thought at the age of twelve when he left home in downstate Illinois to find work in a nightclub band. The closest he got was a succession of cheap barrooms, which he kept more or less clean, for more or less board and room.

Sometimes he thought about the women at the Liberty Towers. In books he read in later years, whores were always wronged maidens with hearts of gold, but that wasn't the way he remembered it for the six months he had lived at Liberty Towers, before that police sergeant conned him into joining the Navy. Of course, by then he had already learned a good deal about whores, his mother being a part-timer and all that. At Liberty Towers, he learned it wasn't generosity that prompted them to throw their money around, but stupidity and an indifference about the morrow. Nor was their line of work—"profession" was hardly the word for a business that required only a few hours of on-the-gob training to master—picturesque so much as degrading and mechanical, mere assembly-line production involving nuts and screws. That they had been driven into prostitution was only a self-delusive fable: they were mostly lazy, shiftless, dishonest sluts who would do anything to avoid decent work, and feared only the day when they would be so old and raddled that there would be no alternative to honest labor. Living in the company of such females hadn't given him a joyous view of civilian life, and it was almost with relief that he had walked through the main gate of Recruit Depot in Norfolk, Virginia, to begin what he thought was going to be a bright new life as a sailor.

Going to sea had been a change, at that, but life was no sweeter than it had been ashore. If he was big for fourteen, he was small for eighteen, and the target of every bully, bugger, and boatswain's mate aboard the battleship U.S.S. *Texas,* to which he had been drafted as a bugler after finishing Music School in late 1943. For Gwillam Forte, the enemy wasn't the Germans and Japanese, although during the next eighteen months he would see action against both, but his own shipmates.

They took advantage of his ignorance by sending him on such fool's errands as fetching five pounds of *beano* from the beano locker—an ancient wheeze inspired by such pronouncements over the public address system as "There will be no man-overboard drill today," and the like. They took advantage of his trusting nature by borrowing money they never intended to return, and cheating him out of the rest of his pay in rigged poker games. They took advantage of his presumed innocence by trying to bend him on in the spud locker, whereupon he stabbed one of the two sodomists in the groin with a potato knife and scared the other into retreat. They won anyway, with perjured testimony before a summary court that got him sixty days in the brig for unprovoked assault.

Not all of Forte's unpleasant experiences aboard the battleship were the result of his shipmates' malice or mischief. Most were due to the conflicts inevitable when one hundred officers and seventeen hundred young men are crammed into a ship making month-long patrols, with little to do but get on one another's nerves. Watch-standers were constantly on the lookout for enemy submarines, a morale-sapping and futile precaution, for the *Texas* possessed no antisubmarine weapons whatever. The ship was slow, ponderous, and uncomfortable. High seas buried its bow beneath the waves, flinging icy sheets of water as high and far astern as the pilothouse; in far northern waters it froze into a frigid mush on one's back and shoulders, and brought on a chill that the hottest coffee couldn't dispel. The ship's pitch was like riding a gigantic yo-yo in slow motion, and could turn a veteran sailor green.

Young Gwillam Forte, weary from constantly fighting the bucking and plunging ship, often seasick, and never more than barely tolerated by his older shipmates, lived a life of lonely misery. He found it hard to believe that anyone could be happy, as one or two of his shipmates actually seemed to be, aboard a man-of-war. He found it even more incredible that this floating concentration camp was once the gem of the ocean. Of course, that was long before his time . . .

In 1912, the year she was launched, the United States Ship *Texas* was indeed the pride of the U.S. Fleet, for it was then the most modern and powerful battleship in the world. Its 27,000-ton displacement was exceeded only by that of the Argentinian battleships *Moreno* and *Rivadavia*. The U.S.S. *Texas* could sail ten thousand miles without refueling—from San Francisco to China and back—make a flank speed of twenty-one knots—over twenty-four land miles an hour—and had a main battery of ten fourteen-inch guns in twin turrets, which could fire shells weighing three-quarters of a ton almost twelve miles. In addition, it had twenty-one five-inch guns as secondary battery and a thicket of smaller guns for close-in defense. The ship was sheathed in steel armor up to fourteen inches thick.

The "Big T" served with the Allied Grand Fleet in World War I, and lived through some historic moments. She landed U.S. Marines at Vera Cruz, Mexico, in 1914, in one of the last unrepentently imperialist actions of the United States in Central America. From a platform on her number two turret, on 9 March 1919, Lieutenant Commander F. O. McDonnell, piloting a

Sopwith Camel, made the first flight from a battleship of the U.S. Navy. A full generation later, the U.S.S. *Texas* served successively as flagship of the U.S. Fleet, flagship of the Atlantic Training Squadron, and with the Neutrality Patrol in North Atlantic waters before the United States formally declared war on Germany in December 1941.

By then, the *Texas* was a venerable twenty-nine years old, overdue for scrapping and replacement by a bigger, sleeker, faster, more heavily armed ship. She got a reprieve when Japan's stunning victory at Pearl Harbor made clear that veteran ships as well as veteran seamen to man them would be needed to do their duty—again—if the nation was to survive.

Her first service was in the North Atlantic on patrol and convoy duty. Then its big guns covered the Allied landings in North Africa. Off Mehdia, Algeria, on 7 November 1942, the *Texas* fired its fourteen-inch batteries for the first time in World War II, against Vichy French ammunition dumps and armored columns at Port Lyautey. When the beachhead was secured, she returned to Norfolk for overhaul. It was there that Gwillam Forte, with his government-issue bugle, reported aboard.

Shipboard routine aboard the *Texas* in Atlantic waters failed to fulfill Forte's conception of naval warfare. Instead of running gunfights against the Germans, there was running of messages from the captain to his junior officers. Instead of the acrid stench of gunpowder, there was the greasy stench of stack fumes. Forte's contribution to World War II, it seemed, would be to stand watch four hours on and eight hours off, and sound Reveille, Mess Gear, Pay Call, Man Overboard, Church Call, Tattoo, Taps, and the several dozen other calls that constitute the entire bugle repertoire. That was all right with him. It wasn't his war.

D-Day, 6 June 1944, found the battleship off Omaha Beach in Normandy, firing three-quarter-ton shells into German shore batteries four miles away, and against troop concentrations and enemy columns moving up to support the defenders. During the nineteen days that followed, the *Texas* fired 891 rounds of fourteen-inch ammunition. It gave much better than it got: off Cherbourg a German 280-mm shell wrecked the bridge, killing the helmsman and wounding thirteen others, the only casualties of the campaign aboard the *Texas*. During the thirty-two years since the battleship had been commissioned, the helmsman was the only man to have been killed in action aboard.

The following spring, while the U.S. Marines invaded and captured the Japanese island of Iwo Jima in the bloodiest and fiercest battle in Marine Corps history, the *Texas* stood offshore with the Amphibious Support Force and bombarded the well-dug-in garrison of 22,000 Imperial Marines with nearly one thousand shells from her big guns. After reprovisioning in Ulithi, in March 1945, the *Texas* steamed north again, to Okinawa, to take part in the largest amphibious assault of the Pacific war. There the *Texas* and other ships of the Fifth Fleet mangled pillboxes and entrenchments the Japanese had been constructing for thirty years, paving the way for beachhead operations by the Marines and Army. Simultaneously, her antiaircraft batteries fought off the Kamikazes that came screaming in out of the clouds, bearing a single suicide pilot astride a ton of high explosive fitted with stubby wings. For the U.S.S. *Texas,* the Battle of Okinawa lasted six weeks. For Gwillam Forte, it would last four. . . .

The second of May, two years to the day since he enlisted in the Navy, began like many another for Gwillam Forte. At three-fifteen in the predawn darkness, "Jimmy Legs," the Navy's master-at-arms, slapped his night stick against the underside of Forte's hammock to rouse him for the four-to-eight watch. Forte rubbed the sleep from his eyes and dropped lightly to the deck from the hammock, rigged seven feet above the division passageway. He unhitched the hammock from its hooks, folded the edges in over the thin mattress, and lashed it into a neat sausage with seven half hitches. He folded it over into a horseshoe and heaved it into the division hammock nest.

Forte groped his way down the darkened, pitching passageway to the division galley, where a big galvanized pot of coffee and a rack of thick white handleless cups awaited the watch. He poured a cup and squatted on his heels beside the others to drink his coffee in the dim light of the single red bulb that illuminated the compartment. Nobody spoke. The warmth radiating through the linoleum deck from the boiler room below induced a sense of weary detachment that made conversation a burden. Anyway, what was there to talk about, when each day was like yesterday, and even more like tomorrow?

After a second cup of coffee, Forte deposited his cup in the rack and shuffled down the passageway to the head, first downhill, then uphill, then downhill again in the never-ending rhythm of the pitching ship. There he shaved and bathed in half a bucket of water heated by immersion under live steam.

At three-fifty, dressed in the uniform of the day, Forte entered the pilothouse on the bridge. Sunrise was forty-five minutes away in this latitude, but the shadows of the watch-standers were already well defined in the light of false dawn. In his high-backed, padded swivel chair, bolted to the deck, the officer of the deck sat facing forward, his cap pulled down over his eyes. He appeared asleep, but Forte knew better. Amidships, the helmsman kept his eyes on the binnacle's illuminated compass card, continually applying minute adjustments to the small brass wheel, so that the ship's swinging bow was never more than two or three degrees off course.

"You're relieved," Forte said to the duty bugler.

The other man nodded and left the pilothouse. There would be just time enough for him to go below for coffee and a cigarette. General Quarters, sounded half an hour before dawn and dusk at sea, would bring him running again to his battle station on the bridge. It was during the twilight of sunrise and sunset that the ship was most vulnerable; in that gray interval, a submerged enemy could make out a ship's silhouette before its lookouts could detect the feathery wake of a periscope, and most ships sent to the bottom by torpedoes were lost during those two perilous periods of the day.

For the next quarter of an hour, Gwilliam Forte stood at the rear of the pilot house, lulled by the hypnotic pitch of the ship, as its bow rose and fell with stately majesty, like a dowager queen acknowledging the cheers of her subjects. Like all watch-standers at sea, Forte had mastered the art of sleeping standing up, with his eyes wide open, even when the sun was high in the sky. Such sleep is neither sound nor refreshing, but so long as nobody spoke to him or made any abrupt movement within his range of vision, he could remain in this state of suspended animation indefinitely. Aside from the steady swish of the windshield wipers and the faint whistle of the wind through the rigging, no sound disturbed his semiconsciousness until he heard the door to the captain's cabin behind him open and a mild voice say: "Good morning, gentlemen."

"Good morning, sir," the OOD replied for all.

"I'll take the conn, Mr. Matthews."

"Aye, aye, sir," the officer of the deck replied, vacating the high chair and saluting.

"Anything to report?" The captain, a gaunt figure in his beribboned blue jacket with the four gold stripes on his cuffs, climbed into the chair and adjusted his binoculars. He slowly scanned the foamy seas.

"Nothing since I brought in the submarine fix from CincPac at 0230, sir."

"Our position?"

"Twenty-six degrees twelve minutes north, 128 degrees thirty-eight minutes east, sir," the OOD replied, glancing at the log. "Our course is 122 degrees, speed eleven knots, zigzag pattern x-ray. All ships on station."

"Weather?"

"Low overcast, breaking up in the north. Wind from the north-northeast at twelve knots. Moderate seas. Forecast is for light rain before noon, sir."

"Very well . . . Sound General Quarters."

"Aye, aye, sir." The OOD nodded to the boatswain's mate, already at the squawk box. "Sound General Quarters!"

The boatswain's pipe shrilled twice, then he cried into the microphone: *"General Quarters! General Quarters! All hands man your battle stations!"* He stepped back, and Gwillam Forte, his left hand depressing the microphone lever, blasted out General Quarters on his bugle.

Before the last note died in the air, the decks reverberated with the pounding of feet as the ship's company dashed for their action stations, pulling on their clothes while scrambling up ladders and forward on the port side, down ladders and aft on the starboard side, to minimize confusion and collisions on the crowded and slippery decks of the still-blacked-out ship. Within three minutes all guns and lookout stations were manned and ready. The destroyers flanking the *Texas* in diamond formation would likewise now be at General Quarters, sonar operators on the alert for the sound of submarine propellers, weather-deck lookouts and others topside with their eyes probing the sullen skies for signs of enemy aircraft. Gwillam Forte, his duty done, eased back into the shadows and resumed his wakeful slumber.

It seemed to Gwillam Forte that only seconds later he heard the shout: *"Aircraft off the starboard bow!"*

The captain's head snapped around.

A kamikaze had emerged from the low clouds and was boring in on the ship. It was no more than half a mile away, and the ship's antiaircraft guns were already filling the sky with flak.

"Hard right rudder!" the captain cried instinctively. Meeting the suicide plane head-on would offer a marginally smaller target than if they turned to port, thus presenting the ship broadside. But it was instinct wasted: the kamikaze would be upon them before the ship could begin to answer the helm.

The helmsman was trying, anyway. He frantically spun the wheel all the way over and held it there with torso-twisting body English.

The kamikaze nosed down toward them in a shallow dive. Gwillam Forte watched the black cylinder as it was buffeted by the bursts of exploding shells, jostled off course but each time swerving back toward the battleship. The flames of tracer bullets tracked its passage through the sky, but incredibly, nothing touched it. The tiny winged torpedo kept coming, growing larger and blacker every moment, until Forte imagined he could see the eyes of the evil little Jap staring through the square windshield into his own, as if aiming the flying bomb straight at him, personally.

The *Texas* began to answer the helm. Its bow swung slowly toward starboard, an inch at a time. The kamikaze altered course and kept coming. It was now only a little higher than the main truck, and so close they could make out the red meatball and Japanese script on the nose of the aircraft. The antiaircraft was coming closer too, the gunfire from other warships crisscrossing through the *Texas*'s rigging. Forte felt sudden panic. If the Jap didn't hit them, stray gunfire would surely do so.

"Clear the bridge!" the captain shouted, his voice barely audible above the din of exploding short-fused shells. The kamikaze was now headed directly, unwaveringly toward them. It couldn't miss. Gwillam Forte dashed for the starboard ladder leading down and aft to the main deck. From the corner of his eye

he saw the captain gripping the arms of his chair, bracing himself for the impact. Forte leapt through the doorway, reaching for the ladder rails.

What happened next he could never quite recall. He could remember looking straight at the kamikaze plane and seeing a bright red flash. That would have been the five-inch shell from one of the destroyers, a piece of its shrapnel apparently striking the control surfaces and causing the pilot to lose control. The suicide plane disappeared from Forte's line of vision, as if it had been wiped from a slate. Though he didn't know it, the craft had winged over and slammed into the sea.

A blinding flash was followed by a huge detonation that rocked the ship, buckling splinter shield around the main-deck 20-mm gun mounts, and raining shrapnel off the ship's armor plate. Gwillam Forte was blown back against the side of the pilot house like a dry leaf in a winter's gale. He passed out.

When he came to, he was lying alone on the steel deck behind a ready box. His mind was still filled with the vision of that huge black bomb homing on him. He tried to rise, desperate to find cover. But in that brief moment of unconsciousness, the deck had become so slippery he couldn't gain his footing. In his disordered mind all he could think of was that an oil line had been severed, spilling its contents all over the deck. But then, he reminded himself, there wasn't any oil line way up there. Ball bearings, he thought muzzily as he again tried to get to his feet. That must be it— ball bearings from . . . from . . . somewhere.

He put out his hand to try once more. Then he understood: he had no hand, only a mangled stump that spurted blood with each beat of a weakening heart. He stared at it dumbly. There was no pain, only an overpowering languor. He wanted to cradle his head in his arms, stretch out in the warm sun on clean white sands, and sleep forever.

Just before he lapsed again into unconsciousness, he

heard from far away the captain's voice. He was yelling, *"Corpsman! Corpsman!"* He had never heard the old man sound so upset.

He was wondering why as the rising sun was swallowed up in a slowly descending curtain of blood, and he remembered no more.

1946-1951

IT WAS A STRANGE FELLOWSHIP, THAT WHICH DEveloped between Gwillam Forte and Otis Creech, for they were as unlike as any two patients in the veterans hospital. Forte was barely seventeen, a triple amputee, morose, uncommunicative, and white. Otis Creech was fifty-five, a giant of a man with seam-straining muscles, full of laughter, and black. Odd as the relationship seemed, their fellow patients would have been even more surprised to discover that its basis was mutual envy.

Creech was an old-timer. He had been in and out of veterans hospitals since World War I, when he had been wounded by shrapnel in the Battle of Belleau Wood and, lying helpless in the mud, nearly smothered in a wave of phosgene gas. Saved by counterattacking Marines and a shift in the wind, he lost a leg above the knee and the use of his right lung. A determined and proud man, he refused to become a charge of the U.S. government. Once fitted with a wooden leg, and having adjusted to a diminished vitality and range of activity, he limped out of the hospital to begin civilian life as an apprentice auto mechanic. In time, he became expert. But time also worked against him, for the strain of breathing on one lung ravaged his heart, and with increasing frequency he had to return for hospitalization. On the eve of World War II he found himself permanently confined in the veterans hospital in Houston, living on pills and potions, waking nights to the throb of a heart that beat with wild and disturbing rhythms, like a jungle drum.

In January 1946, Gwillam Forte was brought on a stretcher into the ward that had been Creech's home so long he felt the pride of ownership. There had been a lot of new faces during the previous two years, mostly young, but a sadder and more hopeless one than Gwillam Forte's Creech had never seen. It was empty of expression, except for the pain registered when the dressings on his stumps were changed. Forte reacted, when he reacted at all, as if he had been heavily sedated and seemed only faintly aware of what was going on around him. He didn't smile, let alone laugh, at the jokes on the Charlie McCarthy or Fred Allen or Jack Benny shows, which convulsed the other radio listeners in the ward. He had no visitors, read no newspapers or magazines, spoke to no one except in necessary reply to doctors' questions and the insistent queries of his wardmates. They would ask him how he felt today, and he said fine. They said it's beautiful weather this time of year, and he said that's fine. They said somebody had just assassinated the president of Bolivia and raped his wife yesterday, and he said fine, fine. His eyes were on the ceiling, but his thoughts were considerably further away. The silent young man seemed to be awaiting only a decent excuse to die.

Otis Creech tried to cheer Forte up. He read the comics to him, and repeated the gossip he picked up in his rounds of the wards. He stole ice cream and cookies from the kitchen and fed them to the lad, who ate as if it were a duty. He reminisced on how it was in the Great War, and goaded veterans of the recent conflict into argument within young Forte's earshot, in the unrequited expectation that he might somehow get involved. In vain. Forte's response was always the same—a nod to show he was listening, and a murmured "Thanks" for services bestowed. Nobody, not even the outgoing Creech, could penetrate that wall of spare civilities. Creech kept trying, with flagging resolution, because he felt it his Christian duty, but he recognized a death wish when he saw it. Privately, he gave the boy three months, six at the outside.

"Too bad about that boy," Creech remarked to a friend several beds down the line one day, when his reading of the news of the day had produced only a suppressed yawn from Gwillam Forte and, a little later, the regular breathing of one fast asleep.

"Yeah," the other agreed. "He don't have much to live for."

"You got it wrong. What I mean is, it's too bad he don't realize he's got *everything* to live for. He's one of the luckiest young men I ever met."

The other veteran laughed. "Ever tell him that?"

"Course not. Way he feels, he wouldn't be likely to agree, let alone understand why I think that way. And that's too bad, because that there's one lucky white boy . . ."

A few days later, when most of the others were still in the dining room, Otis Creech was holding down the steak on the plate with a fork while Gwillam Forte sawed at it with a knife held in his good left hand. Suddenly Forte swung the knife up against Creech's neck, the point at the angle of the jaw and Adam's apple, where the slightest pressure would sever the jugular vein. For the first time since he had been wheeled into the ward, Forte's eyes glowed with life— and an insane intensity.

"What do *you* know about luck, nigger?" he rasped.

Otis Creech swallowed. The knife point pricked the skin. A drop of blood appeared.

Gwillam Forte stared at it for a moment, then threw the knife across the ward. He slumped back against the pillows.

"Oh, so you *was* awake?" Creech said, getting the breath back in his one good lung.

"I was awake. I'm always awake."

"I thought you was." Creech smiled gently.

"You—you *what?*"

"I thought you was awake." He wiped away the drop of blood with his thumb. He inspected it. " 'Bout time you woke up, too."

"What do you mean by that?"

"What I said. You're one lucky boy, and it's time you stopped feeling sorry for yourself and *did* something."

"*Did* something?" Forte's expression was a mixture of incredulity and outrage. "Like *what?* Fight Joe Louis? Or play the piano, or walk a tightrope, maybe?" He sneered. "What do you think I can *do,* nigger?"

Otis Creech's smile faded. "Now, listen here, white boy, if you and I is going to talk, you better think of something better to call me than 'nigger.' I may be a nigger to you, but the only name I answer to is Creech." He looked hard into Forte's angry eyes. Forte just stared back at him. "As for what you can do—well, you may not be able to run a hundred-yard dash, or do card tricks, but you can do about anything else you put your mind to."

"What the hell do you know, nigger?"

"That's Creech."

"That's nigger."

"Well, have it your own way." Creech got up and started to walk away, limping heavily on his wooden leg.

"What do *you* know about me?" Forte's voice followed him.

Creech paused. He didn't hear the magic word. He turned back to the bed. "Don't know anything about you, boy, except that—"

"Don't call *me* 'boy,' nigger."

Creech smiled, showing a lot of tobacco-stained teeth. "Make me a deal."

Gwillam Forte glared stubbornly at the bedsheets. "Okay," he said finally. "What do you *think* you know about me?"

The black man remained silent.

". . . Creech?"

Creech smiled. "Why, not a damned thing, Forte, except that you got two legs and a hand off, and think the world's come to an end."

"That makes me lucky?"

"You're lucky, all right," Creech said with conviction.

"Then listen to this . . ."

Gwillam Forte told Creech the story of his life, what he could remember of it. He told it fluently and well, with a good choice of word and incident. It was something he had recited many times, although this was the first time anybody had heard it beside himself. It was a litany he had composed, and edited, and committed to memory, and told to himself, over and over. If nobody else was going to feel sorry for him, at least he could feel sorry for himself. It wasn't a very long story, considering that it covered his entire seventeen years, but it made up for its brevity by the depressing uniformity of its hardships, disappointments, frustrations, and pain.

"Call that lucky, Creech?" he said bitterly when he finished the morbid tale.

"About the saddest story I ever did hear," Creech admitted. "You sure has had it tough."

"Lucky, huh?"

Creech shook his head.

"Where's all that luck you was talking about, Creech?" he goaded the black man.

"Oh, it ain't gone no place. I never said you didn't have a sad life. All I said was, you're lucky. *Now.*"

"How do you figure that?"

"Well, now, let's look at a young man just starting out in life. He's got a few goals if he's any kind of man. One of them is to serve his country if his country needs him, and to serve it honorably. Well, Forte, you've done that, and you've lived to tell about it, which is more than a couple of million other men did these past few years. Okay. Then he's got to make friends, because you can maybe go through life without friends, but who wants to? You've got a whole ward full of friends right here, if you want them. Then there's the business of making yourself a living, finding security. I know a lot of postal clerks and farmers and truck drivers who work their butts off for forty years, and at the end, what have they got? Debts, is what. They retire on seventy bucks a month from some damned insurance company they've been supporting all their lives, and they die like they been living—like dogs. You—you got any debts? No, sirree. You don't owe nobody nothing. You got *security*. You don't ever have to move from this hospital bed if you don't want to. Three squares a day and a roof over your head and the best medical attention—all free. Those are things men work their lives out for, and most don't get. You've bought and paid for them."

"Sure, but they can walk to work, and play football, and—and they've got two arms and two legs, goddammit. I'd trade places with any one of them."

" 'Course you would. But you can't, don't you see? But that ain't the main thing, Forte. Look at those guys. Every day they spend looking over their shoulder for the bill collector. They live in fear. They aren't free men. *You're* free. You have a hundred-percent disability check coming in every month. You can tell anybody on Earth to screw himself, you don't need his lousy job. You can do anything you want, take no crap from nobody. But most of all, you're young. You've had a lousy life—sure. But life is like the weather—one day cloudy, one day fair. It all averages out. So far, you've had nothing but rain. But now, it's sunshine time, boy—sunshine time . . ."

If Otis Creech thought he had changed Gwillam Forte's outlook with his little lunchtime lecture, he was mistaken. But the ice that enveloped Gwillam Forte's view of the world, and especially of himself, had been cracked, and slowly the thaw set in. He still didn't talk much with his other hospital mates, but increasingly he listened to Creech, and imperceptibly the monologues became dialogues. He also watched Creech with the other men, admiring the man's bulging muscles as he walked among them and wishing they were his own, wondering if he would ever be able to talk so easily, and joke, and make men laugh as Creech did with such grace. And always Creech kept urging him to get out of bed into a wheelchair, and let the doctors fit him with prosthetic legs and learn to walk with them. Forte, afraid they would only make his disability more unbearable—in bed, at least, he was practically indistinguishable from other men in bed—always put him off, saying that when his stumps healed better, perhaps then . . .

During the Christmas season of 1946, Creech's wish that Forte would get out of bed and on his feet—or somebody's feet—came to pass, but Creech wasn't there to witness it. In November, he had died of a heart attack.

For some days, Gwillam Forte retreated into lethargy, his wakeful hours spent staring blindly at the ceiling. The doctors and nurses shook their heads, but resisted the impulse to pay the young man any special attention. They had helped him all they could; any improvement would have to come from him.

Their instincts proved correct. One day he decided that Otis Creech had been right, for wasn't the black man now dead, and Gwillam Forte still alive? He *had* been the lucky one, after all. He stopped picking at his food and started eating again. By the second week in December he was being fitted with prosthetic legs, a simpler matter than it might have been because his stumps were below the knees. On Christmas morning he took his first steps in nearly two years. Just two steps they were, but enough to prove to himself that he *could* walk. That realization was his Christmas gift. It was a Christmas gift to his doctors too: it was the first time they had ever seen him smile.

By the summer of 1947, Gwillam Forte was a different person. No longer frightened, resentful, self-pitying, the child was on his way to manhood. He could get around on his prosthetic legs with reasonable speed and agility, and had mastered the two-pronged hook that served as a right hand to the degree that he could scrawl his signature, use a fork, pull a handkerchief from his pocket and blow his nose—carefully if he didn't want it pinched—and tie his shoelaces. By then, he realized that his disability was only partly physical; perhaps worse was the atrophy of his mental faculties. Since he had run away from home some six years before, he had not attended a single day of school, read a book or newspaper, or taken any interest in what was going on in the world at large. Hitler and Churchill and Roosevelt were names he recognized, and he could locate Germany, England, the United States, and Mexico on a world map, but that was about the extent of his understanding of foreign affairs. His knowledge of other subjects was equally profound. He knew that he was dumb, but considered this a natural consequence of having little schooling, a lush for a father, and a bum for a mother. Mrs. Warren changed his mind about that, just as Otis Creech had changed his mind about being a bedridden invalid.

Virginia Warren was the hospital librarian, a kindly gray-haired woman of sixty whose only son had been killed in Normandy. All the patients were her sons after that tragedy, and none was dearer than Gwillam Forte. To her, he was a lump of clay that wanted shaping, and she began by trying to wean him from the ward poker game that started just after breakfast and continued nonstop until lights out at 10:00 P.M. The Hundred Great Books were her bait. Forte listened politely as she extolled their excellences, dropped *A Tale of Two Cities* she had left for him the moment she disappeared down the hallway, and clumped over to the poker table, where a pair of jacks exerted a more magnetic appeal.

Reflecting on the busted flush of her frustrated enthusiasm, Mrs. Warren decided to lower her sights. Her next offering was *The Three Musketeers,* who also misfired: Forte preferred three of any other kind. By stages, she retreated to *Superman* and *Batman.* They proved to be right on target. Gwillam Forte began to spend more time leaping off rooftops and into outer space, less trying to fill inside straights. Experimentally, Mrs. Warren inserted an illustrated children's version of *King Arthur and His Knights of the Round Table* into the stack of comic books that he was now devouring at a single sitting. He read that, too. Reading, he found to his surprise, had become a habit.

Just in time, for comic books had begun to pall. For them, Mrs. Warren substituted the adventure stories of P. C. Wren, Raphael Sabatini, and Dumas. By the summer of 1948, he had soaked up all the blood and thunder the library contained, and was reading Conrad, Twain, Dickens, and Hugo, at the steady rate of a book a day. His interest in poker waned. Compared with the variety and vitality of the tales he was reading, poker was a bore.

When Mrs. Warren decided the time had come to expand Gwillam Forte's horizons by introducing him to nonfiction, his resistance had disappeared. First she got his feet wet with the great voyages of discovery, then biographies of men who had shaped the world, and finally he found himself immersed in history, where he slowly became aware of the vast panorama that had been hidden in the mists of his ignorance. Whole days and nights were lost to reading. In one such stretch, he went without pause through the entire 817 pages of *The Forty Days of Musa Dagh,* and never afterward wondered why Armenians hate Turks. He marveled at the ease with which he absorbed ideas that he would have loathed had he been subjected to them through

lectures by bored and incompetent teachers. For the
first time in his life, he realized how lucky he was to
have been denied schooling, and only thus acquired an
education.

That education was not achieved by books alone.
The more practical aspects of Gwillam Forte's intellec-
tual development came from the intensive care lavished
on him by patients as well as staff at the veterans
hospital in Houston, beginning with instruction in
poker. For it was at the poker table that Gwillam Forte
learned how men conspire to deceive their fellows, their
strategems of word and expression, the psychological
warfare of bluff and threat and seeming submission, the
construction and baiting of traps—and how to avoid
them—and the myriad other human elements that make
the game of poker a microcosm of the larger game of
life. Gwillam Forte learned it well enough to be able
to make a living at it—honestly, if necessary—on the
outside. His hospital mates had other contributions to
make to his education, too, and once they observed his
appetite for learning, imparted them freely.

John Overholzer, the Army veteran who occupied the
next bed, was a thick-fingered old man who looked
more like a retired bouncer than the certified public
accountant he once had been. In the eleven months
they were neighbors before Overholzer went to the
Final Audit, the old man introduced him to the mys-
teries of creative bookkeeping, and some of the thousand ways to throw sand in the eyes of bank examiners,
IRS snoopers, and other enemies of free enterprise.

C. C. Stong, a chronic drunk with a genius for steal-
ing sickbay alcohol, passed on what he remembered of
his days as a veterinary surgeon in the mornings, before passing out in the afternoons; from him, Forte
learned mainly that he didn't want to become a vet.

"Goatlips" McClanahan, a wily stocks-and-bonds
mechanic who knew all about Wall Street but nothing
about women, having throughout his long life trans-

ferred his profits from the one almost without pause to the other, taught Forte the intricate steps of the financial fandango.

Real-estate operator "Buzz" Battersby instructed Forte in the science of geoalchemy, by which elaborately engraved and wildly mendacious prospectuses, distributed to credulous maiden schoolteachers and Iowa corn farmers, can transmute forty acres of alligator-infested Florida farmland into fifty pounds of pure gold.

Al Barkeley, one-time road commissioner and senatorial campaign manager, lectured Forte in political science by the case method, reminiscing about unmarked envelopes stuffed with twenty-dollar bills, voting the city graveyard, rigging polls, awarding street-paving contracts to the generous faithful, applying muscle to unfriendly editors, making study trips to the French Riviera at taxpayer expense, and other democratic practices not envisioned by the Founding Fathers.

The hardest lesson of all, however, was learning to walk. At first, he could only propel himself clumsily in a cage on wheels, his artificial limbs moving jerkily, as if they had a will of their own. Gradually he got the hang of it, and was able to move with slow but measured steps, aided by crutches. Some months later he abandoned the crutches, at the cost of skinned elbows and bruised ribs when he lost his balance. In a year he could walk with ease and confidence, climb stairs slowly, and bend at the waist to pick up a book from a low shelf without falling on his face. But it took four years before his infirmities and the prosthetics to overcome them became such second nature that he no longer had to think about them. He could then devote his thoughts and energies to making a living, free of the comfortable insulation against real life that the veterans hospital provided.

At five o'clock one humid Texas morning in early 1951, Forte eased out of bed, dressed, and walked out of the ward that had been his home for more than five years. In one hand he carried the canvas bag with the few possessions he had accumulated during his long hospital stay. Outside, just as Otis Creech had prophesied, after the long dark night of infirmity, the sky was filled with sunshine.

APRIL 1994

"WILL," GOVERNOR THOMAS ("CHEROKEE TOM") Traynor said, settling back in his chair and sipping his twenty-seven-year-old bourbon appreciatively, "I've come to ask you a favor."

"Sorry," Gwillam Forte replied, shaking his head. "No can do."

Traynor's glass paused in midair. It wasn't the response he had expected. He and Forte had been friends and political allies for nearly twenty years. Forte's Sunshine Industries, Inc., had helped bankroll Traynor's successful campaigns for the U.S. House of Representatives for three terms and the governorship of Texas for the past two and, he hoped, for the senatorial race five years hence, in the year 2000. The old man on the far side of the polished ebony desk had always been his mentor, protector, and goad to higher office, for they shared common principles and outlook. He couldn't understand why Forte would turn him down now, before he had even heard him out.

"I'll tell you why," Forte said, reading the question on the younger man's face. "You and I know each other pretty well. We've never had any important disagreements, and we've never double-crossed each other.

We're friends. So you don't need to come in here asking for favors, Tom. Just tell me what you want, and it's yours, because I know you wouldn't ask for anything I wouldn't want to give."

Cherokee Tom relaxed. That was more like it. Still, what he had in mind was no simple favor. It involved the expenditure of a lot of money—millions of dollars. Not that old Will didn't have them to spare . . .

Gwillam Forte had, as Traynor knew, walked out of the veterans hospital in Houston almost half a century earlier, with little more than hope and two wooden legs to sustain him. In his bank account was a meager $4,200, accumulated from disability payments and poker winnings over the previous five years. In his mind's eye, however, was the vision of a rapidly expanding Houston propelling him to riches.

For five years he had watched the city growing up outside his hospital window. He had read in the daily press of the postwar baby boom, of the growth of the suburbs, the expansion of American industry beyond the confines of the old cities. Already the government was being pressured by the highway lobby to build a huge network of roads to foster interstate commerce and the future defense of the nation. The auto industry was surging to provide the vehicles to fill those highways, and all the while the railroads were stagnating, their traffic being drawn away by automotive and air transport. The one thing all three methods of transportation had in common was a dependence on oil— even the railroads had switched by then from coal to diesel power—and the oil came, largely, from Texas.

At first, Gwillam Forte had decided that oil was the business for him to get into, and he read voraciously on all aspects of the industry—exploration, production, refining, transportation, marketing, and governmental regulation. But he soon came to the conclusion that the small capital he could scrape up and the knowledge he could bring to a highly technical business would be insufficient to make much of a mark for a long, long

time. On the other hand, oil was bringing people and
prosperity to Houston, and every indicator—especially
its strategic location at the confluence of supply and
distribution—pointed to its emergence as the oil capital
of the United States, perhaps of the world. It would
grow from the sleepy, backwoods town it was in the
late 1940s into a city, and Gwillam Forte intended to
grow right along with it.

The essence of his strategy was to forecast real-estate
movements, get in fast before the smart money concentrated on a particular locality, and sell out before
prices peaked. With his winnings, he would seek out
undeveloped areas in the direction the city was moving,
wait until the trend was established, and sell out again,
striving always for modest profits and rapid turnover.

As he anticipated, his profits were small. But thanks
to the unceasing flood of oil money into Houston, and
the magnetic attraction of the industry for petroleum
workers and service industries, his turnover was very
fast, and his marginal profits multiplied. His negotiations were facilitated by a skill he had acquired during
the war. Aboard ship Forte, attracted by its excellent
coffee, had been accustomed to spending off-duty hours
in the radio shack. There he had picked up international
Morse code, easy enough for one with his musical ear.
After he became a businessman, he found his knowledge
of code a priceless business tool. With a speed key
installed on a ledge in the kneehole of his desk, he
could exchange confidences with a competitor come
calling, then act on it through instructions relayed to
his staff by key, long before the rival could slip away
to a telephone and commit the same duplicity against
him. In this wise he had made many a real-estate coup
whose timing competitors found uncannily precise.
Within ten years, Forte was worth several million dollars, and Houston had not yet begun its period of most
rapid growth, which would follow the Arab oil embargo of 1973, nearly a decade later. When it came,

Forte was ready to parlay his tens of millions into hundreds.

His system was simple. He concentrated on lands near the periphery toward which the city, amoebalike, was constantly advancing. He never bought expensive land, on the theory that property bought at a dollar a square foot would double in price before land bought at a hundred dollars, while at the same time the mere magnitude of the holding would diffuse the risk. When he sold such properties, the profits were only partially reinvested in lands where the next upwelling of investment would occur. The bulk of his earnings he devoted to longer-term, less obvious schemes.

Houston's future prosperity would be based, he was confident, on a one-crop economy—not the traditional cattle business, which even then was relying less on open range than on scientific feeding in small farms, but oil refining and the manufacture of petroleum by-products. The city's accessibility to the oilfields as well as to the Gulf of Mexico and world markets beyond made it the ideal middleman. The cost of transportation of petroleum products to those markets would in large measure determine their profitability. Since water transport was, and always would be, the cheapest, it stood to reason that the best possible land investment in the Houston area was on the Houston Ship Channel, that waterway constructed between the city and the Gulf of Mexico, nearly fifty miles away, which gave promise of making the inland city an important American port. He acquired large tracts of such lands, concentrating on parcels that included the right of way of highways, pipelines, and railroads, when they were still cattle range. Once in his possession, he seldom sold them outright. Instead, he exchanged such lands for equity in the manufacturing and processing companies to be located there. Their advantageous location, he was certain, would give them the competitive edge that would ensure their—and Gwillam Forte's—prosperity.

And so it transpired. By 1985, when he was still a

robust man in his middle fifties, Gwillam Forte was one
of the richest men in America. He wasn't particularly
conspicuous, for while he enjoyed good living, beautiful women, and the exercise of personal power, he
was not identified as the leader in any particular field
of commerce or finance. He had interests in a dozen
oil companies, but controlled none. He owned a chain
of newspapers, including the giant *Houston Herald,*
but the chain ranked only number four nationally. He
had stock in more than forty companies in Houston
alone, but except for Sunshine Industries, Inc., it was
usually as a minority shareholder. Thus he diluted his
risks, avoided managerial headaches, and escaped the
scrutiny of government beagles sniffing about for easy
game. To selected charities, he gave bountifully if not
ostentatiously, insisting on being listed anonymously to
avoid being tapped by professional fund-raisers who
would pocket the larger part of any donation.

For all his power and influence, not one newspaper
reader in twenty had ever read the name Gwillam
Forte, and not one American in a thousand could correctly identify him. Yet those who did know him—the
beef barons and petroleum potentates of Texas, the
power brokers in Washington, and the oil kings of
Arabia—were well aware that Forte was richer and
more powerful than all but a handful of them.

Governor Traynor wasn't one of them, but if his
personal fortune wasn't great, his ambitions were. A
big, heavy-boned, ruddy-cheeked, hearty-mannered
politician of the old school, of the type that had been
common before the trade was taken over by the cardboard creations of advertising agencies, Traynor had
enjoyed a career of successive victories at the polls and
competent leadership in office, the last of which he
hoped would be the American presidency. He was as
honest as his favor-seeking constituents would allow,
rugged enough to stand the campaign rigors of cold
coffee and Styrofoam chicken, and remembered that he
was neither God nor His vicar, but a man who would

be seeking reelection one day, and therefore as thought-
ful about the future as he was diligent about the present.

"Last year, Will," he said, "you urged me to run
for the Senate this fall."

"And you declined. I still think that was a mistake."

"Maybe. It was a matter of loyalty, not votes. After
all, Senator Gunnison helped me get a start in politics. I just couldn't bring myself to run against him."

"Politics is a rough game, Tom. You may have
missed the boat. Gunnison will retire after this next
term, and his party has picked Gallego to succeed him.
That will be one tough Chicano to beat. Remember,
Tom, of Texas's eighteen million citizens, more than
six million are of Mexican origin, and hundreds more
stream across the border every cloudy night, thanks to
the national policy of courting oil-rich Mexico by ab-
sorbing its surplus labor.

The Governor nodded. "That's just the point. It will
take some doing to keep the votes of the native Texans,
yet drain enough Mexican votes from Gallego to make
the Senate, Will. My statisticians and pollsters gave me
a forecast last Friday: I'll need to capture nearly 25
percent of the Mexican vote, plus a full 80 percent of
the native Texas vote, or I can kiss the Senate good-
bye."

"My papers will back you."

Governor Traynor shook his head. "Won't be enough,
I'm afraid. I'll need something dramatic."

"Name it."

"Millenary celebrations."

"Hats?"

"No. Hats is spelled with an *e*. This is the thousand
millenary, spelled with an *a*."

"Spelling aside, I don't follow you."

"Will, my record as governor, however excellent it
might be, would not normally influence the Mexican
vote to any appreciable degree. Gallego would merely
say, Well then, why weren't the Mexicans earning
more?—carefully omitting to remind them that their

pay was three times what their kin made back in Maña-
naland. But I've got one hope. The Mexicans love
color, they love movement—provided they don't have
to generate too much of it themselves—and they love
pageantry. Anyone who feeds it to them in large doses
will be remembered on election day.

"Bread and games?" Forte inquired.

"Right up to their cottonpickin' eyeballs." Cherokee
Tom chuckled. "I'll give 'em speeches—long flowery
speeches full of big words in Spanish, speeches recalling
the illustrious and bloody history of the *conquistadores*.
I'll give 'em barbecues, where they can step up to the
table and gorge themselves on chili and tortillas and
enchiladas and prime ribs of beef until it runs out of
their hairy ears. I'll give 'em parades, and fireworks
displays, essay contests, beauty contests—I'll arrange
for some dark-eyed señorita to win, and crown her myself—and track meets, commemorative medals, lotteries
with two-week expenses-paid trips to Old Mexico. The
works. I'll keep those wetbacks so stirred up they won't
be able to take an afternoon siesta for a year. And on
election day they'll remember who did it all for them—
me."

"Sure, Tom, but so will the native Texans. All that
may remind the pale faces of just how few of us there
are left, comparatively speaking. We don't want to be
reminded. And we won't like the guy who reminded us.
There just might be enough of us to cut into that 80
percent of our vote you need to go over the top."

Governor Traynor smiled, showing the snaggletooth
that was a major asset, in that it kept him from being
movie-star handsome. "Got to keep you all happy
too—right?"

"No other way."

"That's what I'm depending on you to help me do,
Will," the governor said.

"Say how."

"I want to appeal to Texan pride, to the great Texan
heritage. I want to evoke the greatness of our state."

"I can't write a history book if that's what you came for. But I can write a check to a guy who *can* write it."

"You can do better. You can revive a *symbol* of the greatness of Texas, in such a way that it's mere appearance will electrify the electorate—I leave the details to you," he added grandly. "You will make them remember who is preserving that heritage for them—yours truly."

"What symbol is that, O Preserver of Heritages?"

Governor Traynor paused dramatically. "The United States Ship *Texas*—your old battlewagon."

"Tom—you're crazy."

True, the *Texas* was a relic of some celebrity and antiquity. It had been given to the State of Texas after World War II instead of being scrapped, so that sentimentalists could tow it into a berth on the Houston Ship Channel and there, with much puffery and snapping of flags in the wind, christen the old ship flagship of the Texas Navy. But that had been long ago, and the ship had never since been moved an inch from its moorings. Its bottom was fouled with algae and barnacles, and it was in such deplorable condition otherwise that hardly any tourists bothered to visit it these days. As a symbol of the great state of Texas, the citizenry would find it more pathetic than inspiring.

"I couldn't agree more," said Traynor, when Forte confided his reservations. "But it doesn't have to be that way. You can do something about it."

"What, precisely?"

Traynor waved his hand airily. "How the hell should *I* know? I'm just a politician. I deal only in large concepts and the higher morality."

"Uh-huh."

"You, on the other hand, have that subterranean cave you call SD-1 full of overpaid and underemployed researchers and scientists. Not to mention your bank vaults bulging with ill-gotten gains. Put them together, and I'm sure you'll come up with something." He smiled an election-day smile.

"You really think this will work?" Forte asked doubtfully.

"Something dramatic—really dramatic—built around the *Texas?* I'm as sure of it as I am that welfare rolls never shrink."

Forte stood up.

"I'll work on it."

Governor Traynor finished his drink and stood up too. He opened his old brown leather briefcase and took out a scroll, suitable for framing. He laid it on his friend's desk.

"What's that?"

"I knew you'd insist on helping me, Will, so I made it official. This is your commission in the Texas Navy. As of today, you're commanding officer of the battleship *Texas.* Congratulations, Captain."

14 MAY 1994: 10:00 A.M.

STRIDING PURPOSEFULLY DOWN THE PASSAGEWAY TOward the Prosthetics Research Unit of the veterans hospital on Old Spanish Trail in Houston, Gwillam Forte seemed extraordinarily fit for a man of 65. His step was springy, and his clear blue eyes and full head of tawny hair, only now beginning to silver around the edges, were those of a younger man. A plaid bow tie encircled a thick neck that sloped down to the shoulders of a weight-lifter and arms that terminated in hands equally adept at wielding a squash racquet and tying trout flies. His silver brows were too bushy, his slightly crooked nose too long, his smiling mouth too wide, his face too lined, for him to be termed handsome, yet enough lovely women had found him—and, he suspected, his fortune—irresistible for him to have wed, and almost as quickly shed, five of them, and to have loved and lost as many more. He felt as good as he looked, and wondered whether he wasn't wasting his time coming to the PRU for his semiannual overhaul. After all, how could they improve on nature?

Over the years, they had come very close to doing so, he had to concede.

When he made his first big real-estate killing, he had set aside enough money to endow an autonomous prosthetics research unit attached to the VA hospital. The beginnings were modest: a prosthetics technician and a physiotherapist, whose mission was simply to improve the clumsy wood-steel-and-leather contraptions that were then the only substitutes for legs and arms lost by veterans. As his fortunes improved, so did the size and quality of the staff he endowed. By 1975 it peaked with thirty-five specialists, including mechanical and electrical engineers, artists, orthopedic surgeons, neurologists, mathematicians, computer programmers, psychologists, and other experts in a field they themselves created almost from scratch. In distinction to former prosthetic devices, which were basically lifeless appendages, the hands and feet the PRU designed worked by impulses from the central nervous system and feedback from minuscule sensors that replaced the missing tactile nerves.

Early results were as disappointing as the concept was audacious. It took seven years for the first artificial hand merely to clench its fingers on command from the brain and feed back a signal to the brain that resistance was encountered as the fingers met. The problems were legion: materials to duplicate the flexibility of muscle, skin, and connective tissue (a synthetic collagen analogue alone cost University of Texas researchers six years and Forte thirteen million dollars to formulate); a miniaturized power source to animate the "muscles" made of carbon filament, nylon, and other materials—

eventually solved with microminiaturized nuclear-energy packets; a control system that began with crude transistors and evolved into enough microcircuitry to navigate a man to the moon; and the exceedingly difficult task of interfacing the natural nerve endings to a stainless-steel coupling. That alone required more than a dozen painstaking operations for each limb so equipped.

By 1991, it seemed to Gwillam Forte that they could go no further. Each new-year model was only a marginal refinement of its predecessor in terms of strength, durability, appearance, and dexterity. He was impressed when, fitted for a new right foot and calf in 1992, he had discovered that the tactility was so precise that he could thread a needle with his toes, but what was the use of that when he didn't even have to sew a button on a shirt? Already he could dart back and forth on the squash court with a nimbleness that many a younger opponent envied, detect a three-hour chin stubble with his fingertips, play half-forgotten jazz tunes on his trumpet. What more could his scientist have up his sleeve?

Dr. Robert Reeves's hearty greeting as Forte entered the room told him that whatever it was, it must be something special.

"How nice to see you, Mr. Forte," Dr. Reeves said, steering him by the elbow directly into the main laboratory where the white-jacketed staff was congregated around a concert grand piano. "How do you feel these days?"

"I'm—"

"You *look* fine. Never looked better. Have a seat," he said, indicating the quilted leather stool in front of the piano.

Gwillam Forte sat, wondering whether the researchers were under the impression that because he could finger the three valves of the trumpet, he should also be able to manipulate eighty-eight keys.

Dr. Reeves rolled up a small table covered with a

white sheet. On it was a black box. He opened it. Inside was a prosthetic right hand and forearm that exactly matched Forte's own, down to hair and freckles.

Forte shucked his jacket, rolled up his sleeve, and pushed firmly with his left forefinger on the latch that disconnected the prosthesis he was wearing. It dropped to the table lifelessly.

With ether, Dr. Reeves wiped the stainless steel annulus that ringed the stump, inserted the new prosthesis in its grooves, and locked it in place.

"Voila," Reeves said. "I christen thee Gwillam Van Cliburn. Play, maestro!"

Gwillam Forte felt like a fool. Surrounded by thirty-odd scientists, who struck him as 'thirty odd scientists' at that moment, as they seemed intent on embarrassing him, he swung around on the stool to play the one tune he could pick out on the piano—*Star Dust.*

But something funny happened on the way to the keyboard. The moment his right hand approached the keys, it seemed to be endowed with a life of its own. All by itself it began to play. The first chord, to be sure, was from *Star Dust,* but the next was a change of key that transposed Hoagy Carmichael to Johann Sebastian Bach. He watched, fascinated, as his right hand raced up and down the keyboard in a flawless performance of music he recognized as a Bach sonata. His real left hand lay limp in his lap, as useless and uninvolved as Forte himself felt, in contrast to his private enterprising right hand.

A chorus of applause greeted the last notes of the first movement of the sonata, which ended just as abruptly as it began. Personal control returned to the hand. Gwillam Forte, his initial annoyance submerged by the wonder of it all and the obvious pride of the men and women who surrounded him, grinned and stood up to take a little bow.

"Pretty slick, Bob. I must say, I never knew I had it in me."

"You didn't." Dr. Reeves parted the crowd around

the piano and lifted its lid. Inside, in a plastic box between the strings and the sounding board, was a cassette player. He removed it and held it up for inspection.

"Still pretty crude, Mr. Forte," he explained, "but what we have here is a device that transmits instructions to the nerve cells implanted in the artificial hand to trigger certain muscle movements in programmed sequence. The whole thing's in the conceptual stage so far, but we've got a perfected model two or three years down the road."

"What'll it do—put all the concert artists out of work?"

"No, it won't do that. The rapport between the audience and the performer will never be possible to duplicate by electronic circuitry, but it will provide a source of pleasure for thousands of amputees who would like to make music, yet are too young, old, or infirm to endure the grind that distinguishes a top musician. Don't look at it as electronic gimmickry or musical reproduction—we've developed this strictly as spiritual therapy."

"Seems promising, judging by what you've done so far."

"We've only just begun, Mr. Forte. On our drawing boards is a hand that will be able to play up to two hundred concert selections, from sonatas to concertos. All the memories will be contained in the hand itself, and to initiate the recall the performer has only to play the first four notes or chords; the mechanism takes over from there."

Gwillam Forte thought about his real, but useless, left hand lying quiescently in his lap while his artificial one handled Bach. It didn't take much imagination, nor would it take much additional engineering, to coordinate the efforts of two artificial hands to play two-part music. For those unfortunates with two prosthetic hands, it was a long step forward.

"But where does that leave guys like me, with only one artificial hand?" he asked. "How do we play music written for *two* hands?"

It was Reeves's turn to be embarrassed.

"Yes, we've been working on that. So far we've pretty well mapped out the neural pathways from each hand to the corresponding lobe of the brain that processes the electrical impulses controlling the respective muscles. But until we understand better how the two lobes of the brain communicate with each other, sort out their individual responsibilities and capabilities in solving the various aspects of the problem the consciousness perceives as originating from a single modality, we can only surmise—"

"And so forth and so on," Gwillam Forte interrupted dryly. "After I dig my way out of that avalanche of double-talk, I suspect I'll discover that the English translation is 'more money.' Correct me if I'm mistaken, Doctor."

Dr. Reeves coughed apologetically.

"How much?" Forte persisted.

"Well, a team of five neurologists and neurosurgeons, along with the requisite laboratory equipment, and of course the—"

"In dollars."

"Not less than four million over the next five years," Reeves said quickly.

"Will it be worth the expense?"

Dr. Reeves shook his head. "Probaby not."

Gwillam Forte, slipping back into his old familiar right hand, looked up sharply.

Reeves was smiling impishly. "Unless you happen to love Bach."

Forte didn't return the smile. "I don't like Bach."

Reeves's smile vanished.

"But I do like money. There's a commercial future for this hand of yours, Bob, so I'm going to finance the research."

Dr. Reeves licked his lips. He wasn't any more dishonest than most doctors, but he couldn't afford to give Forte any false impressions.

"I'm afraid there isn't much of a—"

"Just think how we could clean up by programming this thing to strangle mothers-in-law."

14 MAY 1994: 8:30 P.M.

DR. WILKIE PHILLIPS CAUGHT UP WITH GWILLAM Forte just as he was leaving the hospital. "Do you have time for a word, Mr. Forte?"

Forte looked at his watch. At four-fifteen he was scheduled to chair a meeting of Stenco, a Sunshine Industries subsidiary that was slowly expiring despite intensive care. He didn't want to miss it, but he would if he paused for a word with Dr. Phillips: the good doctor's words had a way of eating up an afternoon.

"Can it wait until next week?" said Forte.

"Sure, it can wait. Another week *probably* won't kill them.

"Kill who?"

"The twenty-three men on the danger list."

"What's wrong with them?"

"That's what I wanted a word with you about."

Forte surrendered. He always did, for he felt an overwhelming responsibility for the patients at the Houston veterans hospital. In his time of need they had kept him alive and, eventually, hopeful for better days; he could do no less for them. In fact, he did considerably more. To these men, whom he considered family, he gave everything. One of his first large real-

estate acquisitions in Houston was El Caballejo, a
horse-breeding ranch then on the outskirts of the city,
now hemmed in by refineries and factories. There he
held open house for his hospital shipmates—even those
he had never known, even those who had fought in
wars he had been spared. El Caballejo was a spacious,
comfortable spread. The disabled veterans could drop
in unannounced and stay for a day, a week, even a
month, if they liked. There were plenty of inducements
to do so: they had the use of his pleasure craft on the
channel for boating and fishing, the swimming pool,
the bowling alley, the pistol and skeet ranges, library,
sauna, solarium, and stables. Most guests ended the
day at the bar, where drinks were on the house, and
the dark-eyed barmaids weren't quite so hard to get
as they looked. On festive occasions, nearly the entire
ambulatory population of the hospital could be found
at El Caballejo, soaking up the sun, steam, and scotch
and lying to one another about ancient battles they
had fought.

Those whose condition confined them to bed weren't
forgotten. Acting alternately as ombudsman and angel,
Forte made periodic trips to record their grievances and
fight them out with the VA bureaucracy, and apply the
soothing balm of ready cash when the veterans' problems were financial. By the time Dr. Phillips had inter-
cepted him, in fact, he had just put in half a day on
rounds of the bedridden, dispensing the kind of first-aid
the medical profession can't give.

"What's this about the twenty-three men who are—
how did you put it—*dying?*" Gwillam Forte asked
when they reached Dr. Phillips's tiny book-stuffed
cubicle.

Phillips cleared a space on his desk and filled it with
Manila files from a green filing cabinet. They made a
stack nearly a foot high. Dr. Phillips placed his hands
on them, and regarded Gwillam Forte gravely across
the desk. For a moment he said nothing, for though

no obstetrician, he was a devotee of the pregnant pause.

"Mr. Forte," he said finally, "these are the files of twenty-three men who are going to die before their time. The wounds and illnesses that brought them here have long since been stabilized. All are ambulatory, in fair-to-good health considering their infirmities, and yet all have entered a decline that is usually irreversible."

"Why?"

"In layman's language, they believe they have nothing to live for."

Forte nodded. He knew the feeling.

Dr. Phillips opened the top file.

Charley Protock, forty-five, a basket case left over from the Vietnam War. He had been confined to bed for fifteen years, then to a motorized wheelchair, before twenty-first-century technology provided him with prostheses that put him back on his feet, and gave him hands for tasks he had long ago forgotten how to perform.

Barry Burton, seventy-one, an ex-Seabee, had what was left of a small intestine after a Japanese machine-gunner had stitched his belly with nineteen .25-caliber bullets. Thin as a pencil, he survived on soft foods, and walked with a permanent stoop.

Gene Morton, sixty-five, was a two-faced man. The first had been seared away by a Chinese flamethrower at Chosin Reservoir, while the second had been reconstructed from skin of his thighs and buttocks over a period of years. Judging by his pictures, his first had been handsome.

T. D. Roebuck, sixty-nine, Morton's best buddy, was a quiet sort whose face was wreathed in a perpetual half-smile. A former hospital corpsman, his mind had become unhinged during an eighteen-hour bombardment on Iwo Jima in which all but three of his platoon had been killed. Except for a few hours a week, he was perfectly normal; for those few, he was a raging bull.

"Ski" Modeljewski, forty-seven, bore scars of ciga-

rette burns and bamboo barbs over his entire body, but the wounds that never healed were deep within. There he harbored a pathological hatred for the politicians who had surrendered to those who had tortured him for five years, especially the architect of that craven surrender who had been awarded the Nobel *Peace* Prize, for Christ's sake . . .

Only in the details of their personal tragedies did the dossiers of the eighteen veterans differ.

"As you know from your own experience, Mr. Forte, some men so afflicted snap out of their depression in time, and do their best to rebuild normal lives. Others don't make it, and slide into ever deeper melancholy. Some of the older ones here—World War II vets mainly—have been hospitalized so long that their perspectives of the outside world have worn out and disappeared. They're perilously close to becoming vegetables. I've seen this kind slip quietly away. 'Debilities of old age exacerbated by war wounds,' we write on the death certificate, but it really isn't that."

"Then what is it?"

"Challenge," said Dr. Phillips. "They have none. This hospital is like a prison in that security here is total. Here they'll be cared for the rest of their lives. But man is not built to live that way, Mr. Forte. Challenge is a part of nature. It is the constant battle to meet those challenges that gives men strength, self-respect, character. In their youth, these men were strong, brave, useful. Their country needed them. It does no longer, and has found it easier to forget than repay them with the devotion that earned them their wounds. War crippled their bodies; peacetime neglect has crippled their spirits. In cases like these, I sometimes wonder if homeopathy isn't the answer."

"*That* bunch of ass-grabbing characters?"

"No, no—*homeopathy,* not homosexuality. It's a method of treating a disease by using small amounts of a drug that, in healthy persons, would produce symptoms similar to those of the disease being treated."

"You mean these men need a little war?" Forte was shocked.

"Precisely. The best years of their lives—the war years—are behind them. They were terrible, difficult, harrowing years, but they were vital and exciting. The men felt alive. If they could only somehow relive them . . . But obviously that's impossible. For one thing, there's no war. . . ."

True, Gwillam Forte reflected, nor was there likely to be one for a long time to come. To be sure, there had been a time during the middle 1980s when warfare threatened to become the permanent condition of mankind. But then the sun shone through, and in 1987 the guns fell silent throughout the world for the first time since the Japanese invaded Manchuria in September 1931. For eight years peace had presided over the affairs of man, and all signs indicated that it would endure.

In 1980, Forte remembered, there had been only night at the end of the tunnel. The Soviet Union and its surrogates had gobbled up Vietnam, Laos, Cambodia, Angola, Mozambique, Ethiopia, the Ogaden, Nicaragua, and Afghanistan in a few years without any interference from the free world. The Russians were busily at work in El Salvador, Iran, Lebanon, and Thailand, and less conspicuously in a dozen other countries. At one time, American confrontation with the Soviet Union might have stemmed the tide, but in Vietnam the Americans failed to honor their heritage and so encouraged the aggressors. Then President Carter and a nation distracted from self-survival by guilt feelings over Vietnam opposed Russian might not with the force of arms but with sermons on human rights. Unilateral American disarmament in the face of a Russian arms build-up opened a window of American vulnerability that would peak between 1982 and 1986.

President Reagan tried to slam the window shut, but it was already too late: by late 1983 the bear was clambering over the sill. In November of that year,

Russia dropped all pretense of peaceful intentions. Inviting NATO chiefs to Moscow, the Russians gave them a grand tour of defenses the West had suspected but never confirmed: vast underground cities beneath Moscow and Leningrad, with schools, hospitals, bulging granaries, factories, oil depots, and living accommodations for millions; antiballistic missile defenses that could destroy incoming missiles while they were still in the stratosphere; advance-warning measures that in six hours could disperse much of the Soviet population to hardened positions capable of resisting nuclear attack. Those precautions, along with the Soviet's vastly superior ICBM capability, made clear to the West that while Russia could annihilate the rest of the world, the Soviet Union itself was relatively invulnerable. The moral of the demonstration was clear: oppose Russia, and be destroyed.

With supreme confidence that would shackle the world into impotence, Russia embarked upon a program of world-wide hegemony, annexing—generally with a minimum of bloodshed—a few countries at a time. By 1985, Iran, the Arab states, Israel, Turkey, most of black Africa, Mexico, Brazil, Peru, and Ecuador were under Soviet domination. The United States, meanwhile, stood to arms—too strong to be attacked by Russia without risking a blanket of nuclear fallout covering the entire Earth, too weak to interpose its arms in the defense of nations that couldn't, and usually wouldn't, defend themselves. By 1986, fifty-three countries of Asia, Africa, and South America laid their weary heads on the communist bloc. In 1987, England joined the rest of Europe in the communist camp when left-winger Tony Buncombe was appointed Prime Minister. It seemed only a matter of time—and a very short time at that—before the entire world would be enslaved.

But then a seeming miracle occurred. As if the Soviet war machine had run out of gas, the conquests suddenly ceased. The pundits explained that the Rus-

sians had become seriously overextended, and needed
all their armed forces to contain the still-restive conquered nations. It may have been so, for indeed the
world map of September 1987, when the advance of
the Cuban, East German, and Ethiopian surrogates of
Russia abruptly halted, was reassuring to the eye of the
optimist. In terms of land and population, rather less
than half the world was under Russian control. Spared
were seven poor countries—China, India, Pakistan,
Bangladesh, Nigeria, Egypt and Indonesia—and five of
the world's richest—the United States, Canada, Australia, South Africa, and Japan. And not only had the
Russian guns fallen silent; anticapitalistic propaganda
dried up, subversion and sabotage ceased, KGB spying
and assassination became memories.

Military analysts don't believe in miracles. According to them, Russia had advanced as far as it dared.
One more step, they maintained, and the United States
would have been goaded into a preemptive nuclear
strike. Such a strike, with dirty bombs the United
States had thoughtfully manufactured, would have been
fatal, despite all of Russia's careful defense precautions, due to fallout. In contrast, by 1987 Russia itself
had such a preemptive option no longer. With the successful series of *Columbia* space launches, backed by
frantic defense research begun under Reagan in 1981,
the United States had established a chain of laser and
particle-beam antimissile stations in geostationary Earth
orbit. Still, the stand-off would be only temporary. The
Russians were developing Earth-based weapons to shoot
down or otherwise make harmless the American satellites. When they did, the Russian conquest would
resume.

So reasoned the leaders of the West, who decided a
daring new strategy was imperative. The strategy was
obvious: the United States and the four other wealthy
free nations would unleash the tremendous military
power latent in the seven poor countries—comprising
more than two billion souls. Harnessed to the tech-

nologically superior war machine of the West, they
would build an impenetrable wall against future Russian expansion.

Accordingly, the United States initiated a mammoth
rescue operation. Together with its reluctant allies, who
thought that the money would be better spent strength-
ening their own defenses, it poured grain, meat, manufactured goods, technological assistance, and weapons
into the seven starving sisters, who soaked it up like
the parched desert after a summer shower. During the
next seven years, the tempo of aid increased. But so
did the population of the poor, stimulated by the hand-
outs of the West, whose production was immediately
absorbed by the pauper nations' baby boom. The only
legions that materialized were armies of the barefoot,
indigent, and ill; far from being eager to defend themselves, their sole battle was for ever larger subsidies.
To satisfy the demand, the five rich nations could
devote only a shrinking proportion of their production
to their own military defenses.

Not that defenses seemed to matter any longer. Russia, while maintaining its armed forces at high levels
of readiness, did nothing to provoke its neighbors even
when, as in the case of Egypt, surrounded on all sides,
it could have toppled the ruling regimes in a day. Few
dared to guess what was in the minds of the men in
the Kremlin, but judging by their total abstention from
aggression during the past eight years, it certainly
wasn't conquest. . . .

Gwillam Forte considered the problem of the twenty-
three veterans, good men wasting away, according to
Dr. Phillips, for want of a war. Personally, he didn't
subscribe to the theory. He had seen war, and could
recall no single redeeming feature. And certainly, even
among its most persuasive partisans, he had never heard
it recommended as a cure for depression and other
mental illness.

"I've got a fair amount of influence in this state, Dr.

Phillips," he said finally, "but it doesn't extend to the declaration of war."

"Oh," Phillips replied airily, "I wasn't speaking of *war* war, but rather the total engagement of the spirit in some great activity, with the urgency, deadlines, excitement, danger, suspense, the sense of sacrifice and camaraderie that comes with war. Bingo in the hospital morning room is not the answer, Mr. Forte."

The answer came two days later, when Governor Cherokee Tom Traynor called for a progress report on the *Texas* from the captain of the Texas Navy.

"No, nothing concrete yet," Forte confessed. Actually, the matter had completely slipped his mind. The millennium was still six years away, and he was a busy man. "I've been thinking about it, though."

"Good. Any tentative conclusions?"

"Well," said Forte, "the minimum we can do is to restore the ship to the shape it was when in commission."

"I want maximum, not minimum, Will. I want a crowd-stopper, not a static museum piece. You'll have to do better than that."

"Well, how about rigging it up with great metal wings and making it *fly?*" Forte replied with leaden irony.

"Now you're talking, Will. I knew I could count on you for something dramatic. A battleship that flies! By God, Will, you do that and I'll be elected by a landslide. Get on it, and keep me posted. *A flying battleship,* by God!"

"But—" Forte began.

But the governor had already hung up.

Forte replaced the telephone gently in its cradle and gazed out the window at Houston fifty-seven stories below him, spreading out almost as far as he could see. He should have known better than to play word games with a politician.

For the first time since Governor Traynor had

broached the subject, he really thought about it. Thought came hard, because his memories of the *Texas* were bleak and heavy, and he had spent years trying to obliterate them. But gazing out the window of his skyscraper office, looking into the future six years distant, a picture of the *Texas* transformed began to take shape. To remodel the old hulk that lay rusting in its berth at San Jacinto National Monument into the image that was forming in his mind would be no easy task. It would take money, imagination, dedication, gigantic effort—the moral equivalent of war.

Suddenly it came to him. Cherokee Tom, Dr. Phillips. Two problems, one solution.

19 MAY 1994

THE BATTLESHIP WAS NEARLY A CENTURY OLD, AND looked its years. Its gray paint was peeling and flaking, and leprous patches of rust spread up from the water line. One of the foremast stays had rusted and parted, and now trailed in the stagnant water of the basin, festooned wth algae. A tampion had been stolen from the muzzle of one of the fourteen-inch guns, and a wad of newspaper had been inserted in its place to keep out the rain and dust. In the muzzles of the casemate five-inch .51-caliber broadside guns, birds had nested, and their droppings were liberally distributed across the turrets and decks. Bilge waste pumped from the double-bottoms streaked the basin waters and cast up the musty odor of neglect and old age. From the fantail the flag of the State of Texas hung tattered and limp from the ensign staff, while on the mainmast the

American colors were snarled and strangled in the lines. Candy wrappers, cigarette butts, and crushed Styrofoam cups littered deck and dock. A single Chicano family strolled listlessly on the quarter-deck.

"Beautiful," Ski Modeljewski commented.

Gwillam Forte made no reply. He led the party of veterans up the gangway onto the quarter-deck.

It was the first time he had come aboard in the forty-nine years since he had been wounded on the bridge. He was too busy to indulge in nostalgia, he always claimed when someone suggested he visit the old ship; the truth was that he had consciously put out of his mind all recollection of his past when he left the hospital, and wanted no reminder of it. Strangely, seeing the Texas for the first time since 1945 did not evoke the dread and repulsion he was sure he would feel. It evoked no emotion at all. His only thought was of how *small* it was, where once it had been his world.

When in uniform, the proper procedure on boarding a naval vessel is to stop at the brow, salute the flag on the ensign aft, then make a quarter turn to the right and salute the officer of the deck on the quarter-deck, and ask permission to come aboard. Out of uniform, Forte wasn't sure what he should do, especially since no officer of the deck had commanded the quarter-deck in almost half a century. Still, some vestige of naval protocol made him pause at the brow, face aft at attention, then the quarter-deck, before stepping aboard. To his surprise and annoyance, the deck was surfaced with concrete—he later learned that this had been done to withstand the scraping and scuffing of cowboy-booted tourists—where once it had been a velvety camouflage gray.

"We'll start back at the fantail," Forte told them when the twenty-three others had come aboard. "The fantail is the rear of the ship, in case the exdogfaces and other inferior species among you were about to ask. Since the purpose of this tour is to acquaint you with the ship and get suggestions from you as to how it can be fashioned into a really proud symbol of a proud state come the Millenary Celebrations six years from now, we're going to take our time and see it all. The fact that some of you never set foot on a battleship is no disadvantage: you'll bring a fresh perspective, and maybe some originality to the project. If any of the terms that come up baffle you, just ask me or one of the other old tars, and we'll be happy to share our superior wisdom. This way, men."

Assembling them beneath the twin barrels of the number 5 fourteen-inch turret, Gwillam Forte gave his party the benefit of his researches of the previous evening, when he relearned data about the U.S.S. *Texas* that had been long and thankfully forgotten.

"For all you landhogs who've never sailed blue water," he said, "let me give you a quick rundown on the *Texas*. This is the former U.S.S. *Texas*, BB35, authorized by the Congress in an Act of 24 June 1910, keel laid 17 April 1911, launched 18 May 1912, commissioned 12 March 1914 in Newport News, Virginia. In a representative fighting year—1943, say—this ship carried a complement of 100 officers, 85 Marines, and 1,625 enlisted swine. It displaced 34,000 tons, had a length of 573 feet, a beam of 106 feet, and was 132 feet from the foretop to the water line. Its two counter-rotating engines could push this big loaf of bread through the water at up to twenty-one knots, but it usually moved at about ten nautical miles per hour, the speed of a middle-aged jogger who's just spotted a mugger closing in. At that pace, it could sail halfway around the world without refueling.

"It could also hoist a lot of iron into the air. It has ten fourteen-inch guns like these two above our heads, in five turrets, shooting three-quarter-ton shells up to fifteen miles. In addition, it had something like thirty-five smaller guns, ranging from 20-mm antiaircraft guns to five-inch broadside batteries, lobbing fifty-pound shells up to ten miles.

"Now, reading from the fantail forward, you see

two after-turrets with two naval cannon each, then the mainmast fourteen-inch battery with a catapault for the OS2U Kingfisher on top. The Kingfisher flew about one hundred miles an hour when scared; it took a brave man to fly her, and a skilled one to land in the curving wake of the ship. Then you have the ship's single stack—smokestack to landlubbers—the mainmast, and finally the two forward turrets.

"A man-of-war is a self-contained community, a floating fortress that can wage war or run away from it. To keep a ship functioning efficiently requires many specialties, only a few of which are directedly concerned with shooting off all that impressive armament. Here on the main deck you have the gunnery office, bakery, galleys, spud locker, butcher shop, armory, air castle, admiral's cabin, and other compartments easily accessible to the ship's company on the lower decks. On the superstructure deck of the foremast, above the main, or weather, deck, is the captain's cabin, gear locker, fruit locker, paint locker, and the motor whaleboats in their cradles. You—"

"Whaleboats?" Protock said. "You were hunting *whales?*"

"Only by accident, when we ran into one asleep on the surface. These whaleboats you see here, though, are direct descendents of the two-prowed craft whalers used two hundred years ago. Okay, up the ladder on the foremast is the signal bridge with the navigation office and the radar motor room, while at the next level are the combat-information and fire-control centers. Above them are the navigation bridge and chart house, radio shack, and pilothouse, and above that is the flag bridge, where the Admiral can keep his eye on the whole task force. Above all the rest, you can make out secondary battery control, forward battle lookout, main battery control, and finally, up on top, the radar antenna.

"All that stuff is in the foremast. In the mainmast toward the stern you find radar and fire direction apparatus, and the secondary conn from which the ship is controlled in case the pilothouse is knocked out of action—Any questions so far?"

There were—lots of them—but Gwillam Forte refused to answer the one uppermost in the minds of the twenty-three men until later that afternoon, when they had made a complete circuit of the ship, from the pilothouse to the engine rooms, and were back at El Caballejo having a beer to wash away the dust of the long hot day.

"Okay, Will, the suspense is killing us," Ski Modeljewski said, wiping foam from his lip. "When are you going to tell us why you dragged us out into the hot sun to spend the day looking at that floating scrap heap?"

"A little respect from the white-hat jungle," Forte said severely. "I'll have you know that you're speaking about the ship I love and, as it happens, command. Allow me to introduce the commanding officer of the flagship of the Texas Navy: me. All rise."

From the assembly came a chorus of raspberries.

"All is now clear," drawled Jimmy Rawlins, a Viet vet who had been hit by a castrator mine, but because he was uncommonly tall lost only two legs instead of his manhood. "You are captain of a ship without a crew. You want to press-gang us into the job. Wouldn't that be cute—a crippled ship with a crippled crew."

"Is *that* what this is all about?" Zeno Defrees asked. "Because if it is, I demand a promotion. When I was hit aboard the old *Enterprise,* I was a machinist's mate second. Guarantee me three stripes and I'm game."

"You'd sign up just to be machinist's mate *first?*" Ski asked. "You must be around the bend."

"I was thinking," Defrees said stiffly, "of the three stripes of commander."

"When you clowns are finished," Forte said, "I'll tell you the deal. In six years, as I mentioned, that ship will be part of the Texas Millenary Celebrations. It's going to be fully restored. I need your help to do it."

"What do we know about reconditioning a ship, Will?" a voice complained. "We're disabled vets, not shipyards stiffs."

"Now, this is not going to be a matter of a coat of paint and shining up the brasswork," Forte said, ignoring the interruption. "I could turn loose a gang of shipyard types six months before the events are to begin, have them chip the paint, rerig the standing gear, brighten up the brass, but with all that taking place for months before, where would be the drama on opening day?"

"You want drama?" said Roebuck.

"That's what I want."

"Then have the old rust bucket towed away and sunk some dark night, and offer a big reward to the finder. Every skin-diver and shrimp fisherman in the southern U.S. would be gaffing one another trying to find her. The blood would attract the sharks, and—well," he concluded lamely, when he saw Forte regarding him with narrowed eyes, "you want drama."

"What I thought of was announcing, come opening day, that the *Texas* was being retired, that it would be towed away to the breaker's yard on the morrow, and that everybody who wanted to pay last respects to this symbol of the state—and partake in a gigantic, free barbecue—should come down to see her off on her last cruise.

"Imagine the scene. . . . Hundreds of thousands of Texans line the banks of the Houston Ship Channel. Some are indignant, others philosophic, others merely curious. Tugs plod solemnly up the channel in two columns, swing in toward the *Texas*'s berth. A bugler mounts the gangway, climbs the ladder to the bridge. The crowd is hushed, tears mist the eyes of the old salts, the very wind is stilled, as he puts the bugle to his lips to play a funereal *taps* over the ship, soon to die.

"Instead, from the bugle comes the electrifying blast of *Attention!* A moment later the call is followed by *Assembly!* and from every hatch pour sailors in dress whites. They sprint down the deck to their muster stations and silently form, rank on rank, as their officers appear, swords drawn, to take command of their units. A Navy band materializes, marches to the forecastle, and plays the national anthem.

"As the last notes die away, the voices of the multitude stilled, the band strikes up 'Anchors Aweigh.' The crew breaks formation at the run, heading for its getting-underway stations. Lines are cast off from bollards and cleats. Engine room telegraph bells tinkle. A spume of black smoke spurts from the stack. The deep-throated horn sounds once, its echoes reverberating across the silent, expectant horde of Texans.

"The ship shudders from the vibration of its engines coming alive. The water of the slip churns as the great brass screws begin to turn. The ship backs down out of its berth, picking up speed as it swings around in the middle of the channel and slows to a stop.

"The turrets of the big fourteen-inch guns train to broadside. They slowly elevate to forty-five degrees. As one, the ten guns fire, a tremendous blast that rolls the ship over until its port side is awash. It rolls back, steadies, then another salvo thunders out across the assembled populace, smoke rings from the muzzle blasts floating lazily toward shore. Another, then another—twenty-one in all—are fired, the salute of a great ship to the state it symbolizes.

"On the twenty-first salvo, the upper deck undergoes a miraculous transformation. From bare masts streams a cloud of bunting, and suddenly the ship is dressed from stem to stern in flags all the colors of the rainbow. But this is not all: before the reverberation of the last salvo fades, the ship itself is transfigured. Its dull, dirty gray is obliterated in a flash, as if by a thousand brushes, and the ship is a gleaming white.

"A cheer goes up from a million throats on both

sides of the channel as the U.S.S. *Texas,* its engines res-
ponding to a full head of steam, squats stern down in
the water and races away at thirty knots, headed for
the open sea. . . .". Forte paused.

There was silence.

"Aw, come *on,* Will," somebody said.

"I've discussed it with the scientists of my research
staff. They assure me it can be done. It will need hard
work, high standards of performance, dedication, time,
money—but it can be done. In six years. If I can get
the men . . ."

Again, silence.

Ski Modeljewski looked around the room at the faces
of his friends and shipmates. He shrugged. "Well," he
said, "I always *was* a sucker for lost causes."

JUNE 1984

THE SUBTERRANEAN WORKSHOPS OF SUNSHINE INDUS-
tries had been built in the scary days of the early
1980s. At the time, it seemed that the Russians had
solved the American missile defense equation, that they
could drop their ICBMs with assurance that they would
atomize everything American right out to the horizon.
Russia itself, thanks to an efficient antiballistic missile
system that had been extended from mere point defense
of major cities ever farther into the hinterland, had
less and less to fear from America's nuclear might.

By 1984, Gwillam Forte's men had been digging in
for four years. Not having mountains that they could
hollow out, as the Swiss and Swedes had done to protect themselves, their stores, and industry, Forte deter-

mined to burrow underground. At first it seemed an impossible goal to excavate millions of cubic meters of rock and earth far enough beneath the surface to be invulnerable to megaton bombs. A team of economists and scientists said the costs would bankrupt Sunshine Industries before he installed even a tenth of SII's manufacturing capacity twelve hundred meters down, considered the minimum depth necessary to dissipate anticipated shock blasts. Forte didn't argue with his experts: he paid them to be right.

But one night while gargling with the salt-and-soda mixture he favored over over-the-counter frauds, a balloon blossomed in the bathroom mirror. Inside was a glaring light bulb. He paused, and looked thoughtfully at the gargle water.

The next day he called in his geologists and told them what he was looking for. Poring over geological maps of the area, they soon found it. Encouraged, Forte instructed his mechanical engineers to conduct an energy survey of the mainly petroleum-related industries along the Houston Ship Channel, with special attention to flared gas and other waste heat. Some weeks later they returned with an exhaustive two-volume study. On their heels came Forte's chief civil engineer, who listened with skepticism as Forte outlined his plan.

"Stifle your doubts, and talk to the men who will do the work," Forte told him. "Determine whether they can do it. If they can, bring back two figures: the cost, and the completion date."

"Right."

Twenty-two days later, a weary chief engineer brought to Forte the required two figures. Forte studied them with a frown. The sum was large—even by Forte's standards $78.8 million was a lot of money. And the date was a lot further in the future than he had anticipated. Nevertheless, he nodded and said: "You're in complete charge. Bring it in under budget before this date, and you'll get a bonus of double the savings. Exceed the target date or go over budget, and you're fired."

Forte kept his word. He usually did. The project came in $1.2 million over budget and twelve days late. The chief engineer was fired. Still, he had been on the payroll longer than the experts who said the subterranean workshops were an economic impossibility: they had all been kicked out the day work began, and from that day on Forte never allowed an economist on the premises.

Forte's solution had been just that—a solution. Observing the salt and soda dissolving in the glass of warm water, he reasoned that the same process might work on a larger scale. His geologists confirmed the presence of a suitable site 1,450 meters below his El Caballejo ranch property beside the Houston Ship Channel. There, seismic surveys of oil exploratory companies in the 1920s had turned up a number of salt domes, although precious few of them sat atop the hoped-for reservoirs of crude. Forte's mechanical engineers had likewise discovered promising energy sources in the millions of BTUs flared off in petrochemical plants and refineries that extended some thirty miles along the channel.

At a modest investment, Forte was able to buy up the flare gas and pipe it to a steam-generation plant constructed above the salt dome under the ranch property. Superheated water was forced down a drill pipe into the dome, where it liquified the halite deposit, which was then forced up by the same pressure through a second pipe to the surface. The hot brine was evaporated and purified in stills and sold to chemical, glass, and agricultural industries in which Forte had interests. Had the brine recovery been planned as a strictly money-making proposition, the project probably would have lost money. But speed was Forte's purpose, and the fact that the excavation was made close to the break-even point was considered a financial success.

Into the enormous chambers excavated nearly a mile

underground, Sunshine Industries installed almost its
entire manufacturing capacity, its offices, research center, library, fuel supplies, raw-material stockpiles, warehouses, electric generators, leisure and sporting facilities, air conditioning machinery, food and water re-
serves to last the entire work force for three years, and
dormitories extensive enough to house the workers
and their families twice over. The transportation system
alone was equivalent to that of a town of twenty thousand, with electric buses running on regular schedules,
a small electric railroad for heavy equipment and supplies, and even a radio-taxi service for executives. According to defense experts, it was the ultimate in bomb
shelters, invulnerable even to zero-error hits by mega-
ton-yield nuclear missiles. To be sure, it was impossible
to forecast casualties from blast effects, but the facilities themselves would survive, even should everything
else in the United States be destroyed.

So would its secrets, which ranged from gaseous
storage batteries, lasers, ion-drive vehicles and other
high-tech products being tested in its laboratories, to
arcane theories of submarine and satellite warfare developed by SII researchers, along with designs for hard-
ware to carry them out, for SII was a prime U.S. defense contractor. As such, security was virtually absolute. Admission to the underground offices and workshops was via one of two entry shafts after a thorough
security check of the individual, who typically spent
an entire week at work below the surface, followed
by a week of total freedom at home. Those who talked
about their work outside quickly discovered they had
no work to talk about. Thus, over the years, a work
force was built up that was relatively small, efficient,
healthy, and very well paid. Working conditions in the
cavernous factories below ground were excellent: no air
pollution, very little noise, absolute temperature and
illumination control, and performance goals that kept
workers, who were shifted around from one job to another to counteract boredom, constantly challenged to

produce. It was a tough shop, but a happy ship. The loyalty of the workers to Forte was correspondingly fierce and possessive.

He depended on it now as he assembled the engineering chiefs who would be responsible for the rehabilitation of the U.S.S. *Texas*. One would take charge of propulsion, another of instrumentation, a third of armament, a fourth of paintwork, and so on.

"Keep always in mind," Forte warned them, "the purposes of this job. They are to regenerate the U.S.S. *Texas*—make it the fastest, leanest, cleanest, most exciting ship afloat, while preserving its outside appearance unchanged, and to ration the work so as to stretch it out for five and a half years, to coincide with the Texas Millenary Celebrations in January 2000. You will schedule the work to produce a crescendo of excitement, a tempo that will pick up as the TMC draws to a close. That's vital. These war veterans must feel that they've got to keep humping to get the work done on time. That feeling of urgency will keep them alive and productive. To me, that's more important than getting the old ship rebuilt. Anybody who lets slip that the work can easily be done in two years will hear from me. The words he will hear are 'good' and 'bye.'" His blue eyes rested on each of his engineers in turn.

"These men will have direct responsibility for getting the work done, and you'll devise work schedules so they can handle it. But there'll be no free rides. See that they have plenty to do."

"Seems to me like this is about three parts ego-building and one part ship-building," one of the engineers grumbled.

"Your proportions are correct," agreed Forte. "Now get cracking."

The U.S.S. *Texas,* as a state monument, was open to the public seven days a week. Enough tourists still came to make impossible any overt work on the ship if secrecy was to be preserved. A major overhaul on a 34,000-ton vessel under the very noses of the visitors

without them suspecting it was obviously impossible—
until Gwillam Forte thought of a way.

"Tunnel," he ordered.

They tunneled.

A Mountain Mole was hired away from its more
prosaic role in the construction of subways and was
lowered piecemeal into the underground cavern of
SD-1. There, within the walled, guarded confines of the
transportation-pool area, it was reassembled, then
moved to the point on the perimeter of the chamber
nearest the ship channel.

The engineer in charge mounted the ladder to the
cab and switched on main power. Brilliant lights sprang
to life, revealing a machine as big as a two-story house.
The front of the Mole was a huge steel ring, bristling
with diamond-tipped titanium-steel teeth the size of
wheelbarrows. The engineer touched a button, and the
giant ring began to rotate. He pressed a lever, and the
283-ton monster clanked forward on six caterpillar
treads until the cutting disk touched the wall. A sheet
of protective blue glass slid up to cover the windows
of the Mole's control room. The engineer's hand de-
pressed a switch. From within the ring, a multitude of
laser beams pierced the limestone wall with eleven-sec-
ond bursts of energy. The intense heat was followed
by bursts of liquid CO_2. The din was like the explosion
of cannon, as the differential expansion of the rock
caused it to star with a million minute fissures.

The diamond-tipped teeth of the rotating ring now
bit into the crumbly rock as if it were just so much dry
bread. When the ring reached the limit of the fissured
stone and struck the native bedrock, a sensor retracted
and shut down the rotating mandible.

Horizontal conveyor belts at ground level, meanwhile, were carrying the spoil in a continuous stream
to the rear of the Mole, where electric rail cars hauled
it away to skips. The skips, in turn, raised the broken
rock to the surface. The Mole then ground forward—

the upward gradient was one-in-ten—on its huge steel-shod feet to take another bite.

The air was filled with churning rock dust despite a constant stream of water across the drilling surface, and the noise of the clanking, whirring, sparking, thundering machinery was so intense that the Mole's attendent workers, some 140 per shift, wore hardhats with earmuff speakers and throat mikes, in addition to respirator masks against the rock dust.

Operating around the clock, three crews drilled an average of seventy-two linear centimeters a minute, driving a circular passage 5.8 meters in diameter. The spoil truckers worked fast to keep up with it, as did the concrete crew, which braced and cemented the floor and walls of the tunnel behind the Mole. In their wake came the track-layers and electricians, putting down twin standard-gauge railways—traffic would proceed in both directions when the tunnel was completed—signal system, fresh-air tubing, bundles of electrical cable, and overhead lighting. Bringing up the rear was a gang laying pipe for fresh water and others for sewage and liquid-waste disposal.

It took ten days to drill the 9.1 kilometers from SD-1, as SII's underground complex in the salt dome was called, to the edge of the basin where the *Texas* was berthed. Two weeks after the first trucks rumbled away with spoil, the last carried its load of rock to the skip. By then, some 250,000 cubic meters of rock had been excavated and hauled to the surface, put on barges, and shipped twenty kilometers downstream to Galveston Bay for dumping in deep water. The quantity was sufficient to cause comment from environmentalists. Gwillam Forte's press representative explained it away by saying that it came from a tunnel to a nearby salt dome, where SD-2 would soon be built.

An airtight passageway now was extended through the remaining rock and silt separating the tunnel from the *Texas*'s slip. In order to prevent a breakthrough from flooding SD-1 at the base of the steep tunnel, an airtight caisson punched through the remaining rock and was jacked forward. One steel section at a time was added to the rear of the caisson, until with a metallic *clank!* it closed against the hull of the battleship two meters below the water line, invisible from the surface in the murky waters.

Divers welded the connection watertight. The caisson's air lock opened so metal workers could cut through the battleship's six bulging layers of protective hull armor, which had been added in 1925 to protect her from torpedos. A continuous passageway now connected SD-1 with the engine room of the U.S.S. *Texas*.

The first man to go aboard was Gwillam Forte.

In the engine room, he addressed the assembled veterans, engineers, and technicians: "As you all know, only certain areas of the ship are open to the public. As of now, hatches leading from those areas to this will be welded shut. Under no circumstance is the public to get the idea that any work is going on down here. To make sure they don't, in future we work night shifts only." He paused. "The future starts now."

28 DECEMBER 1997

HOW BRIEF THE FUTURE MIGHT BE GWILLAM FORTE had learned forty-two months later, when he was summoned to the White House for a secret conference with President Wilson Wynn and eight fellow moguls of the American press, radio, and television. Together, the nine media men sitting around the polished ebony table in the cabinet conference room had daily access to more than 97 percent of American readers, listeners, and viewers. President Wynn rightly considered their influence crucial in the formation of American public opinion. How the nine men felt about any public issue was how, ultimately, the American people would be persuaded to feel. Usually the nine were divided, and thus Americans were divided, and politicians like Wynn exploited such divisions to win high office. But today, Wynn was praying he could unite them: the nation's future, no less than his own, depended on it.

"I have asked you here today, gentlemen," the President began, "to seek your support of an important foreign policy initiative. How important it is, and the secrecy you should attach to it, you may judge from the absence of anyone but the ten of us in these discussions. No tape recording is being made, and I shall ask you to take no notes and to keep what will be said here confidential. Anyone who does not agree to maintain confidentiality may leave before I proceed."

He waited. No one stirred.

"I am happy to know I can count on you all," Wynn said with a cryptic smile. "Let me begin by remarking that most of you have been generous with support for my foreign policy during my first administration, without which I doubt that I would have been reelected last year, considering the primacy of foreign policy issues. I now thank you collectively, as I have previously thanked you individually, for that vote of confidence, gentlemen." He nodded to each of seven of the nine, who smilingly acknowledged his gratitude. "However, honesty obliges me to confess that perhaps—only perhaps, mind you—this foreign policy has given birth to disaster."

Seven smiles faded from seven faces, and were transferred to those of Gwillam Forte and J. D. Pascal, the eighty-eight-year-old New England press lord who had bitterly, consistently, and long repudiated the premises of America's one-world foreign policy.

"Disaster?" the owner of CBS exclaimed. "How can

you even suggest that a policy that has bought us ten years of peace is a disaster, Mr. President?"

"That is all it is, so far, David," the President replied equably, "—suggestion. The suggestion comes from my service chiefs, and I've asked you here to help me examine it. If you think it has merit—which, I might add, my political advisers do not—then I hope you will have some ideas about how we can prepare the American public for a drastic change in official United States policy, for that will be a first priority. If, on the other hand, you think the criticism has no merit, I hope you will give me the ammunition with which to shoot it down."

The President leaned back in his high leather chair and regarded his steepled fingers.

"The watershed in recent international relations was, I am sure you will agree, the abandonment of world conquest by the Soviets just ten years ago. Since then, the guns have remained stilled, although Russia's war readiness remains at high pitch. That, of course, doesn't alarm us, since both Russia and the United States have achieved nuclear parity and the capability of destroying each other's ICBMs the minute they leave their launching pads, by means of satellite-based weapons in geosynchronous orbit. If we need fear Russia at all, it is that nation's conventional offensive weapons that we must look to."

"Then we can quit worrying, Mr. President," interjected Frank Twigg, the dynamic young chairman of a Washington-based chain of eighty-three large American dailies. "My group has recently completed a survey of American opinion about the strategic forces of the two great powers. American opinion is inescapable: 63 percent of Americans believe Russia would be creamed if it tried to invade the United States today, against only 8 percent on the other side and 29 percent 'don't know.' After all, the Russians have no new secret weapons—at least that we know of—and without such weapons they could never launch the two-ocean amphibious assault that would be necessary to subdue this country. Besides, if they tried, using their full military strength, their unguarded satellite countries would immediately revolt. That's confirmed by a poll we took only last month—81 percent of Americans affirm it."

"You speak of today, Frank. What about tomorrow?"

Twigg shrugged. He was a newspaperman. Today was what counted.

"Consider what happened ten years ago," the president said. "Russia could have conquered the United States then—and if not the United States, at least South Africa, Japan, Australia, and Canada. Yet it did no such thing. Why not?"

That was a moot question, one that evoked the strongest and most varied opinions, because short of reading the minds of the men in the Kremlin, no one could be sure. Fear of a universal holocaust in which they too would be consumed, territorial indigestion, a triumph of the Russian peace party over the hawks, dissension within the Kremlin, a fight for leadership that immobilized all parties—these were some of the theories advanced for the halt to Russian imperialism.

"But my military and naval analysts have finally agreed on a more complex scenario. They believe that what most of you maintain—that the Russians feared a nuclear war that would exterminate humankind—is substantially correct. Russia feared that if it attacked the last of the few reliable allies the Americans possess—South Africa, Canada, Australia, and Japan— the Americans would, in desperation, push the button. So far so good. But what, then, about the countries they *could* have taken with impunity, but did not—Egypt, Bangladesh, Nigeria, Indonesia, Pakistan, India, and China? Why did they leave these inexhaustible sources of manpower and armies for the free world to exploit?

"According to my service chiefs, because they were sure, having dealt with such Third World countries for decades without benefit to themselves, that far from being a blessing, the backward nations would be the graveyard of the West."

"Nonsense!" roared Bernard Davis, the television king of America and the second most powerful man in the room.

"You think so, Bernie? Well, we've poured a steady stream of wheat and trucks and building materials and arms into these seven pauper countries for the past ten years, and what have we reaped besides an enormous internal and external debt? We've got 700 million more mouths to feed than when we began a short decade ago, and we've subsidized armies that couldn't beat that of Paraguay in a stand-up fight. I'll grant you, they have a lot of field marshals and beautifully tailored uniforms and rows of fruit salad on their chests and put on impressive parades, but *they can't fight!"*

"They need time," said Davis aggrievedly. This was his beloved Third World the president was knocking. "After all, Rome wasn't built in a day."

"We're not building Rome. We're trying to build armies. We've failed. Today, having strewn our food and technology and matériel on foreign sands, we're barely able to defend ourselves against a conventional amphibious attack by Russia and its armies of slaves. That's not theory; that's fact."

"But Russia is peace-loving," Davis said soothingly.

"They keep saying so," President Wynn admitted. "But do you believe them?"

"Of course, because they keep demonstrating it. Look at South Africa. They could have knocked off South Africa any time they wanted."

President Wynn's distinguished patrician face was creased in a scowl. What Davis said was all too true.

"Still, my analysts feel that this whole scenario was constructed deliberately to weaken the West. The Russians *knew* the pauper Third World would make no contribution to free-world defense. They *knew* the Third World's exploding population and demands to feed it would impoverish us—as they have. In time, we will be too weak, at the rate we're going, to resist a determined push. A little shove will do, and the U.S. will crumble."

He licked his lower lip. He could see that his words were making little impression, except on Forte and old Pascal, who had been saying the same things as long as he could remember. With the others, ten years of peace was hard to argue away.

"Is this why we've been called together?" said Dr. Werner Spoke, the scholarly chief of the Continental News Service. "Is it to inform us that we are so weak that a Russian attack is imminent?"

President Wilson Wynn shook his head. "No, on the contrary, I have received new proposals from the Russians. We have examined them, and while on the surface they seem most attractive, we believe they carry the seeds of national disaster."

"Let's hear the good news first, Mr. President," said Davis tartly.

"Very well. The proposal is quite long, complicated in the Russian manner, and detailed. But it boils down to this: the Russians propose the total demilitarization of the Third World—plus their poor possessions such as Poland and England as well as those that are technically our allies, such as China and India."

The men around the table nodded. The better-armed, better-organized Russian satellites would be a greater loss to Russia than America's client nations would be to the United States. A distinct plus for the United States.

"Next, Russia proposes the conversion of its arms industries to the production of plowshares, pen wipers, petroleum pipe, and other products for peaceful purposes. Russia will assume the burden of supplying the entire Third World with capital and consumer goods."

"*What?*" Spoke exclaimed. "But that's *wonderful*. What do we have to do in return?"

"In return, we too convert our arms industries to peaceful endeavors. But we will supply fertilizers, de-

salination plants, seed, and other products and processes for the agricultural sector of the world, and
intensify our own agricultural production at home and
in Canada and Australia."

"Then that *is* wonderful," said a grinning Dr. Spoke.
"It is indeed the millennium."

"So the Russians claim," President Wynn remarked
warily. "But how do *you* figure it, Dr. Spoke?"

"Isn't it obvious? We have, as you justly remarked,
Mr. President, exhausted ourselves in producing arms,
building materials, and other necessities for the Third
World. We could use a rest. Russia is giving it to us
by assuming the burden of providing for the growing
needs of the world's poor. We, on the other hand, are
preeminent in food production. By concentrating on
this, an American specialty that no one in the world
has come close to equaling in efficiency, we can supply
all the food mankind requires. The two hands wash
each other—Russia providing capital and consumer
goods, and the United States the wherewithal to eat."

"Yet—"

"But there is another dividend even more vital," continued Spoke, declining to yield the floor. "Neither can
exist without the other. Russia cannot wage war against
us without losing its daily bread. It would starve in six
months. We, for our part, could not be enticed into
martial adventures, because we would no longer have
the capacity to produce arms. Whoever thought up the
Russian plan is a genius, and I take off my hat to him.
Always providing, of course, that there will be mutual
inspection to be sure that the terms of the agreement
are carried through."

"Oh, yes," the president said, "there are provisions
for mutual inspection, all right."

"You seem, nevertheless, to have reservations," Bernard Davis noted. "Care to share them with us?"

"I'm thinking about the United States becoming an
agricultural nation. I'm not sure I like the idea."

"Thomas Jefferson did," Davis shot back.

"Thomas Jefferson lived two hundred years ago. Times have changed."

"For the worse. It's time we went back to the soil."

"Six feet under?"

"Ah," said Dr. Spoke. "So there's more to the story. I might have known it was too good to be true. What's the catch, Mr. President?"

President Wynn rubbed his jaw. "We're not sure. But we're suspicious. Leopards don't change their spots, and Russians who have been shooting their way down the road to expansion for four hundred years don't suddenly stop and build rest houses. I'm thinking about their proposed fleet visits, and I don't like the idea at all. Neither do my service advisers."

"Fleet visits?"

"Yes, this is another part of their proposed package. The concept is an ancient one, actually—an exchange of hostages. The idea is that if either party tries to dishonor its undertaking, the other has a hostage to deal with, in this case the whole country."

"I don't understand," said Davis.

"I'm not sure I do, either," Wynn sighed. "The way it is supposed to work is this: a large portion of each nation's fleet will visit the other nation's ports each summer; a trial visit this summer I have already authorized, by the way. Presumably, the courtesy calls will help dispel suspicion by letting the crews meet the people on a person-to-person basis. Another part of their mission will be overflights as an element in the inspection procedure to ensure that no covert arms build-up takes place. But mainly, as the Russians envision it, the fleets will be able to take immediate punitive action if they detect any sign of aggressive movement on the part of the other side, and this option is designed to inhibit such aggressive action absolutely."

"Well," Spoke said, "that sounds fair. In fact, it sounds great. What possible reservations could you entertain about such an intelligent suggestion? It's failsafe."

For a long moment the president didn't reply. Then he leaned forward, his hands clasped before him on the table. His expression was somber. "I have reservations about the whole agreement—even the name they proposed for it: the Washington Protocols. The Russians even give us the benefit of naming the agreement after our capital. Like everything else in the agreement, its uncharacteristic of the Russians. They never give *anything* away.

"Take the economic clauses of the protocols. Why are they willing to relieve us of the burden of supporting the Third World, when our misguided philanthropy is bankrupting us very nicely without their help? Why are they trying to save us?"

"They've decided that peace is preferable to war," Davis concluded. "Not a very difficult concept to understand."

"For us—not for Russians. Their whole history is built on aggression, from Alexander Nevski in the thirteenth century right down to the present day. It's in their blood. Then note their plan for the division of labor: the Russians take over manufacturing, we take over farming."

"Quite right, too. We farm better than they do, that's all," commented Davis.

"We manufacture better, too—if you exclude what comes out of Detroit. But you can easily switch manufacturing capacity from consumer goods to arms, from automobiles to tanks. You can't switch from rutabagas to rockets."

"True, Mr. President," Spoke countered, "but such a conversion to armaments would take several years, and its very first stages would be detected by our inspection. Could—"

"Perhaps," said the president, cutting Spoke off, "I should confide in you what my staff thinks will happen if I sign and the Congress ratifies the protocols: for the first few years, everything will proceed precisely as the Russians outline. We will concentrate on agriculture, the Russians on manufacturing. The living standards of the whole world will benefit, for nearly one-third of the world's gross national product is presently consumed in military preparations. Meanwhile, the fleets exchange visits without incident or observed enemy build-up. This state of affairs lasts four or five years— long enough for our industry to run down, to pass beyond the point of no return, to be plowed under like a rank weed. That of Russia will have grown commensurately while their farming, to be sure, languishes.

"At this point, we must ask ourselves: how long does it take to build a national industry from scratch? Five years? *Ten?* And how long does it take to plant the fields and reap a crop? *One* year.

"Now then, at some point the Russians, conscious that we are no longer capable of manufacturing the means to defend ourselves, on the short *or* long term, begin to rearm, quite openly. Naturally we halt our grain shipments. But the Russians have carefully withheld large portions of their grain and stored them in underground silos for just such a day. They can survive eighteen months or two years without additional shipments, and meanwhile they are replanting the Ukraine.

"Their fleet, in American waters at the time, now is in a position to cover the Russian invasion—an invasion not of Russians but of South and Central Americans who have been under training ten or fifteen years. Their weapons will be the simplest—rifles, pistols, grenades—because remember, the arms industry has been dead for five years. But such weapons, which the United States no longer manufactures, will suffice to permit the invaders to swarm up through Mexico in their millions and overrun the United States and Canada. Any trouble spots will be dealt with by the aerial cover of the Russian fleet, which—"

"Which would bring instant reprisals against Europe by *our* fleet," Dr. Spoke said triumphantly.

"Very true, but of no significance in strategic terms.

After all, we have no army on Russia's doorstep ready to invade. Then too, would Russia worry if our planes killed several thousand, or several million, Europeans? Just fewer mouths to feed when the conquest of the United States is complete."

"What you have outlined is pure conjecture," Bernard Davis said acidly. "Not one of these catastrophes need happen. Admit it, Mr. President."

The president admitted it.

"On the other hand, they *could*. On form, the Russians can be expected to pull something very much like what I have just outlined. And if it did, gentlemen, the United States would cease to exist."

Dr. Spoke cleared his throat. "I agree with Bernie here, Mr. President. We must distinguish two things: the *certainty* of peace and prosperity now, so long as guarantees are made and enforced, and the *possibility* of Russian betrayal at some nebulous future time. The advantages so obviously outweigh the potential—note well the word 'potential'—handicaps that, in my opinion, we have no choice but to accept the protocols. And rejoice!"

The president seemed to shrivel in his high-backed chair. He had invited the men in the hope that they would heed his appeal for caution, for a deliberate and exhaustive examination of the protocols, before the clamor of the American people for the instant eternal-peace fix stampeded the Congress and himself into signing what he believed would be the death warrant of his country. The issue was too serious to be decided quickly. But now, he knew, it would be. If he failed to release the terms of the protocols very soon, the Russians would leak them to obtain a cheap propaganda victory. He would be branded a warmonger for having tried to suppress proof of the Russians' pacific intentions. The peace-at-any-price partisans would in either case be mobilized by the seven men who had so vigorously supported the salvation of the Third World. The ensuing pressures on him to sign would be irresistible. If he didn't, against the unanimous opposition of the nation, he would likely be impeached.

The irony was that, though his instincts said to be wary, cold logic said there was nothing to fear. As Spoke pointed out, the alternatives were present peace and prosperity, and the possibility of betrayal at some vague future date. By then, the Russian regime might see the benefits for all mankind of part one of their carefully contrived scheme to conquer the United States—if that was what it was. Besides, whatever he thought personally was immaterial in the face of the unanimous accord of the people of the United States: he was their voice, and he would be a traitor to his trust if he said no to a peace agreement they—or at least these seven men who told them what to think—believed in.

The voice of Dr. Spoke recalled him from his reverie.

"I'm sorry, Werner," he apologized, "I was thinking about . . . What were you saying?"

"I merely asked, Mr. President, whether copies of the Washington Protocols will be released any time soon?"

President Wynn smiled sadly. There was his answer. The news. News was what mattered, not the security of the nation.

"I'll tell my press secretary to give you copies," he said, "right after lunch. It will be for immediate release."

28 DECEMBER 1997: P.M.

LUNCH WAS STRAINED AND AWKWARD. THE PRESS LORDS were plainly anguished as they endured course after leisurely course, each trying to contrive an excuse that would permit an early departure so as to break the news of Russia's magnanimous offer before his rivals. CBS, pleading that rich desserts and coffee gave him heartburn, was the first to take his leave. One by one, the others were quick to follow. President Wilson Wynn and Gwillam Forte, who had spoken but few words during the morning's discussions, were left alone in the Executive Dining Room.

"It occurs to me, Will, that with all the flak flying around I didn't get hit with any from you. That's a novel experience."

Forte shook his head. "I'm afraid, Mr. President, that's because as yet I have nothing to shoot at. You advance one theory, the others the precise opposite, to account for the Russian initiative. Either, it seems to me, could be right."

"But you agree that it's Russian *intentions*—not protocols, declarations, guarantees—that count?"

"Of course. But, as usual, we have no way of knowing what they are. No one has yet succeeded in bugging the Kremlin."

Wynn smiled, the crafty politician's smile reserved for the boys in the back room. A voter, having seen that smile, would have automatically cast his vote for Wynn's opponent, on the grounds that no one with a smile so cagey, so cunning, so sly, could possibly be

75

entrusted with the destiny of the great open-faced
American people.

"We've done better. We've got a piece of the Kremlin—right here in the White House."

"What?"

"'More coffee, sir?'" came a grave voice at his elbow.

Forte looked up. He had thought they were alone.
The tall gray-haired man with the silver tray looked
down at him with an expression at once deferential and
cool.

"Uh—no thanks," Forte said, wondering how much
the man had heard.

"No?" the man in the steward's jacket said. "Well, in
that case you won't mind if I have a cup. It's quite
good. Made it myself."

With that, he filled the cup at the place next to
Forte, put down the tray, and settled comfortably into
the chair beside him.

"Who the hell's this?" Forte demanded, turning to
the president.

The president chuckled.

"Allow me to present Nikolai Vasilievich Grimm,
former admiral of the Red fleet. Nick, meet Gwillam
Forte."

"You're supposed to be dead." Forte pushed back
his chair and turned to face the other man. "Missing at
sea. I read your obituary—last July, I seem to remember."

"Typical Soviet disinformation." The man in the
white jacket shrugged. "I can assure you that I'm
alive."

"I also remember your face. It wasn't the one you're
wearing now," Forte said coldly.

"If it were, I could scarcely have become the president's favorite steward. Plastic surgery, of course."

Gwillam Forte turned to Wynn. "I don't suppose . . . ?"

The president shook his head.

"No doubt whatsoever. This is Nick Grimm, no
question about it. He's been under interrogation eight

to ten hours a day since he defected, and the information he's given us has been confirmed many times over. Besides, I've known Nick for years, and I saw him before the surgeons got to work on him. He—"

"Allow me to explain, Mr. President. In brief, Mr. Forte, as a Ukrainian of German descent, early in life I decided that frank, cold opportunism was the only way to survive and prosper in my land. That was my path, and it took me to the top. I married in cold blood, joined the Communist Party in cold blood, curried favors with the Politburo in cold blood, betrayed friends when it was in my interest, corrupted superiors and then blackmailed them to advance myself. In short, the portrait of a successful Party man. I'm afraid you won't find that I conform to American standards of morality, but then I wasn't living in America. The important point is, I survived—survived and reached the top."

"Then why aren't you still there?"

Admiral Grimm took a cigarette from the silver box on the table and lit it. He blew twin streams of smoke from his nose and regarded Forte thoughtfully. "I'm getting old. Backstabbing is a sport for the young and fleet of foot. I could feel the breath of the ambitious on my neck, and it gave me a chill. I'm unusually susceptible to chills, I might say. So before the wishes of my subordinates could become reality, I arranged for my own demise—aboard a nuclear submarine of which, I am happy to report, I am the sole survivor of an explosion conveniently close to Charleston, South Carolina.

"Nick proposed a deal," the president said. "We'd give him a new identity and a discreet but very lavish future. And for this he'd allow us to pick his brains."

"Treason, in other words," Forte remarked.

"Ah—the very word I've been looking for." Admiral Grimm snapped his fingers. He chuckled. "I don't have to justify my life to you, Mr. Forte, only to myself. And I can tell you that if treason always paid off so handsomely as mine has for the United States, you'd advertise for traitors like me in *The New York Times*."

"What he says is true," President Wynn affirmed. "He has given us information of enormous importance."

"Such as?"

"Such as the hypothesis I attributed to my service staff, concerning a possible Russian attempt to invade the United States in four or five years via Mexico, using a Soviet fleet in American waters as cover."

"It's not a hypothesis but a fact," Grimm interjected. "I was one of the chief planners of Project Lime Kiln, as it is known in the Kremlin. The target date is the fifth of July, 2001, but the exact date depends on the degree of obsolescence and attrition of American arms that could oppose the onslaught. Already, in anticipation of the signing of the protocols, a steady stream of soldiers—Russian, German, Turkish, and Bulgarian, mostly—is flowing toward assembly points and training camps in Central and South America. When the time approaches, they will move north in small groups, form into divisions, and roll over the border of Mexico on a broad front into Texas and California. We—the Kremlin, that is—anticipate the subjugation of the United States and Canada will be complete by the following summer."

"Has this man's story been thoroughly checked out?" Forte asked the president.

"Yes—again and again. He's been subjected to truth serum, lie detector tests, voice-stress analysis—every method known to science. Furthermore, in the six months he's been with us, the predictions he's made—such as the movement of East Bloc soldiers into South American camps—have been right on the money. I wish I didn't have to believe him, but I must."

"All right, then—it's all true. Why are you telling *me*? Why didn't you bring in Grimm and have him say his piece at the meeting this morning? Instead of sounding the alarm against the Washington Protocols, at this moment my colleagues are preparing media campaigns in its favor."

President Wynn nodded somberly.

"Naturally, I considered it. In the first place, it wasn't until *after* Grimm received his new identity that he divulged the information you heard today. If I had confronted them with Grimm today, they'd have insisted he was a ringer sent by the hawks—his or ours—to sabotage Russia's peace proposals. After the series of operations, even I couldn't prove he was really Grimm, you see."

"Your assurances were good enough for me."

"That's why I confided in you, Will, and not them. They are press and television tycoons, neither pure nor simple. They've seen and heard and manufactured lies all their lives. It's their profession. Why should they believe me?"

It was a good question. Forte wondered whether he was believing any of this himself.

"But there was a greater danger," President Wynn went on. "The danger was that they *would* believe that it was Grimm, that he had defected from Russia with the connivance of the Kremlin hawks and was intent on sabotaging the peace process. They would feel even more compelled to trumpet the virtues of the protocols than they already are. And even if they did go along with my plea to counsel reason and due deliberation on the part of the American people, give them time to understand the dangers inherent in the protocols, it would only give the Russians the leisure to formulate an alternative strategy—once they knew Grimm was alive and talking, as they surely would, given your colleagues' propensity to share their secrets with the world."

Forte's head felt as though stuffed with cotton wool. The president's words had registered, and they seemed to make sense, but the tableau—the president of the United States, a defected admiral of the Red fleet dressed as a waiter, and a triple-amputee industrialist from Texas, all sitting cosily around the table talking about World War III—greatly disturbed him and confused his thoughts. President Wynn and he were old acquaintances, but hardly friends, having stood on the opposite side of almost every public issue in the twenty-five years since Wynn had emerged on the national scene. So what was Forte doing there? And why was Wynn confiding in him?

He asked the questions, but as is usual with politicians, President Wynn eschewed the straightforward reply.

"Nick," he said, turning to where the Russian lounged in his chair, apparently as bored and aloof as a boyar watching peasants being flogged, "what would it take to make the Russians abandon Project Lime Kiln, make them pull in their horns and leave us the hell alone?"

"The same medicine that has always worked with the Soviets—a good punch in the mouth," the admiral drawled through a cloud of smoke.

"Where did you learn English like that?" Forte asked.

"As a lieutenant in the Soviet Navy, I became an illegal—I used faked papers to enlist in the U.S. Navy. Spent six years on cans and flattops. I could pull my time on you, Mr. Forte."

Forte regarded Grimm thoughtfully, more at sea than ever.

"Be specific, Nick—what can we do about the Russians?" the president repeated.

"Very well." He took the cigarette from between his lips, flicked off the ash in his coffee cup, and took a deep drag.

"From earliest times, the Russians have been a conservative people, like peasants everywhere. They're not risk-takers. They prefer the certainty of suffering to the risks of revolt. They bury their rubles and kopeks under the apple tree rather than gamble them on a turn of the cards. They'd rather fight a bear than grapple with

a new idea. In war, they never take the offensive unless they are three hundred percent sure of winning.
By July 2001, they will be in that pleasant situation if
you sign the Washington Protocols. It's as simple as
that."

"And if I don't?"

"But you *will*. Thanks to the press campaign of Mr.
Forte's colleagues, which will cater so sedulously to the
Americans' craving for peace, you'll have no choice
but to sign."

"In that case, there's no way to avoid a Russian invasion in 2001."

"There *is* a way. The Soviet fleet will arrive six or
seven months from now on the trial summer cruise.
The Soviets will be on their best behavior, to convince
the Americans of their peaceful intent. If this façade
can be shattered, if the Americans can be made to see
that the pearly smile conceals a sharp set of bear's
teeth, then perhaps your countrymen will forget their
television programs and ball games and Big Macs long
enough to put their defenses in order. Only a dramatic
incident, an incident that lays bare Russia's true character, can save your country now."

"A dramatic incident," Forte mused. "Like what?"

"Do you recall the *Panay?*"

"No."

"No. That would be before your time. During the
Japanese struggle to conquer China in the 1930s, the
invader found the presence of American warships on the
China station an annoyance and an embarrassment. As
a hint to keep their distance, a Japanese warplane 'ac-
cidentally' dropped a bomb on the U.S.S. *Augusta,*
killing a sailor. Their 'apology' was accepted, but the
Americans remained. Another incident was arranged,
the bombardment of the American river gunboat, the
Panay, on the Yangtse. In this incident, two American
sailors were killed. Again an 'apology,' but the agres-
sion was so blatant that it produced a nationwide wave
of outrage, entirely unanticipated by the Japanese. The

American anti-Japanese policy, the embargo on arms and oil, the internment of Japanese during World War II—all these had their inception in the bombing of a simple gunboat."

"I'll take your word for it," Forte said. "So what?"

Admiral Nikolai Vasilievich Grimm reached for another cigarette, took his time about lighting it, and let the silence build. Finally he looked Gwillam Forte in the eye.

"If such an effect could be produced by the bombardment of a riverboat, just think what one might do with a battleship."

8 JANUARY 1998

IT HAD BEEN THREE AND A HALF YEARS SINCE GWILLAM Forte set foot on the U.S.S. *Texas*. His hospital shipmates superintending the ship's rebirth were disappointed and resentful of his seeming disinterest in their work, he knew, but though he kept scheduling inspection trips, somehow they never materialized. Something about the ship made him nervous and apprehensive. Every time he thought of visiting it, a foreboding shadow seemed to close out the sun.

But since the conference with President Wynn a week earlier, he knew he could avoid the *Texas* no longer. The ship had been given one last mission, and it was up to Gwillam Forte to make her ready.

At 7:30 A.M. on the first raw, dirty, windy day after the White House conference, the kind of day that would discourage casual visitors, Forte's limousine pulled up to the *Texas* basin. The only figure visible on deck was that of Ski Modeljewski, in charge of hull painting. His chilled, cigarette-scarred face and hands, Forte reflected, bore a striking resemblance to the pitted, blue-gray exterior of the ship itself—except for the ironic smile that greeted him.

"About time you came for a look-see, *Captain.*"

Forte made an apologetic gesture. "You know how it is with us tycoons, Ski—affairs of state, momentous decisions, nations trembling at our every word—"

"And your secretary trembling on your lap—sure, I understand. Well, how's she look to you—the ship, not the secretary?"

"Same as always," Forte replied truthfully. "Awful."

Ski beamed. "If it looks the same after forty-one months of hard work, we're doing pretty good. Want a rundown?"

"That's what I'm here for."

"Right." Ski led the way down the gangway to the concrete pier. Beneath his hooded parka his shoulders were hunched against the cold drizzle. He extended a hand whose gnarled and misshapen knuckles said all there was to say about the methods of Vietcong interrogators. "If you look close at the water line," he said, "you just may notice how clean it looks below the surface. One group of engineers said that after we refinished the ship's bottom, we should attach fake algae and barnacles, make it look natural. But we took a vote, democratic-like, and I decided that the water is dirty enough to conceal any possible contrast with the way it was before."

"Anyway, why *fake* barnacles and algae?" asked Forte. "As I remember, the real stuff needed no encouragement."

Ski looked at him appraisingly. "You *are* out of touch. I'd better start at the beginning . . ."

In the beginning, a special access chamber was constructed and attached by an accordion umbilical to the tunnel air lock. This umbilical extended out to the bottom of the ship, where the chamber was held flush against the hull by electromagnets; a neoprene seal kept the water out once the accordion tube was pumped dry. The work crew then entered through the air lock, set up tubular-steel stages, and began the painstaking job of replacing the bottom paint.

The old paint was removed with organic solvents. The steel side and bottom plating, rough and pitted through nearly a century of corrosion, was ground down to the smooth texture of an optical lens. The rivets holding the plating to the hull stringers were drilled out, and replaced by the titanium equivalent of tree nails, holding the plates together by pressure, having been turned out .04 mm larger than the holes into which they were driven. Their exterior projection was then ground down to the level of the surrounding plate. Finally, an enormously powerful electrical charge was applied to the titanium plug and steel plate, causing a mutual migration of molecules from one metal to the other and resulting in a superstrength bond. When each section of hull was finished, it had the glassy smoothness of a funeral director's smile.

To this surface was applied, by ionic exchange, a very fine coating of an epoxy resin that not only excluded contact between metal and water but was itself only a few molecules thick. The surface was so smooth—far smoother than the polished steel beneath—that hull resistance was practically eliminated. The frictionless, laminar flow of water around the ship's hull, engineers computed, would increase the speed of the *Texas* by more than twelve knots at maximum speed, with no increase in power. The epoxy alone, bonded to the polished surface of the hull, in effect boosted the ship's speed more than fifty percent.

As for algae and barnacles, there were none to befoul the ship's bottom, causing a turbulent flow of water to reduce the vessel's speed. They couldn't survive, let alone reproduce, in the basin's waters, thanks to time-release canisters of algacides and molluscicides now anchored at intervals in its depths.

The stagnant water of the ship's basin was, as Ski noted, sufficiently murky to obscure the bottom's transformation from all but the most careful observation. The ship's exposed superstructure was another story. Similarly treated and covered with epoxy resin, it received several other coats of paint, the last one of the same old dirty blue-gray with which it had started.

At least, so it seemed. The blue-gray paint was essentially the same in optical reflectivity and grain, but chemically it was a totally new product, devised in the research labs of Sunshine Industries, Inc., especially for the *Texas*. Gwillam Forte himself had given his chemists the seed of the concept, from which grew a whole plant dedicated to the paint's manufacture. He had remarked one day to his chief chemist, Dr. Tom Lee, when they were discussing the exterior paint, that resonance might be the answer.

"You know that old gag about the soprano who hits A above high C, and the mirror shatters?"

"Sure."

"So make a paint that will shatter and flake off, when it's subjected to a high-frequency sound wave."

The chemist suppressed an urge to laugh. "You may be a crackerjack businessman, Will," he said, "but as a scientist . . . You see, glass is a noncrystalline but rigid substance that can, it is true, resonate when excited by the proper sound frequency. If the amplitude is sufficient, then the glass may indeed shatter. Paint, on the other hand, displays the essential features of a hot fudge sundae in this respect. There is no single frequency at which it will resonate. Given its structure, there can't be."

"Then change the structure," Gwillam Forte suggested coolly. "Change it fast, and change it right. I want a paint that can be made to flake off completely, instantly, and without residue. If resonance isn't the answer, then find out what is." He regarded the scientist with wintery eyes. "I'm counting on you, Dr. Lee."

Dr. Lee knew from the experience of others at SII

that if he met the challenge, his career would be secure. If he didn't, of course there was always his widowed sister's chicken farm. Dr. Lee loathed chickens.

Perhaps because of this aversion, he worked his staff round the clock until they perfected a paint that, surprisingly enough, did what Forte demanded. When subjected to a 180,000-volt jolt of electricity, it instantaneously atomized in the air.

". . . so that when the captain pulls that switch on the bridge," Ski was saying, "the whole damned ship is suddenly transformed from the dingy-gray monster you see now to a gleaming knight in shining armor. Just be wearing rubber-soled shoes when you pull that switch, though, or you'll be spread in a thin layer over southern Texas."

"Sounds great, Ski," Forte said abstractedly.

His mind was elsewhere, on the troubling cloud that had appeared the week before out of Russia. Time was now a crucial factor because of Russia's recent moves on the diplomatic front. The Millenary Celebrations were already a dead letter so far as the *Texas* was concerned, but a more important fate awaited it—if there was time.

"I suppose you're pretty near to finishing up?" he said.

"I'm on schedule, if that's what you mean. Need twenty-seven more months. The hull is completely repainted. Some of the rigging and superstructure has been treated. The rest remains to be done."

"Any problems?"

"Not really. Of course, we can't work topside on the scale we did below the water line. Up here we have to do a single square-meter patch at a time, under cover of darkness."

"What would you need to finish the job in, say, six months?"

"Ten more crews like the one I've got. Why?"

"Just asking . . ."

The engine room was Forte's next stop. Six Bureau

Express three-drum oil-fired boilers had been installed when the ship was converted from coal to oil back in 1925. They provided steam for two sets of four-cylinder triple-expansion engines that, even at the time they were newly built, were inferior to the steam-turbine engines used by most European navies. But fidelity to the original, not efficiency, was what Forte desired when the renovation began. Therefore the boilers, engines, and auxiliary gear had been dismantled piece by piece and removed to the SD-1 workshops, where the machinery was cleaned, repaired, and painstakingly reconstructed.

"Looks fine," Forte observed as he inspected the various improvements that had been wrought in the engine room. "How much time do you need to wrap it up?" he asked T. D. Roebuck, the man in charge.

"Twenty-six months. Right on schedule," he said proudly.

"If we put the engine room repairs under forced draft, how long would it take to put her back into commission?"

Roebuck considered.

"Oh, maybe thirteen or fourteen months. Why?"

"*That* long?" Forte was dismayed. Various other improvements could be dispensed with, but a ship couldn't move without engines.

"You see," Roebuck explained, "some of the connecting rods were in such sorry shape from metal fatigue that they flunked the tests last November. We could put them back as is, but they might fail if we ever got real steam up."

"Replace them."

"Can't. Spares don't exist for these old model engines."

"Then have them manufactured."

"We've looked into that. The only plants in this country capable of turning out shafts like these are backlogged with high-priority orders for the new missile frigates the Navy is working on."

"You're telling me we aren't going to get this old ship underway in under a year, no matter what?"

"That's what I'm telling you, Will."

"Thanks, T. D. Thanks a lot."

Forte's mood was still sour as he sought out Lincoln Bellamy, in charge of deck and bulkhead reconditioning.

"It was more complicated than I thought it would be," said Bellamy, when Forte asked him how the work was going. "For one thing, I had to go to your chemists for help."

"That's what they're paid for. What was the hitch?"

"You'll see. Now, take this stretch of deck. This is what I had to work with."

Kneeling, Gwillam Forte inspected the gritty gray surface. He grimaced. If it was a sacrilege to paint gleaming white holystoned oak decks, what had hell in store for those who slapped a layer of concrete on top? He rose.

"Nastiest gunk I ever saw," he said.

"Let's go sit and I'll tell you about it."

Forte followed Bellamy to two squat, fireplug-sized iron bitts around which hawsers were looped, holding the ship immobile in the slip.

Bellamy glanced casually toward the foretop, where a lookout scanned the mist-shrouded area around the ship.

The lookout could discern no sign of life except the two men sitting on the bitts far below him. He extended his arm, thumb up.

Bellamy nodded.

A sizable section of the deck at their feet was suddenly enveloped in a flash of blinding fire so hot it singed the nylon hairs on the back of Forte's right hand. When the smoke cleared a moment later, a neat square patch of concrete deck had vanished. In its place was pristine white holystoned planking.

"How the hell did you do *that?*"

Bellamy chuckled contentedly.

"You should have seen your face, Will. You looked as surprised as a senator who's passed a lie detector test."

"For a second I thought the Other Place had opened up and the Devil come to take me."

"That figures, because we had one devil of a time working it out. It was easy to remove the concrete and to sand down the deck to the original bare wood. But then we somehow had to transform the whole deck from concrete to white at the same moment the hull was transformed to white. The chemists said it couldn't be done."

"They always say that."

"Yeah. The hull paint, they said, ionizes and is dispersed by an electric charge. It wouldn't work with a wood base like oak. Anyway, they couldn't duplicate the toughness and texture of concrete."

"So?"

"So I threatened to take the problem to an outside consultant, quoting you as authority. After that they got to work. In a couple of months, they came up with this stuff. It *looks* thick and it *looks* as if its bonded to the deck. But actually it's several distinct layers of material. On the bottom, the holystoned deck, then on top of it a very thin vylar film. To the vylar film is bonded the top 'concrete' layer you see—about three-hundreths of an inch thick. When the top layer is ignited electronically, it flares up with considerable heat and flame, as you saw, but the vylar film protects the oak deck from scorching during the instant the heat and flame needs to disperse in the atmosphere."

"And the vylar film?"

"It decomposes in the heat of the burning 'concrete.' An instant later it crumbles to dust. In fact it's the vylar dust, not smoke, you saw just now. Nobody better be on deck at the time, though, or they'll have a hot foot they'll never recover from. . . ."

And so it went for the rest of the day. Forte inspected the main and secondary batteries, the AA batteries, radar and fire-control stations, bridge, and pilothouse. He inspected the motor launches and whaleboats and captain's gig and admiral's barge, and the hundreds of pieces of equipment and living and working spaces that had once accommodated two thousand men. The work had been done meticulously and with considerable imagination, and most of it was right on schedule.

In two years, at the present rate of progress, the *Texas* would be ready for the Texas Millenary Celebrations that Governor Traynor had recently decreed.

But if President Wynn had his way, in six months the ship would be at the bottom of the sea.

As he left the ship that rainy afternoon, Gwillam Forte still had not decided which would be its fate.

9 JANUARY 1998

"YOU'RE SAID TO BE THE BEST IN THE BUSINESS."

The four men on the other side of Forte's private bar in the depths of SD-1 smiled deprecatingly, but nobody raised a voice in protest. They *were* the best. Their combined salaries of more than $1.3 million a year, five doctorates, seven columns in *Who's Who,* and two Nobel Prizes attested to it. At various times in recent years, they had all occupied high government posts, and their Top Secret clearances had been one of the requisites for the consultancies Forte had offered them at fees they couldn't refuse.

Two of them had asked for Scotch on the rocks, one a glass of California white wine, and the other for any brand of non-American beer available, which proved

they were men of discernment as well as intellect.
Forte poured the drinks, wiped his hands on a towel,
and got right down to business: at something in excess
of three thousand dollars an hour, their time was too
valuable for chitchat.

"You've all read about the Washington Protocols?"
The four nodded.

"What do you think of them, Professor?" he asked
Dr. Edward T. Curry, the oldest and most distinguished
among them, a man recently retired as vice-president
for research and development for one of America's
leading aerospace companies.

"My wife is the political scientist in the family. She
thinks the protocols are the berries. Babbles about
'peace in our time' and similar nonsense."

"I gather you don't agree?"

Dr. Curry harrumphed. "Unmitigated imbecility.
Even from one's wife. Man is an aggressive animal—
one of the very few that fights merely for the fun of it.
Monday night football is proof. There won't be peace
in our time or anybody else's time, especially if the
president signs those protocols."

"Why not?"

"It sticks out a mile, doesn't it? The Russians shift
their agricultural labor to manufacturing, giving them
the capability to produce plowshares—which can
quickly be forged into swords. Meanwhile, we're all
down on the farm wading through pig shit to grow
grain for them, which they'll squirrel away for *den Tag*.
How can we be so dumb as to swallow that bilge?"

The others drank to that, none more deeply than old
Oxonian Dr. Herbert Chilton Fallows, naval architect
and strategist, who ventured a discreet "Hear! Hear!"
and begged to add that it wasn't just the economic
arrangements that disturbed him.

"Look here," he said, taking a cocktail napkin and
placing it flat on the bar. "Here's the United States,
surrounded mostly by sea. Here comes the Russian
fleet. According to the protocols, each year they will

visit Seattle, San Francisco, San Diego, Houston, New Orleans, Charleston, Washington, New York, and Boston." With his pen he inked nine dots on the periphery of the napkin.

"And which nine ports does the United States fleet call at in the Russian domain?" He took another napkin, and supplied it with nine dots, mostly at one side. "London, Le Havre, Oran, Barcelona, Naples, Pireaus, Istanbul, Tel Aviv, and Tripoli. Kindly observe the difference. The Russian fleet calls at points that almost surround the United States, no part of which is more than one hour by naval aircraft from one of these ports. Our fleet, on the other hand, never approaches the heartland of Mother Russia, which is several thousand miles inland. This bestows on them the capability of all sorts of mischief denied to us."

"Such as?"

"Oh . . . sneak atomic attacks from their carriers; sowing atomic bombs in the shallows on both coasts, so that radioactive mists would blanket the continent; poisoning our ground-water supplies with botulism or anthrax—any number of unpleasant things, in fact."

"Then we're agreed that the Washington Protocols shouldn't be signed?"

"Yes, I think we are," said Professor Hamilton Reed, whose specialties were higher mathematics and computer technology. "But they will be, you know. The nation wants it, and Wynn and his Congress will slide down the bear-greased poll of public opinion despite what I understand are their private reservations."

"Right," Forte said. "Now, the legislative timetable calls for Congressional hearings on the protocols beginning in March, just two months from now. Then while the Congress is in summer recess, the Soviet fleet arrives—the first of June, I believe—in Seattle. It will spend ten days in each port, coming to Houston the first week in July. The fleet winds up in Washington late August, when the Russian premier is to meet President

Wynn for the signing ceremony, after which the Senate is expected to ratify the protocols overwhelmingly.

"All this is contingent, as I see it, on the outcome of the fleet visit. Obviously, the Russians are going to behave like little Soviet gentlemen, to show America what fine, trustworthy fellows they are. But if we can jostle them off balance, make them show themselves for the cynical and nasty types they really are, the United States public will have second thoughts about the protocols. If they do, Wynn won't sign. It is imperative for our national security, as you all concede, that he does not . . . Gentlemen, I have asked you here to help me plan a surprise party for the Russian fleet."

He told them about the *Texas*, how it was being reconditioned to take part in the Texas Millenary Celebrations, and how it might, with their expert assistance, be the goad that would make the Russian bear say *Ouch!* and bare its claws.

"My God!" Emilio Salvatore protested. The physicist was on leave from the vice-presidency of the Warfare Systems Division of Allied Aircraft Corporation. "You're not talking about sending that old hulk out against the Russian fleet, are you? That would be an act of war."

"Not if it isn't armed."

"Then how—"

"What I want is a demonstration that *looks to them* like an act of war. The ship will roar out among them, at very high speed—speed, gentlemen, will be your number-one concern—shooting its guns in all directions. Its sudden appearance will disconcert, and its speed will discombobulate and terrify them in its unexpectedness, and the gunfire will, I fervently hope, prod them into firing back, before they realize that the barrage consists of blank saluting shells, and that the apparition of the ship among their fleet is merely a big Texas *hello!* I'm depending on surprise to stampede them into shooting off everything they have and sinking the old *Texas* before they tumble to the fact that it was only an elaborate and boisterous welcome."

The four men sipped their drinks, alone with their thoughts.

"Yes, that might work," one said finally.

Another added: "We'll film the whole hilarious episode and blanket the TV networks."

"They'll look like asses," said a third, "and what's more, villainous asses."

"Christ," Professor Reed said, warming to the idea, "I can see it now—that huge white ship whipping in between the columns of Russian men-of-war like a PT boat, flames leaping from its muzzles, the gunners— say! If the Russians are supposed to *sink* the *Texas,* what about the crew? Who would volunteer to sail her?"

"You, my dear Professor," said Forte gently. "You'll sail her. You and your little black boxes. There won't be a drop of American blood shed aboard the U.S.S. *Texas* and, if our idea works, anywhere else either, for a long, long time."

18 JANUARY 1998

SALT DOME-1 WAS ASWARM WITH TALENT, WITH AN admixture of genius and a leavening of imaginative madness. Much of the talent and genius had been accumulated over the years by Sunshine Industries, Inc., to fulfill its manufacturing commitments to the U.S. government in the fields of advanced weaponry, communications, high-speed surface transportation, and submarine propulsion. The pool of brains and tech-

nological skill had been augmented during the past
week by teams of bright young men—and a handful
of creative crackpots—temporarily seconded from their
regular work by the four experts Gwillam Forte brought
in to ramrod the *Texas* conversion, phase two.

Over the years, the SD-1 work force had settled down
into a comfortable routine, cushioned from layoffs by
long-term government contracts, made complacent by
high pay and ample time off, and deliberately paced
rather than hurried in order to assure the highest standards of production and quality control. Into this secure
world the outsiders came like a blast of arctic wind,
blowing away established methods and procedures,
sprinting rather than strolling, speaking in phrases
rather than sentences, holding frenzied corridor con-
ferences, drinking gallons of coffee, banging away two-
fingered at computer terminals far into the night, and
arguing and pleading and cajoling with, overruling,
ignoring, sneering at, commanding, warning, evading,
lecturing, and defying their nominal superiors according
to mood, their insubordination excused by the vast
amount of sound work they produced. They were forever building models—clay and mathematical and
balsa wood, proposing, testing, perfecting, and rejecting
theories, and leaving masses of shredded paper, dis-
carded hypotheses, empty coffee cups, and wounded
feelings in their wake.

Gwillam Forte, striding through the drafting rooms,
past the test stands, model basins, instrumentation center, and especially the canteen and bar, where it seemed
the really important business was being transacted, was
invigorated. He didn't know precisely what was going
on, but *something* was, and his scientists assured him
that the *Texas* would go down, not only in glory beneath the waters of the Houston Ship Channel as
planned, but in the annals of naval history as a ship
absolutely unique: a man-of-war that sank the enemy's
foreign policy without firing a shot.

On that point Forte had been adamant. There must

not be so much as a bullet hole in any of the Russian ships for them to cite as provocation for sinking the U.S.S. *Texas*. Nor could there be any armament capable of doing the slightest damage aboard the *Texas* when it slid down into the depths, for the depths of the channel were so inconsiderable—despite dredging so it could accommodate megatankers—that it would be easily accessible to inspection by frogmen.

"But there's the rub, Mr. Forte," demurred Emilio Salvatore, the young weapons specialist at a conference convened to discuss the subject. "There must be weapons aboard capable of inflicting major damage or your scenario won't hold water."

"No dice," Forte said firmly. "If we shoot real bullets at the Russians, they'd have every excuse to defend themselves by shooting back. That's the whole idea—that they sink a *defenseless* ship. A ship with guns popping off using real ammunition is scarcely defenseless."

"Very well, sir," Salvatore said, with the air of a professor explaining a simple truth to a backward pupil, "let us examine your scenario step by step and see where it leads us. As the Russian fleet steams slowly up-channel, in column formation because of the relative narrowness of the channel, and at respectable intervals to maximize the impact of the naval display on the spectators, the *Texas* breaks out of its basin. It—"

"That's right," Forte said, warming to the sight in his mind's eye. "It cuts its mooring lines, and backs down into an interval in the line of Russian ships. Then it takes off at high speed—how fast that will be we still don't know—and starts weaving among the slow-moving Russian ships. This calls for an extraordinary degree of maneuverability, by means also under discussion. But the *Texas*'s high speed, its cutting in and out among the Russian ships, firing blanks and making a terrific din, are going to spook the Russians into firing back and sinking the ship pronto."

"Why?" said Salvatore mildly.

"Why what?"

"Why are they going to fire back?"

"Because we're shooting at them, of course."

Salvatore coughed politely. He was a small, self-effacing man, dressed neatly in striped seersucker suit and a bow tie. His hairline mustache, smooth black hair, and Latin good looks were reminiscent of the 1920s gigolo, but his great romance was with weapons even more lethal than women.

"I beg your pardon, Mr. Forte, but your knowledge of surface warfare seems to date from World War II, if you will pardon my saying so. You see, these days a ship's commanding officer doesn't observe smoke issuing from enemy gun barrels, then immediately order his own to commence firing. First of all, he would be astounded, and certainly amused, to see anything as archaic as a naval cannon shooting in his direction. What his reaction would be when no explosion followed is difficult to predict, but I would assume that he— even a humorless Russian—would consider it a species of joke. Ordinary guns are too slow, too puny, to be a factor in today's warfare, you see. In any case, he would not order his own weapons to commence firing on the basis of visual evidence."

"And why not?" said Forte, his eyes narrowing.

"Because, had any projectile been fired, he would have a report of its origin, azimuth, and point of impact almost instantly from his radarmen, who are charged with tracking flying objects so that they can compute the trajectories of their own missiles to silence the batteries that fired at them. The Russian captain, lacking such a report, would check to see why he didn't receive it. The answer would come forthwith: because no projectile had been fired. In such a case, Mr. Forte, do you think that the captain would fire upon the *Texas?* Or would he, rather, conclude that he had, for whatever reason, been subjected to a series of realistic sound effects?"

Forte growled something unintelligible. He didn't like

being made a monkey of by a young twerp, especially in front of dozens of assorted staff, who were carefully avoiding his eye while they waited to see whether reason or pride would triumph.

In the winter of his life, Gwillam Forte had learned that pride, like summer, goeth before the fall.

"Very well, Mr. Salvatore, what do we do—spit at them?"

"Yes."

"What?"

"Just a little, mind you. You are the prime contractor for Elbows, and—"

"Now hold *on* a damned minute," Forte said, starting out of his chair. "We're not putting any Elbows on the *Texas*. Get that straight. Those gadgets are still in the Top Secret category, and even if the U.S. government permitted us to use them—which they wouldn't— I'd refuse. I want the Russians to sink the *Texas,* not vice versa."

Forte sat down, agitated by the thought. He had allowed Sunshine Industries to bid on and accept the contract for the electron-beam weapons before he realized just how destructive the things could be. In the testing cells, one of the circuit breakers failed at peak strength, and the beam had drilled a hole forty centimeters through the concrete protective shield and severed a technician's arm before they could shut down main power. And that had been only the first of a series of mishaps. Elbows made him nervous, and the less he had to do with it, the better.

"The scenario, as you've outlined it, Mr. Forte," Emilio Salvatore was saying, "leaves few alternatives to Elbows."

"No soap."

"If you'll kindly let me explain," the little Italian said with sudden asperity, "you'll understand what is involved."

Forte nodded curtly. He'd been made a fool of once; there was no reason to compound the folly.

"Real projectiles and missiles are excluded, for reasons we both know and appreciate. What does that leave us? One: lasers, which are relatively ineffective in the dense atmosphere. Two: proton guns, which the Russians possess, but on which we are only now making a beginning. Three: electron weapons, which we have fully developed."

Forte started to speak, then thought better of it. He sat back in his chair and moodily nibbled his artificial right index finger.

"Electron weapons are, as you know, quite lethal at short ranges. With sufficient power, they become correspondingly lethal at longer ranges. Now, Russian particle detection sensors are pretty well developed, but their instrumentation aboard ship is not integrated to the same degree as ours."

"What does *that* mean?"

"That means, one device discriminates the bearing of the beam, but another one entirely then locks onto the beam and calculates its strength. A third computes the range. It does this by measuring the width of the 'hole' that is burned through the air by the beam. Theoretically, this hole is of uniform width, from muzzle of the electron gun to target—that, after all, is the rationale of the weapon: an intense concentration of electrons along a single axis. In reality, the second-generation Elbows SII manufactures still has not been able fully to reduce the shotgun effect—that is, the beam spread—to zero. Therefore the farther the beam travels, the wider the 'hole' it burns in the atmosphere. The path is thus conical, not cylindrical, although the flare can be measured in angstrom units per meter. So you see, by measuring the width of the 'hole,' you can compute the range. That's simple enough, isn't it?"

Gwillam Forte said he understood, which indeed he very nearly did.

"Well, then," said Salvatore, smiling, "let's put one of your Elbows aboard the *Texas* and see how it works. As it passes the target ship, it shoots a stream of electrons. The beam, if focused correctly at a sufficiently close range, would burn a hole right into the Russian ship. But we deliberately leave the beam *not* focused. The shotgun effect is pronounced. The scattered electron beam burns no holes through anything, though it would give you a hell of a suntan, I'll admit. But notice, the power is the same, and the Russian detection apparatus registers that the incoming beam is at full strength and from such and such a direction; both these data are entirely accurate. Simultaneously, the third detection apparatus measures the range of the enemy ship by computing the width of the electron beam. The beam is degraded, wide; therefore the computer—which assumes the beam is focused—comes up with a much longer range—say, three thousand meters instead of three hundred—for the American ship. Are you with me, Mr. Forte?"

"Sure." Forte nodded.

"Of course you are. Now, then, all three data are transmitted to the bridge instantaneously. They tell the captain that a lethal charge of particles, from such and such a direction, is being directed at his ship. The range is still too great, however, for the beam to do any great damage.

"Now, the captain sees the *Texas* with his own two eyes, and his eyes tell him that it is closer—a lot closer—to three hundred meters than the three thousand the range finder reported. And it is firing a lethal beam at his ship. Something's wrong, but what? Either his radar ranging device is haywire or the focusing element on the Elbows firing at him is out of adjustment. He knows instantly that the radar report is wrong—his eyes tell him so. But, on the other hand, the spread of the enemy beam cannot be ignored. Why would an enemy deliberately fire an ineffective beam? Therefore, he reasons—and all this goes through his head in a split second—the enemy will quickly see that its beam is not having the desired deadly effect, and will adjust the beam's spread to zero, at which instant the Russian ship will be incinerated or cut in two.

"The Russian captain must act, and act at once, to save his ship. He'll order his own proton guns into action, and worry about second thoughts at some future date. *Ecco!* The *Texas,* hit by dozens of proton guns, goes to the bottom. Mission accomplished."

He folded his arms, and waited for Forte to voice the obvious objection.

It took some time in coming. Forte sat in his chair, his eyes on the floor, rehearsing the sequence of events. He went over what Salvatore had said three times. There didn't seem to be any holes in the argument.

"Yes," he said slowly, "maybe what you— *Hey!* What about the frogmen who'll go over the wreck after the *Texas* is sunk? If we fired projectiles, the empty shell casings would be evidence."

"True."

"Then how about the Elbows? They're a hell of a lot bigger than a shell casing."

"True. In fact, the Elbows carousel is about the size of a large wastebasket. Mostly electronic gear and wiring. It weighs exactly eighty-three pounds five ounces. We haven't decided on how to do it, exactly, but we're working on it."

"Working on what?"

"How to get rid of the Elbows units, of course."

"Can't be done," Forte said categorically, glad to find an objection to using the beam weapons.

"On the contrary, we have four foolproof methods already designed and under test. Merely a matter of choosing the best one. As a matter of fact, I thought of a fifth only this morning."

"While drinking it?"

Salvatore laughed dutifully. "You see, when the ship sinks, a water-sensitive timer set for, say, twelve hours, begins running. The Russians won't send down frogmen immediately, for fear of running into booby traps. They'll wait until daylight. So we'll have all night to get rid of the Elbows carousels. When the twelve-hour time period elapses, at two in the morning, say, an encapsulated balloon inflates from a bottle of compressed helium gas. When fully inflated, it will trigger explosive bolts to fire, severing the Elbows carousel from its foundation on the deck. The balloon shoots to the surface, with the carousel on its tether, and right on up into the dark night sky. The prevailing winds carry the carousels far inland. There a second explosive charge, set to go off at twenty thousand feet, distributes the wreckage over five square miles of farmland, safe from detection by the enemy. Of course, it might kill a few cows. How does that sound?"

"Pretty fancy, if somewhat hard on the cows. Do you think it will work?"

" 'Oh, it'll work all right. I tested it this morning in computer simulations. But the other four ideas are better. The point is, whichever one we use, the Russian frogmen will find nothing to justify having sunk the *Texas*. That's what counts, isn't it?"

"It is."

"Well?"

Forte smiled grimly. "Shoot!"

19 JANUARY 1998

SPEED.

One word said it all. Without blazing speed, the sudden apparition of the *Texas,* even with Elbows blazing, wasn't likely to inspire the panic that would ensure a furious Russian bombardment. And only the sinking of the flagship of the Texas Navy would arouse the bitter condemnation of Russia that President Wilson Wynn was counting on to support him in his rejection of the booby-trapped Washington Protocols. Speed they had to have.

They didn't have it.

This realization became depressingly clear as the team of naval architects and propulsion experts, led by Dr. Herbert Chilton Fallows, toured the engine and boiler rooms of the *Texas*. T. D. Roebuck's assessment that it would be twenty-six more months before the propulsion train was again operative was borne out by the extreme disorder of the below-decks spaces. Huge valves, snarled hosing, gear boxes, stacks of pipe, parts of a disemboweled turbine, chain hoists, a disassembled pump, and severed multi-colored wiring hanging from the overhead formed an almost impenetrable jungle of litter in the narrow passageways through the machinery. From a boiler a cloud of acrid smoke issued as welders labored to reinforce the lining where hairline cracks had appeared. At a makeshift table of two-by-fours, three engineers tried to make sense of a blueprint. In the next compartment, a shipfitter was heating a two-gallon coffee pot with a blowtorch. To a layman's eye, everywhere was confusion, disorder, pools of water from overhead leaks, work half done and abandoned. But to Fallows and his companions, everything made sense and seemed to be proceeding with an efficiency they could do little to improve upon. In their mind's eye, they could visualize what it would look like twenty-six months hence. It would be a vast improvement over previous design and performance. Still, it wouldn't be anything like good enough. Despite all the innovations and refinements in the engine room and laminar-flow hull, the old *Texas* wouldn't steam at above thirty-five knots flank speed. That was fast for even a new man-of-war—but not fast enough, by a long shot.

Back in SD-1, Fallows convened his assistants in the cafeteria. He pulled a crumpled paper from his pocket. "Got this from the naval attaché at our embassy in Moscow, via Washington this morning. Says: 'Best information now available indicates Presidium will send newly formed Seventeenth High Seas Fleet to American waters on courtesy visit preceding signing of Washington Protocols. Seventeenth Fleet consisting of newest and most powerful Red units, presently includes the following: the super–battle cruiser *Karl Marx,* 76,000 tons; helicopter carriers *Beria, Yezhov,* and *Zinoviev;* aircraft carriers *Dzerzhinsky* and *Andropov;* six missile cruisers; twelve Kura-class destroyers; and a communications ship, two fleet tankers, two mine sweepers, one amphibious support ship, three attack submarines, and four supply ships. The auxiliaries are expected to lie off shore and take no part in port calls. Updates will be filed as compiled.'

"That's our competition, gentlemen: twenty-four of the most modern, fastest ships afloat, not counting support ships—Serdyuk, you're the house expert on the Soviet Navy. What is the speed of the fastest ships that will come calling?"

The small, bald, bespectacled Ivan Serdyuk put down his coffee. "The Kura-class destroyers are the fastest afloat. They've been clocked at fifty-three knots in a moderate sea. Analysts believe they can make up to sixty knots. Even the *Karl Marx* can exceed thirty-three knots, and it is the slowest of the ships you've named."

"And the *Texas may* make thirty-five knots," Fallows said. "Well, there's the problem in a nutshell. Unless we can somehow put a much larger press of canvas on that old scow, somehow beef up the speed fifty percent or more, we won't be doing the job we're being paid to do."

Bitter laughter greeted his solemn words.

"You're asking for heaven—tomorrow," one of his assistants commented drily. "Increments in speed of this type of ship have been at the rate of about one knot every seven years over the past century, as you know better than anybody. Yet you want us to add something like thirty knots to the speed of that bloody bucket of rust within four months. With all due respect, Dr. Fallows, you're barmy."

Fallows nodded. "You're right—I'm barmy. Still, we're going to do it. Start thinking . . ."

In the nonstop brainstorming sessions that continued through the week, the first thought upon which all could agree was that the present propulsion system had to be scrapped outright. For one, it could not be reassembled anywhere near the deadline. And even if it were, the screws weren't designed for higher speeds: whatever gain was achieved in increased speeds of shaft rotation would be canceled out by cavitation. One engineer, with a taste for overkill, had even computed that, with a shaft speed sufficient to propel the ship at only twenty-nine knots, the vibration of the screws would shake the ship apart.

Something radically different was required. Furthermore, whatever solution was found had to be absolutely and irrefutably practical, for while there would be time for computer-model simulations, there would be none for scale-model tests. It had to be right the first time.

A bright young engineer, Leften Stravrianos, a refugee from Turkey, came to the morning conference one day with the galley proofs of a yet unpublished scientific paper that purported to prove that extremely high-speed air jets, thrusting downward from the periphery of a vehicle, would replace the heavy, inefficient plastic aprons used in ground-effect machines. According to the paper's calculations, there appeared to be no theoretical limit to the weight such GEMs could support.

"That's antedeluvian," Fallows scoffed. "It's been tried in laboratories and in the field. It doesn't work. If I had time, I could spend two or three hours telling you why it doesn't— Next screwball, front and center!"

"You've got a closed mind, boss," Stavrianos said stiffly. "Look, this is really the stuff. Instead of directing the jets downward at ninety degrees, they're angled inward 3.7 degrees. The proper deviation from the vertical was discovered when the researchers tried fore-and-aft deviations. So far, they haven't been able to establish any theoretical basis at all for the results, but talk about synergism, why—"

"Here, let me see that," Fallows said impatiently. He grabbed the paper from the young man's hand and rapidly scanned the dense lines of text. At first, he punctuated his reading with a muttered "Twaddle," or "Nonsense!" or "God preserve us!" But after a time he fell silent, absorbed in the experimental data. He strode over to the nearest computer terminal and busied himself for the next ten minutes checking out the computations in the article.

"Well, I'm a monkey's uncle," he confessed finally. "That is something else. Interesting—very interesting. I'll hang on to this for a while, Leff, if you don't mind."

"Then we use it?" Stavrianos's smile brightened his dark Mediterranean countenance.

Dr. Fallows sidestepped the question and addressed the group at large. "According to the author of this paper, some broad named Dr. Faith Hamilton—that's why I checked out the figures—I never take anything on faith—the speed and direction of the jet streams is such that when the main thrusters' air jets touch them, it curves back on itself hyperbolically, producing a turbulence that piles up under the machine in what seems to be a very controlled—and better yet, controllable—manner, supporting it as gently as if it were riding along on glass. A real magic carpet, *if* we can believe the experimental data. The math is all right, I can attest to that. But the real kicker is this: la Hamilton says that it takes only 22 percent of the energy expended by a state-of-the-art GEM to produce the maximum hypothesized speed." He returned to the computer keyboard and made a few entries. "Unless I'm way off base, this could work on the *Texas*. We could squeeze speeds of nearly fifty-eight knots out of the old wagon, depending of course on the size of the power plant. And it would operate, naturally, across dry land as well as water, although I'd hate to be within a country mile when that baby started through a forest of ponderosa pine." His smile was wistful as he visualized the old battleship plowing across the landscape like a giant bulldozer from another world.

"We use it?" said Stavrianos again.

"No."

"But you just said—"

"I said, 'Unless I'm way off base.' Despite the consuming faith of all present in my infallibility, I *have* missed guesses—oh, perhaps once or twice in a long lifetime. But this—it's never been tried outside the laboratory. What if we convert the old *Texas* to a GEM and it just sits there, making noises like a vacuum sweeper? If that happens, the Russian fleet won't be the only thing red around here— Any other geniuses to be heard from this morning?" he inquired sweetly.

There was, as usual, no shortage of them. One proposed to convert the *Texas* to a hydrofoil. Mount huge blades that could be deployed horizontally once the ship was in the channel, and then conventional power could be applied to raise the ship up on the blades, reducing water friction against the hull to the extent that speed would be increased nearly threefold. He had the figures to prove it.

Dr. Fallows examined the figures and pronounced them beautiful.

"Trouble is," he went on, "you're talking about a five-year project."

First there was the question of designing, testing, forging, and fitting the huge underwater foils, a task of much greater magnitude than simply forging new connecting rods, and one that could hardly be carried out in secret. Second, the machinery to manipulate huge blades at high speed didn't yet exist. Third, where would the fins be installed? Installation would require transfer of the *Texas* to a graving dock, for no floating drydock in service could accommodate it. Russian satellites would pick it up before it left its slip, and where would the surprise be *then?* And finally, even if the foils were installed, and a computerized guidance system developed to control them, even if the ship were assumed to be balanced without dock and sea trials, there still remained the matter of propulsion.

Propulsion. They always came back to it, empty-handed . . .

A week passed. Ten days. Two weeks, and they were no closer to a solution than when they had begun. Dr. Fallows, hounded almost daily by Gwillam Forte, finally had to confess that not only had no solution been found, but none was in sight.

"There must be," Forte said.

Dr. Fallows shook his head.

"Atomic power?"

"Well, of course, there's atomic power. But there is no shipboard power plant available in the United States that is big enough for the job. To produce the speed you require in the 34,000-ton *Texas* would take a power plant big enough to propel a 90,000-ton aircraft carrier. None is now abuilding."

"Submarine power plants?"

"Too small. All committed under current construction programs, anyway. You ought to know—you're a prime contractor."

Gwillam Forte considered the problem. "It's a question of priorities. I could go to the top."

"Still wouldn't solve the problem. As I said, the submarine power plants haven't the capacity we need."

"Would *two* of them do?"

"No."

"Four?"

Fallows broke into a smile. *"Now* you're talking. Could you really get four released?"

"It all depends on which the White House wants first—the *Texas* or those subs. Let's say, for the sake of argument, the *Texas* wins the toss. What then?"

"What stage of completion have they reached?"

"Two are in the test stands down here in SD-1. Two of the other five under contract are in the sub-assembly stage. They could be ready to install in two months or ten weeks."

"That's cutting it pretty close, but we could do it. . . . What next? There's only one way to go, Will. Conventional screw propulsion is out, and so are all the attractive but hopelessly esoteric alternatives my staff has been brainstorming. We have to go with the tried and tested."

"Which is?"

"Jet propulsion. Water jet. We can obtain the requisite power from the four reactors with a good margin to spare, I should imagine, although of course I haven't made any calculations yet. We'll install huge water intakes at the bow, and impeller turbines amidships, to shoot the water in two streams out the stern under tremendous pressure. For guidance, we remove the rudder and put in bow and stern thrusters port and starboard, also working on water jets. It's quiet, efficient, and, compared with the other ideas floating about, easy to install, as it minimizes parts and engineering. Need a lot of manpower, though."

"You'll get it. Can it achieve the speeds we need?"

"Yes, I'm glad you asked about that, because there's a piece of the puzzle that we've been pushing around that really doesn't fit the way you've been thinking."

"Oh?"

"It's this business of top speed. First, we must remember that all the Russian ships are going to be limited by the speed of the slowest. That's the *Karl Marx,* which can make a bit better than thirty-three knots. The top speeds of the other ships, since they will all be staying together in column formation, is irrelevant."

"That's true."

"Another thing: the *Texas* won't be encountering them on the high seas, where they will be going at top speed. On the contrary, they'll be in relatively narrow, calm, protected waters—the Houston Ship Channel. They'll be ascending the channel in stately procession, so that the natives can get an eyeful. That means at a relatively low speed—say, ten or eleven knots. Any craft moving at a speed three times that will seem to be flying. If the old *Texas* barrels through the Soviet fleet at fifty knots—and with nuclear power and water-jet propulsion I see no problem in attaining that—it'll look like a speedboat among coal barges."

"But you do think it'll work?"

"Hell, Will, I don't know. I'll certainly give it the old college try. Do you think you can get the White House to spring those nuclear power plants?"

"Hell, Chil, I don't know."

"But you'll give it the old college try?"

"Don't know how—never got past the seventh grade."

28 FEBRUARY 1998

"Hobe Caulkins is outside, sir. He'd like to speak with you."

"Tell him I've gone to Alaska," Gwilliam Forte grumbled.

"I told him that yesterday."

"Good. Tell him I'm still there."

"I did. He saw you get in the elevator this morning. He wants to welcome you back."

Forte sighed.

"Send him in."

He rose from behind his desk as a young man who looked as though he had just put down his hoe and dressed in his Sunday best shambled into the room. His brown hair was carelessly slicked down, his ankle showed a lot of white sock below the cuffs of blue trousers, and a button was missing from his beige sports jacket. He had freckles across the ridge of his nose, which went perfectly with the Huckleberry Finn grin and the wholesome aroma of country bumpkin. Forte wondered why he bothered with the yokel act: everybody knew he had graduated summa cum laude in political science from the University of Texas, bruised many a linebacker who imagined all quarterbacks to be fragile, and was a damned smart newspaperman.

"Have a chair, Hobart."

"Thanks, Mr. Forte." The cheerful young man sat down and draped a long leg over the arm. He looked around the spacious modern office. "Redecorated your office again, I see."

"Gives my secretary an excuse to get off the couch from time to time. What's on your mind besides the new décor, Hobe?"

Caulkins laughed apologetically. "Well, Mr. Forte, I've run into a little problem, and I thought you might be able to help me with it."

"Shoot," Forte said, wistfully wishing he could. Hobe Caulkins was the cleverest investigative reporter in Texas, and where he went, trouble followed. In his wake floated the debris of an implacable curiosity— divorces, hasty resignations, indictments, libel suits (rarely won), fist fights (rarely lost), sudden disappearances, suicides, and consent decrees. Anything that smacked of scandal was grist for his grinder, and the fatter the victim, the sharper the ax. He had never taken on Gwillam Forte before—not because he feared his connections or the clout of Forte's own *Houston Herald,* but simply because Forte had a reputation for straightforwardness and indifference to public opinion. Forte had never dodged the unpleasant truth that in business, as in love and war, where there are winners there must be losers. Forte did whatever was necessary to win, and made no apologies about it.

"Got a list of names here." The young man dipped into an inside pocket and extracted a notebook. "Thought you might be able to tell me something about them." He flipped it open and slid it across the glass-topped desk.

Forte glanced down the list. It contained twenty-one names, the names of veterans-hospital shipmates he had put in charge of the *Texas* restoration two years earlier. The only omissions were those of Lester Bates and Haig Gargurian, who had died the previous year.

"What about them?"

"Do you know them?"

"They're patients at the veterans hospital over on Old Spanish Trail. Yes, I know them."

"Anything special about them?"

"Plenty. They served their country and paid for the privilege with their limbs and their health. Their country has rewarded them with bed, board, and amnesia. The usual Tommy Atkins treatment—garbage disposal, American style."

"Tommy Atkins?"

"Kipling. Tommy Atkins is the nickname for the British soldier, and Rudyard Kipling had things to say about civilians 'making mock of uniforms that guard you while you sleep,' and how in peacetime 'it's Tommy this and Tommy that, and "Chuck him out, the brute!" But it's "Savior of 'is country," when the guns begin to shoot.'"

"Before my time. What else can you tell me about them?"

"Nothing."

"But they're working for you."

"If you want to know anything about them," Forte said, feeling his lips tighten, "they're the people to talk to."

"They won't talk to me."

Forte shrugged.

Hobe Caulkins's eyes hardened. "It's going to be that simple, Mr. Forte. They may be involved in activities adversely affecting the national interest. And that involves you, because they are on your payroll."

"So are approximately 8,300 other people, at latest count. Are you suggesting that Sunshine Industries, Inc., is working against the national interest? Because if you are, you should tell the Department of Defense right away: I have $2.3 billion in prime defense contracts, and you wouldn't want them to worry, would you?"

"I wouldn't know about—"

"I'm busy, Caulkins. Get down to cases or get out."

Caulkins retrieved his notebook and flipped a page. "Okay. These twenty-one men are veterans of foreign wars. They all have horrible, disabling wounds. They range in age from forty-three to seventy-eight, and have hope neither of full recovery nor of leading full, useful lives on the outside.

"Second, for some time they've been observed passing regularly through the main gate to your La Porte property. On that property is located Sunshine Industries' underground manufacturing and research facility, SD-1."

"Not to mention the barge landing on the Houston Ship Channel, a 65,000-barrel-per-day refinery, a cat-cracker, and a PVC factory. Not a horse- and cattle-breeding spread, El Caballejo. After all, that property's 960 acres."

"But we both know they're going down to SD-1, don't we, Mr. Forte?" Caulkins winked conspiratorially. "And in the bowels of SD–1 you do atomic research and weapons development."

"That's classified information." Forte's stomach muscles were tightening.

"Sue me. You can always claim I was a Russian spy. Third, I've discovered that the nearest relatives of every one of these veterans I've checked on have been receiving substantial cash payments each month.

I guess I don't have to tell you the checks are drawn on Sunshine Industries, do I?"

"Where did you get that information, Caulkins?"

"Informed sources."

"Care to name them?"

Caulkins laughed good-naturedly. "With all due respect, go to hell, Mr. Forte. Where was I?"

"Fifth," said Forte, with a malicious twinkle in his eye, "as in that bottle of Scotch over in the bar, in case you need inspiration."

The newspaperman studied the ceiling. "Fourth, my informed sources tell me that five of these veterans have developed a sudden interest in atomic energy. They've been boning up on the subject from reference books in the VA hospital library. . . . How'm I doing, Mr. Forte?"

You're getting warm, thought Gwillam Forte, getting cold as the implications of what Caulkins was saying sank in. There was nothing he had said so far he could use as a basis for a story, but there was enough to encourage him to continue prying. Forte had to head him off at the pass.

"So, what does all this signify to you, Caulkins?"

Caulkins scratched his head in feigned perplexity.

"Damned if I know. But a lot of interesting explanations spring to mind, which I owe to my readers to check out."

"For instance."

"Waaal, let's try this one for size— Everybody knows how you feel about the Washington Protocols. Your editorial writers froth at the mouth every day, making dire predictions of the demise of the West if they're signed. One of the provisions you most object to is that the protocols promise a tremendous revival of American agriculture, which everybody else believes to be a useful and sensible international division of labor, but which you pretend to see as the death of American industrial might."

"First sensible thing you've said today. Please continue."

"Now, if you wanted to sabotage the protocols before they had a chance to justify their promise of lasting world peace, what I've found out would go far to demonstrate that such a program of sabotage exists."

"How?"

"The veterans—they're expendable. They know it, and are willing to trade the last few painful years of their lives for assurance that their families will be well provided for after they die. You've been making that provision. Next, their sudden interest in atomic energy. Atomic radiation is invisible, and damned dangerous; Houston is the major American port of origin for overseas shipment of wheat and other food grains. Put these two facts together, and you get the suggestion that these men are somehow involved in secret research— probably as guinea pigs—to poison that grain with atomic radiation, perhaps in order to sterilize the Russians and others who eat it, or give them cancer, and thus permit the gradual, painless, and undetectable elimination of those peoples you insist are our enemies. Your guinea pigs would—"

Forte gestured impatiently. "Quit talking nonsense. All this you're saying is plain preposterous, and you know it." Inwardly, Forte sighed with relief. Caulkins was only guessing. But at least he hadn't guessed the *Texas* connection. That was the important thing.

"Well, of *course* it's preposterous," Caulkins admitted easily, "but it's only one theory among many. One of them's got to be right, and none of them are pretty. I'll keep digging until I uncover the one that fits all the facts. Then I publish . . ."

The newspaperman's face was suddenly grim, and Forte knew why. Fear was a participant in every Caulkins interview. Digging was precisely what could not be permitted. The danger to national security of premature disclosure, by so much as a minute, of the *Texas* plan, overrode every personal consideration.

Though Forte respected, even liked, the young man immensely, for a moment he contemplated calling in several of his competent assistants and instructing them to take Mr. Hobart Caulkins to a remote and private place, and there keep him until sometime in August.

But there might be another way . . .

On the speed key in the kneehole of his desk, Forte's right hand began tapping out terse instructions. He knew Caulkins's character well. Money had no attraction for him. But he loved good living—excellent cuisine, praise of his column, creature comforts—and especially the company of lovely women who gave him these things. Before Caulkins had finished reminding Forte of the implications of the revelations he intended to make, Forte's instructions were already being carried out.

"Well, now, Hobe," Forte said when the other settled back in his chair, his face flushed from his own eloquence, "that's some program. I wish I could convince you you're wasting your time."

"I'll bet you do. And now, if you'll excuse me, I'll be getting along to work on it. I've found that when I start floating a few facts in my column, readers begin phoning in. First thing you know, the dam breaks, and somebody's catching the next plane to Brazil. Hope it doesn't have to be you, Mr. Forte." He rose. "Thanks for seeing me."

"Would it help if we paid a call on those fellows to see exactly what it *is* they're doing at El Caballejo?"

"Oh, sure." Caulkins snorted. "I'll come back next week, and we'll drive out to see the production your scriptwriters have put together. No thanks."

"We'll go out right now, if you prefer."

"Huh?" said Caulkins, his hand on the doorknob.

"Miss Barker," Forte said over the intercom, "would you please bring in the medical files of those twenty-one veterans who have been coming out to El Caballejo lately?" He turned to Caulkins. "You'll want to look these over before you talk to the men. Data for your story."

"Yes, I guess I'd better have all the facts." Caulkins's tone was wary. He didn't know what Forte was trying to pull, but so long as Forte wasn't left alone to stage-manage his meeting with the veterans before it actually came off, he didn't see any harm in playing along.

Forte glanced at his watch as the svelte Miss Barker brought in the files and put them before Hobart Caulkins. It was twelve-fifteen.

By twelve-fifty Hobe Caulkins had leafed through fifteen of the files, occasionally jotting down notes in his book. Gwillam Forte continued his own paperwork, only occasionally glancing at his watch and noting with satisfaction that the minutes were slipping by. He calculated that preparations at El Caballejo could be completed within two hours at the most: the men could be mustered from the *Texas* inside of twenty minutes, and the other players in the drama he had ordered up for Hobe Caulkins summoned from various parts of Houston within an hour and a half. Already more than half an hour had passed. He went back to his company reports with the reassuring feeling that all was going well.

At precisely one o'clock a discreet knock on the door told him that the lunch he had ordered by speed key—he customarily ate nothing at noon at all—had arrived from the caterer.

"Come in!"

A uniformed waiter pushing a cart, followed by another with a table draped in crisp linen and a third with a straight-backed chair, entered in single file.

"Oh, I'm vairy sorry, sair," said the *maître*. "I deed not know you had ze company zees lunchtime. Shall I eenstruct the *cuisiniere* to send anozair—"

"No, Gustave, that won't be necessarry. I had a bit of an upset stomach this morning, and I'm going to settle for a bottle of soda water."

"C'est dommage! Because for lunch today we have brought you *Courgettes à la Grecque, Salade Cauchoise, Petits Soufflés aux Fromage, Raie au Beurre Noir, Queue de Boeuf aux Olives Noires avec des Épinards à la Crème,* and ferry special for you, zee—"

Gwillam Forte waved his hand.

"Take it away, Gustave," he said, observing Hobe Caulkins' trying not to drool. "Can't bear the thought of food."

"But, Monsieur—"

"Absolutely not."

"Perhaps your guest . . ." Gustave ventured.

Gwillam Forte seemed to remember that he was not, after all, alone. "Oh, sorry, Hobe—I didn't mean to—"

"Quite all right, Mr. Forte," Caulkins said stiffly.

"Would you care to—that is, if you don't mind taking potluck."

"Wouldn't think of it."

"You can snack while you're reading the rest of those files, Hobe. Got to keep Gustave honest, you know. Besides, it's a shame to waste food."

"Well . . ." Caulkins tucked the napkin under his chin and pulled a chair up to the table. "My mother always did tell her boy Hobe that it was a sin and a shame to waste good food . . ."

At El Caballejo ranch an hour and a half later, Hobe Caulkins stepped out of the elevator on the basement level, and into a hash fiend's vision of an Arabian Nights harem.

In the center of the room a fountain sprayed scented, multicolored water into the air, its mist mixing with the aroma of expensive cigars whose smoke floated languidly about the room in swirling layers. The floor was carpeted with a lush pile so thick that walking was like wading through water. At one side arose a convivial medley of tinkling glasses, the full-throated voice of a man telling an off-color story, the giggle of appreciative female laughter.

Caulkins could just make out, through the smoke

and flashing lights interrupted by opaque slashes of absolute darkness, the figures of seven people. In a cluster at the long mahogany bar were two men—old men—and five women.

And what women! Unconsciously, Caulkins licked his lips. He had never seen five such lovely creatures all at once outside a chorus line. In fact, judging by their meager attire and abundant bosom, they may well have just stepped down from the stage. Everybody seemed to be having a wonderful time.

On low leather divans scattered around the room, a lot of interesting business seemed to be going on, but the lights were so faint that it was impossible to tell just what it was. Caulkins now appreciated the wisdom of the flashing lights, apparently directed toward new arrivals to distract their minds while they were getting into the spirit of things.

There was definitely no lack of spirits, as was evident when Gwillam Forte led him to the bar and invited him to name his poison. The glass shelves behind the bar were fully five meters long and contained every alcoholic beverage Caulkins had ever heard of, and a good many he hadn't.

A young shapely woman wearing high heels and not much else appeared at his elbow with a large tray of coronas, diplomaticos, partagas, belvederes, pyramides, cheroots, Madrigals, Havanas, and other aromatic cigars. He chose an aristocratic Montecristo, accepted a light from the grave, white-waistcoated barman, and took a deep draught of the incredible smooth-textured Scotch the barman produced with the next flourish. He felt it might clear his head of the perplexing thoughts that were chasing one another through it.

He had been so *sure*. All the evidence, all his clever deductions, had pointed to the existence of some diabolical conspiracy in which these men—he had already identified several present from their pictures in the dossiers supplied by Forte—were involved. And yet the evidence was wrong.

For the men, supposedly engaged in dark doings, were here—engaged in dark doings, all right, but hardly of a sinister kind. As if to drive home the falsity of his inferences, a sudden lull in the music allowed to slip through a snatch of conversation, or rather proposal, followed by a quick assent as a couple rose from their cushions and went unobtrusively toward the door at the far end of the room.

"Where does that go?" he asked, although the answer was self-evident from the tenor of the whispered suggestion he had overheard.

Instead of Forte's reply, another caressed his ears.

"Three guesses," intoned a husky, sardonic voice behind him.

He turned—and nearly fell off the barstool. Tall, with flawless skin and a regal bearing that could only have been the fruit of ballet training, she was at once erect and as supple as a serpent. Her lustrous eyes studied him with smoky suggestion, while the rise and fall of her breasts, with the majesty of the tides in the Bay of Fundy, mesmerized him.

"Say!" she said with a sudden, excited look of recognition. "You're Hobe Caulkins!"

He admitted it, shyly.

"Meet your greatest admirer in Texas—Lorry Vine," she said, extending a slim-fingered, exquisitely modeled hand. He took it, and felt an electric tingle pulse through his body. No woman had done that to him since he had learned about sex behind the barn at eleven in the morning of his life. He didn't hurry to release the hand.

"I just *love* your exposés," she was saying.

"You *do?*"

"Sure. Professional respect, you might say. I'm in the exposé business myself. Maybe you've heard of me—Lorry Vine?" Her lips parted in a suggestive curve, revealing almost too-perfect teeth.

Caulkins's heart was hammering hard enough to fracture a rib. With effort, he wrenched his eyes from her heaving breasts, and instead reexamined his assumptions. Obviously, he had done Gwillam Forte a grave injustice. These men had been in the last stages of depression not too long ago, according to their medical records. They could look forward to nothing but a lonely, bitter end. Forte, well known for his concern for his shipmates, had presumably observed their declining condition, and resolved to do something about it, in his inimitable, flamboyant way. What else could explain all this?

Caulkins felt like a fool. But he was a fair man, and he owed Forte an apology. He turned.

Forte wasn't there.

He turned back to Loretta Vine. *She* hadn't disappeared, at least.

"Where's Mr. Forte?" he asked.

Loretta Vine slid up on the barstool beside him. Her skirt parted to reveal a thigh—smooth, silky, swansdown soft—and one millimeter of bare hip. She didn't seem to notice his eyes on it. She looked at him for a long moment before answering. "Does it matter?" she whispered.

23 JUNE 1998

AT TEN-THIRTY ON THE EVENING OF 23 JUNE, GWILlam Forte kicked off his shoes and sank into his favorite armchair overlooking Houston from the big picture windows of his fifty-eighth-floor downtown penthouse. Reflecting on the day's activity, he decided that it had not all been unproductive.

It had begun at dawn with a flight to Austin for

breakfast with Governor Tom Traynor. Forte hadn't
looked forward to the interview, because he knew he
was going to have to lie to his friend, and while lying—
like dying—is one of life's realities, it made neither
experience more pleasant.

After their third cup of coffee, Governor Traynor
pushed back the breakfast dishes and unrolled the first
of the tight cylinder of plans and blueprints Forte had
brought along.

"What's all this about?" he said, running his eye
over the *Texas* deck diagrams and hull profiles, with
the specifications of each written in neat draftsman's
script in the margins. "You know I can't make head or
tail of all this."

Gwillam Forte pointed to the lower diagram. "That's
new. Those four nuclear reactors will power the ship.
We've eviscerated the engine rooms, removing boilers,
engines, drive shafts, and masses of auxiliary equipment to accommodate them. The rudder and screws
were also eliminated, as you see. Cleans the hull up
considerably."

"But those reactors are tiny little things," Traynor
protested. "Removing all that mass of metal must affect
the weight of the ship. Won't it ride higher in the water,
make it top-heavy, threaten it with capsizing?"

"Oh, yes, you can't make head or tail of all this,"
said Gwillam Forte with a wry face. "Like hell you
can't. But you're right. We've compensated for the re-
duction in weight by adding extra concrete and steel
shielding around each of those reactors. The weight
and balance remain substantially the same."

"And where did the reactors come from? I suppose
they were just lying around SD-1."

"More or less. They were made for the new 19,000-
ton Reagan-class submarines, but the Bureau of Ships
upgraded their tonnage to 27,000 to accommodate the
Ranger ICBMs the Air Force couldn't squeeze into
their budget. The new pig boats require larger power
plants, so the Department of Defense told us to put

these on ice. What safer place to store them than on a battleship?"

It was the first of what would be a whole parade of untruths that morning, but Cherokee Tom, being only part Indian, accepted it without reservation. He slapped Forte on the back. "You're a sly one, Gwillam. What if they send an inspector to check up?"

"I'll buy him off with a box seat at the next Oilers' game . . . Now, these four reactors will drive turbines pumping water in through bow scoops and expelling it at high speed through subsurface ports astern. Maneuvering is by means of bow and stern thrusters, port and starboard. They divert a portion of the propulsion stream, giving a turning radius and maneuverability like that of a speedboat."

"And speaking of speed . . . ?"

"Don't know yet. This can only be estimated so far by computer models. But we calculate speeds of up to sixty-two knots."

"That's one hundred kilometers an hour," marveled the governor. "If that doesn't grab the crowds, I don't know what will."

Maybe, thought Forte dismally, the sight of the *Texas* sinking beneath the waves of the channel under the proton guns of the Russian Seventeenth High Seas Fleet? He longed to tell his friend that the *Texas* wouldn't be around for any Texas Millenary Celebrations, that it had been drafted for a more important role in the national destinies. But of course he couldn't. President Wilson Wynn had entrusted him with the responsibility of creating an incident that would goad the Russians into a fatal belligerency, and that was a secret even the governor of Texas couldn't share.

Still, he felt mean and ashamed as the governor poured over the plans for the ship, discussed details that would by next month be completely academic, and praised Forte for the tremendous sacrifices in time and money he was making for the State of Texas.

"Don't thank me, Tom," he said, rolling up the

diagrams and unrolling another in its place. "I'm only doing what a normally patriotic American would do in my place. Don't forget that, when the time comes to remember."

"Never fear, Will," said Traynor heartily. "Now, then, what's all this?"

"The assembly site for the Texas National Guard."

Governor Traynor looked blank.

"Refresh me."

"You mentioned how beautiful it would be if the Texas National Guard could somehow be rung in as an honor guard for the *Texas?*"

"Yes, but what—"

"And you said you'd leave the details to me?"

"Sure. On the other—"

"Well, this is what my men have come up with during the past twenty months. I thought it would be a nice surprise for you."

"It's that, all right." Traynor laughed. "But what is it? It looks like a bunch of underground pipelines."

"It is—people pipelines. . . . When you came to me four years ago with your *Texas* brainstorm, you'll remember I had to obtain a Mole—one of those enormous machines used to bore subway tunnels—to provide access from SD-1 to the *Texas* basin about nine kilometers away."

"I remember."

"At the time we began, I put a study team to work out your suggestion about the Texas National Guard as honor guard for the *Texas*. This is the plan the team worked out. And today, the first phase of that plan is a reality—the 'pipelines.'

"The team first of all surveyed the channel banks between which the *Texas* will cruise upstream toward the city center. When the channel was deepened a few years ago, you may recall, most industry along the banks relocated some hundreds of yards inland in accordance with the new industrial development master plan. The banks are thus relatively unobstructed for a stretch of nearly three miles. Along each bank, come next June—just a year hence—will be erected grandstands twenty-eight tiers high. They will have a clear view of the channel. They'll be provided with parking facilities to the rear, equipped with food services, rest rooms, first-aid stations, and crowd-control officers' quarters beneath the stands. The whole complex will take 3,200 men five months to construct, and when it's all finished, and the TMC opens on the first of January, 2000, it will accommodate 2.8 million people simultaneously. You get first choice of seats."

"Fantastic!" exclaimed Governor Traynor. "I—I don't know what to say."

Say it ain't so, Joe, Forte thought sadly, because it ain't going to be. The plans were sound enough, but what's the use of a bowl without the cherries? By next June, the *Texas* would have been on the bottom of the channel for eleven months.

"That's what's going to be on top, although construction hasn't started yet, of course. What you're looking at is underneath the channel, and it's already completed. That Mole cost me a lot of money, and when we finished drilling the tunnel to the *Texas,* my staff was given the job of finding other uses for it. They got together with the TMC team and came up with this: two sets of subterranean tunnels running the width of the Houston Ship Channel, just ten feet below the bottom. The two sets are about one hundred meters apart—something to do with the geophysical properties of the bottom, although the separation is of no particular importance. Each set consists of three stacks of three tunnels, nine in all. Each tunnel in the set is separated from the next by only a few feet. Each tunnel is 5.8 meters in diameter."

"Making a total of eighteen tunnels beneath the channel," mused the governor. "I suppose it *would* take that many to transport 2.8 million people from one side of the channel to the other."

"People, hell," chuckled Forte. "No visitor is going to get near these tunnels."

"Huh?"

"One other detail will give you the tip-off: the center tunnel of each three-tier stack is provided with toilets, mess halls, emergency aid stations and a communications center."

Traynor shook his head. "No help, I'm afraid."

"In the dark, eh? Well, so is the public. Until the TMC's opening, nobody will be aware of their existence. Keeping the secret has been the toughest part of the project so far, in fact, because we had to shift something like 1.5 million cubic meters of soil from those tunnels, barge it down to Galveston Bay, and dump it during hours of darkness. When I think of the state and federal regulations we broke, I—"

"I'll square the rap for you, Will, if you'll just tell me what all this is in favor of."

"The Texas National Guard, Your Excellency—what else?"

"You're going to put the National Guard in those tunnels?"

"Right. A few companies at a time, from assembly points outside the city the night before the ceremonies begin. When the stands are full of your constituents, and you've cut the ribbon and the oratory declaring these proceedings open, the band will strike up 'The Eyes of Texas,' and from those tunnels will materialize the Texas National Guard. Ten abreast, one division will march up one side of the channel before the reviewing stand, the second division up the other, flags snapping in the breeze, cymbals clashing, Texans cheering. Can you visualize it?"

"Yeah," said Traynor in a reverential whisper. "I can see it. I can *see* it." He turned to Gwillam Forte and stuck out his hand. "I think you've just assured my election to the United States Senate, Will. I don't know how to thank you."

"Forget it, Tom," Forte said.

And he meant it.

Back at Hobby Airport in Houston at 10:30 A.M., Gwillam Forte found Station KATY–TV's news helicopter, *Fubar,* gassing up to cover a condominium fire in Pasadena. Since the *Houston Herald* owned the television station, and Forte owned the newspaper, he was able to persuade the pilot to drop him off at SD-1 en route to the fire, sparing the use of his private helicopter. He hadn't got rich by throwing his money around.

In that section of SD-1 devoted to the *Texas* project, he met by prearrangement with Emilio Salvatore in the model chamber, a large room occupied by two scale models of the U.S.S. *Texas* in cradles, side by side. Constructed on the scale of one to forty, they were nearly fifteen feet long, with the foremast truck lights reaching almost to the level of Forte's shoulders. To casual inspection, the models were identical, but close study would have revealed differences. Differences were the reason for the models: one represented the *Texas* before work had begun on her while the second incorporated every change, however minute, made since then. The technical men feared that small alterations in appearance dictated by the renovation, which might not be noticeable from day to day, in time would be noticeable in aerial photographs or to Russian high-resolution satellite reconnaissance from space. So long as the changes were, taken together, minuscule to the unaided eye, Forte's experts judged that they would not be detected, by friend or enemy.

"Notice anything?" Emilio asked, when the two men were alone.

Gwillam Forte looked from one model to the other. He shook his head.

"Look closer," prompted the weapons expert. "Look at the deck mounts for the Elbows carousels."

Forte bent down and inspected the tiny circular arrays of pale blue dots at intervals along the main deck, where the carousels would be anchored the night before the Russian fleet appeared on the Houston Ship Channel. Again he shook his head.

"Good," said Salvatore with satisfaction. "On the outboard side of each carousel, we've replaced sections of the scuppers with strips of a cobalt-manganese-nickel steel alloy. Rub it with your fingers."

Forte did so with the tips of the fingers of his artificial right hand, the more sensitive of the two.

"Feels rough."

"In full scale, that roughness resolves into thimble-size protuberances. They throw up a powerful magnetic field."

"What's the point?"

"I got to thinking, what if the Russians, instead of sinking the *Texas* out of hand, zeroed in on the Elbows? That's a possibility, you know, if they aim at the source of the electron beams firing at them. Then the Elbows would be knocked out, leaving the *Texas* afloat, and no international incident to torpedo the protocols."

"That's a risk, I suppose, but one we have to take."

"No, we don't. If they can't knock out our Elbows, they'll have to gun for the weapons platform—that is, sink the ship. The magnetic devices make sure they do."

"How?"

"Simple. These magnetic strips are energized by the ship's nuclear generators. When an enemy proton beam locks onto an Elbows carousel, it triggers activation of the magnetic field just in front of it, and the incoming particle beam is deflected."

"If it's deflected, it would hit another part of the ship."

"That's the idea, isn't it? But in reality, the deflected particles will do very little damage. Think of a powerful water jet directed against the side of a building—in this case the magnetic field: the jet breaks up into a shower of droplets that can drench you, but not knock you off your feet as the jet can."

"And what about our Elbows beam, when it hits that magnetic field?"

"Same thing. It's dispersed in a shower of relatively harmless radiation. But remember, that happens only when the enemy's proton guns are firing directly at a carousel. With seventy-two carousels firing at once from the *Texas,* in self-defense they'll have to sink the ship fast. Or, so they'll think in the panic of the moment."

"I see. Have you tested this setup?"

"Yes. We've installed a command station aboard the flag bridge on the *Texas*—well camouflaged and magnetically shielded in case of malfunction of our own Elbows. We've had a series of night tests at each of the carousels using an experimental proton gun of a design similar to the Russian model. The system works like a charm . . ."

But so did that of the Russian Seventeenth High Seas Fleet, Gwillam Forte reflected at his penthouse office in the *Houston Herald* building that afternoon, as he scanned the press reports of the fleet's visit to San Francisco, where it was currently anchored. As in Seattle, the fleet's previous port of call, the keynote of the Russians' behavior, in fact, *was* charm.

Russian sailors went ashore on liberty, in parties of ten, under the command of a commissioned officer and an English-speaking political adviser. They were immaculately turned out, politely attentive to the descriptions of the sights they were shown, drank nothing stronger than lemonade, and spoke, when they spoke at all, only in Marxian clichés about the brotherhood of man and the solidarity of the working masses. They toured museums, parks, and zoos, attended ball games—where they applauded both winner and loser impartially—ate sea food at Fisherman's Wharf, exposed yards of stainless-steel teeth to press photographers, and were always back aboard ship by nightfall. The local ladies of the night had no part of their custom, nor did the sin-and-skin palaces, waterfront bars, and gambling hells, the sailors pleading—honestly if disconsolately—short liberty and low pay.

Their reception by the burghers of Seattle and San Francisco had been equally restrained and aloof. These cities not only had experience with sailors long at sea and far from home but a growing suspicion that the Washington Protocols, which would be ceremonially signed at the conclusion of the fleet visit some weeks hence, were somehow booby-trapped. The East Coast press had been so unanimous in praise of the protocols that West Coast conservatives were convinced they must be dangerous. As a consequence, they treated the Russian sailors as they would messengers of death—with respect, but a respect filled with cold foreboding.

Between the Russians and the Americans, after two Seventeenth Fleet port calls, there had been neither friction nor affection, and Gwillam Forte, perhaps alone among Americans, didn't like it. The natural buoyancy of sailing men, which bubbles to the surface on liberty in fun and laughter, shattered beer halls and fistfights, dames and demolition, hangovers and fractured limbs, was being suppressed both by the ships' officers and their American hosts ashore. If the visit to San Diego proceeded with the same decorum and lack of incident, the U.S.S. *Texas* plan was in jeopardy. After all, the American people were not likely to believe the prim and mannerly men of the Soviet Navy capable of cold-bloodedly sinking a defenseless old man-of-war that had steamed out to offer them hospitality and greetings on behalf of the State of Texas. It would be completely at variance with the Russian behavior that they had already experienced first-hand. That the behavior was a well-rehearsed sham they would not pause to consider. The image, Gwillam Forte decided, would have to be altered, and at once, to conform with the true Soviet nature.

After Seattle and San Francisco, the Russians would expect the same coldly formal reception in San Diego. They would be prepared psychologically for a correct and civil welcome, but without smiles, friendly toasts, escorted tours, invitations to dine *en famille*.

Forte chuckled. They were in for a shock.

At four-ten that afternoon, Forte's Gulfstream IV rolled up to the VIP gate at the San Diego Airport. Waiting on the tarmac was Mayor Archibold Grace, who was there to do Gwillam Forte, a man he had never met but knew by reputation, a favor. He was more than willing to grant it sight unseen, for Gwillam Forte was known as a man who paid his debts most handsomely.

"Mr. Mayor," Forte said, stepping out of the plane and taking the other's proferred hand, "I'm Gwillam Forte, a man who's very much obliged to you for consenting to receive him on such short notice."

"Delighted, Mr. Forte." Grace beamed. "Welcome to our fair—"

He broke off as a pair of lovely long legs appeared in the doorway of the plane, and a moment later a breathtaking young woman in a linen suit of dazzling white descended, with a smile that made Grace forget that he was years past dreams populated by such lovely women.

"Lorry, may I present His Honor the Mayor, Mr. Archibold Grace," said Forte, leading her by the hand to hizzoner. "Mr. Mayor, this is Miss Loretta Vine, my social secretary."

Mayor Grace took her hand. He was an experienced shaker of hands, and managed to hold on to hers until they were inside the airport conference room seated

in club chairs opposite his, where he could keep
Loretta Vine fully in view.

So delicious was the sight of those long, slender,
well-bronzed legs that his mind kept wandering from
Gwillam Forte's presentation, although his politician's
instincts told him that Forte's words were sound and
reasonable. From time to time, when Forte paused,
Mayor Grace would nod encouragingly and make
noises of understanding and assent, and then let his
thoughts graze on greener pastures, just barely retain-
ing the thread of Forte's discourse.

In fact, Forte had come with a very reasonable request. It was that the City of San Diego show a rather
warmer and more human face to the Seventeenth High
Seas Fleet than it had been accorded in Seattle and San
Francisco. His motives in making the request were
strictly business: certain clauses in the Washington
Protocols, not yet made public, concerned trade concessions the Soviet Union was considering to benefit the
American economy. These concessions might be rescinded if the chill in their reception in American ports
continued. On the other hand, if the Russians were
really warmly received from now on—which Forte had
taken upon himself to ensure—all Americans would
benefit from Russia's gratitude. Washington, in turn,
would favor in the award of government contracts
those who facilitated this patriotic purpose.

The mayor saw, and saw clearly. Yes, of course he
would make the Russians feel welcome. Indeed, he
would immediately convene a committee of the heads
of colleges, social service agencies, fraternal organiza-
tions, civic groups, chambers of commerce, voters'
leagues, and the like and devise a program of official
and unofficial entertainment that would make the Russians realize they had found a second home. He would
lay out a welcome on as lavish a scale as Gwillam
Forte could wish. There was just one thing . . .

"Send the bills to me," Forte said. He had been waiting for the bite. "I'm an exsailor, and the drinks are on the house. I know what it's like to hit a great liberty port like San Diego without a pair of greenbacks to rub together. I want these young men to enjoy themselves to the hilt—get drunk, dance with the bears at the San Diego Zoo, see flicks being made in Hollywood, applaud the seals at Marineland applauding them, go dune-buggying on the Mojave Desert, loll on muscle beach at La Jolla, roll a joint, spend the night in the comforting arms of an understanding woman— Miss Vine will introduce a note of professionalism into this aspect of the operation to keep San Diego's maidenhood, so to speak, intact—in short, they're to have a week that will be the high point of their lives even if they all make admiral."

"Well, Mr. Forte," said Mayor Grace doubtfully, "the way you put it, it's going to run into a lot of money. We've had a lot of experience with fleet visits to San Diego, you know. The breakage, the . . ."

His voice faded as he strained to read the check Forte was writing on the briefcase balanced on his knees. Forte signed it with a flourish and handed it over.

Grace, who had read the check upside down, regretted he hadn't poor-mouthed with greater conviction, for the sum barely exceeded the rough estimate he had mentally made of the likely cost of the fleet visit. Then he read the check right side up, and saw that he had missed a zero.

"Well," he said, *"Well!* That's very handsome of you, Mr. Forte."

"I'll get it all back, with interest," Forte promised. "A week-long, nonstop, no-holds-barred party, for every man in the Soviet Seventeeth High Seas Fleet, from Admiral of the Fleet Grell down to Seaman Third Class Ivan Ivanovich—agreed?"

"When they leave port, they'll be so high they'll be lucky if they come down this side of Denver," Mayor Grace promised.

"You're sure you can handle it?"

"A lead-pipe cinch."

"Because if you need any help, Miss Vine can stay for a couple of weeks for moral support."

"On second thought . . ." Mayor Grace grinned like a little boy in ice-cream heaven.

It was nine-fifty Houston time when Gwillam Forte alighted from his plane at Hobby Airport, alone, and boarded his chopper for the heliport atop the *Herald* tower. As working days went, it was only slightly more vigorous than usual, but what it lacked in incident it more than made up for in expenditure. Still, it was money well spent. If the Washington Protocols were signed, it would be the beginning of the end of an independent United States, as well as the freedom and fortunes of all those who lived within its borders. He had done his part. Now all depended on Mayor Archibold Grace—and Lorry Vine.

He looked down on the lights of Houston from his fifty-eighth floor eyrie. That wasn't quite accurate, he reflected—with Lorry Vine in charge of the entertainments, the fate of the Soviet Seventeenth High Seas Fleet was chiseled in stone.

27 JUNE 1998

FORTE, DR. ED CURRY, AND DR. HERBERT FALLOWS were shucking off their white lab coats and hard hats in the shower room of the nuclear test area when they heard the commotion. A moment later the door burst open and a man stumbled in, shoved along by four stern-jawed security officers. He collapsed on the floor, a rivulet of blood trickling down his forehead, another larger stream from his nose. His face was puffy and bruised, and one sleeve of his white overall was torn at the shoulder.

Forte looked interrogatively at the security men.

"Spy, sir," said one of them, who also guarded his words.

"Let's have a look at him."

Two of the security men hauled the recumbent one to his feet. Clipped to his lapel was the standard SII radiation plaque, and beneath it a plasticized identification card. The picture of a sallow, fat-nosed man with pale-blue eyes matched his face. The name on the card was Izard T. Opal.

"Mr. Opal?" Gwillam Forte asked the man, who was sagging between the guards, as limp as spaghetti *al dente*.

Opal opened a puffy eye. "You'll answer for this, Forte."

One of the guards casually elbowed Opal in the ribs. He gasped with pain.

"*Mr.* Forte to you, cheese-head."

Opal set his lips in a firm line.

The guard repeated his recommendation, punctuating it with a sharp rap of his night stick on Opal's elbow. Opal fainted.

When he revived, his arm was throbbing with pain and his rib cage seemed to have caved in. Obduracy, he decided, must wait until he could try it on someone more impressionable than Gwillam Forte.

"This is illegal," he said through tumescent lips. "The law is explicit," he continued, warily eying the man with the sharp elbow and leaden night stick.

"Absolutely," Forte replied. "At the shaft head of SD-1 there is a sign that says 'Authorized Personnel Only.' You are here illegally."

"The law says—"

"The law down here is these gentlemen who have been interviewing you. I suggest you tell me what they wanted to know."

"Or else?" Opal said sarcastically, his nerve returning with the use of his arm. "You'll have your goons work me over some more?" Automatically he flinched, and felt foolish when nothing happened.

Forte laughed.

"They were just auditioning you for the company lacrosse team, Mr. Opal. You're free to leave."

The two men released him. Opal shook the wrinkles out of his rumpled clothes and drew himself up to his full five feet five inches.

"Thank you," he said stiffly.

He turned on his heel and marched out the door toward the principal manway, just around the turn in the passage.

Gwillam Forte and the others put their lab clothes in their lockers and were about to go when Izard T. Opal returned.

"They won't let me in the lift," he said plaintively. "They said that only authorized personnel are admitted."

"I warned you," Forte sighed. "This plant's strong on authorization. You need it to get into work spaces, to get a drink of water or a bite of food, to use the toilets. However, you're free to walk up and down the corridors, Mr. Opal."

Forever, Opal thought desperately. The old man's manner was mild enough, but beneath it was steel. He might last five or six hours treading water in this sea of hostility among men with elbows like pickaxes, but in the end he would have to capitulate.

Forte saw submission surfacing in Opal's watery eyes. He waited.

"I want to make a statement . . . My name is Izard T. Opal. *Dr.* Izard T. Opal, Regional Safety Engineer, Nuclear Regulatory Commission."

"Oh? What happened to Gluyas Grant?"

"You mean Gluyas *Gant*," Opal replied, sidestepping the trap. "He—ah—resigned. I was his assistant. I replaced him."

"I see."

Gluyas Gant was an uncommonly decent man and a fine engineer. If this little man got his job, it was probably through the usual government application— the application of a knife between the shoulder blades. The suspicion put an edge on Forte's voice.

"Then why didn't you come down here the way Gant did—apply for permission twenty-four hours in advance and pick up an escort at the manway head?"

"Because twenty-four hours is all you'd need to cover your tracks."

"What tracks?"

"Unauthorized hot-water emissions. You'd divert the hot water to another outlet. *Not* exploring this possibility was the kind of sloppy work that got Gant fired."

Opal had the earmarks of the authentic government snoop, but then so would a Soviet spy.

"I.D.," Forte snapped to one of the assistants who performed such chores.

At the nearest computer terminal, the assistant punched in the appropriate code.

"Step right up, Mr. Opal," invited Gwillam Forte. "You're on the air. If you're NRC, you know the procedure."

Opal went through the steps with accustomed ease. He sat down at the console, faced the screen, and intoned: "Izard T. Opal, Ph.D. class of 1988, State University of New York, South Bronx campus." He then turned his face to present a profile to the screen, at the same time placing his right hand flat on a glass plate beside the keyboard.

After an interval of a few seconds there appeared on the screen a series of still images showing Opal in various kinds of attire, ranging from swimming trunks—he had singularly unlovely fat knees—to street wear, with and without a hat. This was followed by a brief sequence showing Opal walking. A print-out then noted that his voiceprint and fingerprints checked, as did the analysis of his sweat and breath. "Subject," it said, was "confirmed as Izard T. Opal, born 12 January 1965, white Caucasian, blue eyes, brown hair, height 165 centimeters, weight 71 kilograms. Burn scar right forearm. Presently employed as Regional Safety Engineer, Texahoma District, Nuclear Regulatory Commission."

Opal turned to Forte with a self-righteous smirk.

"Satisfied?"

"Not since my fifth wife divorced me."

"Can I go now?"

"Let's talk about the hot-water emission first. Where did you detect it?"

"You know where," Opal replied nastily. "Nothing happens at Sunshine Industries you don't know about. But for the record, the temperature gradient in the Houston Ship Channel, as recorded by satellite infrared detection, indicates clearly that you're pumping cooling water into the channel just beneath the keel of the so-called flagship of the Texas Fleet. Gant didn't think of checking there."

"But *you* did. Now, that's what I call smart."

Opal beamed. His eyes came alight with smugness,

arrogance, and a flash of something else. Forte recognized it instantly: the unmistakable gleam of greed.

Forte relaxed. Once Opal proved he was in the pay of the NRC and not the Russians, Forte knew he had nothing to fear. By the time the violation citation for unauthorized emission of hot water had penetrated the successive layers of bureaucratic flab at the NRC, the *Texas* would have been at the bottom of the channel for months. But Forte's sudden perception of Izard T. Opal as a man who could be reasoned with made the solution to the problem even simpler.

"Let's go down to my office," Forte said with a wink, "where we can have a drink and discuss this matter like civilized human beings."

Izard T. Opal's ready acceptance of Forte's invitation told him he had not erred.

Later that afternoon, Dr. Fallows encountered Forte in the command center from which the computerized, crewless *Texas* would be directed in the "battle" against the Russians. Forte, like a boy with a new slingshot, was ensconced in the padded command chair, his helmet chin strap buckled tight, blipping the enemy as the Russian ships appeared in computerized simulations on the 360-degree panoramic screen that formed the wall of the circular chamber. The helmet incorporated variable-magnification lenses, an eye-tracking device, and microcircuitry that coupled eye movements with those of the servomotored Elbows carousels. The principle was ancient, the device having first been used by American helicopter gun-ship pilots in Vietnam as far back as the late 1960s, but as embodied on the *Texas* it was much refined. The thirty-six carousels on the port side of the ship swung around as one to the target at which Forte's eyes were directed, almost as quickly as his eye could move. He had only to press the firing pickle in his right hand for a stream of simulated electron beams to zap the targets that had engaged his eye.

"Who's winning?" an amused Dr. Fallows asked. He rather enjoyed playing with toys himself.

"I always win," Forte said, unstrapping the helmet. "It's the only principle I never violate."

"Even with Izard T. Opal?"

"Especially with Izard T. Opal."

"How much did he cost you, Will?"

Forte started to reply, then thought better of it.

"I think I'll pass that one, Herb. If I told you, you'd want a raise."

1 JULY 1998

DURING THE LAST DAYS OF JUNE, THE MOOD OF TEXAS turned sullen, paranoid, mean and a little crazy, and nowhere more so than in Houston.

Loving couples fought knock-down, drag-out battles. The rape rate quintupled; women ceased going abroad at night unless accompanied by an armed escort, and on the streets during daylight hours ostentatiously clutched black cylinders of Mace in sweaty hands. In schools, students were openly rebellious and teachers more than usually indifferent to their depredations, which in one case involved hallucinating seventh-graders, at midmorning recess, torching a Good Humor man and his truck. Local industrial production was off 36 percent due to absenteeism. The drunk tank at the city jail had to be emptied twice daily to make room for new arrivals. Automobile collisions, hit-and-runs, casual shootings, coronaries, teen-age runaways, petitions for divorce, wife-beatings, suicides, and armed robberies multiplied at a record rate. On 30 June,

Cherokee Tom Traynor put the Texas National Guard on alert to back up the local police and the Texas Rangers, already on duty in Houston.

For perhaps the only time since 1845 were the citizens of Texas in such close accord as to the cause of their discontent. Then it had been the approach of General Santa Ana's armies; today it was the approach of the Russian fleet.

Texans, echoing the editorial stand of the *Houston Herald* and other Forte-owned newspapers and television stations, had been at best suspicious of the Washington Protocols, at worst absolutely hostile. This was but natural, considering the composition of the population. White, Protestant, cattle-rasing, oil-drilling Texans reflexively rejected any position embraced by the Eastern establishment, and few initiatives had been so rapturously hailed by the establishment as the Washington Protocols. The Chicanos, Koreans, Vietnamese, Indians, Chinese, and recent immigrants who made up the rest of the state's population had too-recent experience with Russian policy to want to have any further connection with it. The views of both old and new elements were reinforced by the hair-raising accounts of the Soviet Seventeenth High Seas Fleet's "good-will" visit to San Diego during the last ten days of June.

The twenty-four ships anchored in San Diego harbor on the evening of 21 June, and the senior commanders were received at a sumptuous banquet ashore by a delegation of city fathers who assured them that San Diego, unlike Seattle and San Francisco, was waiting to greet officers and men like the prodigal son returned. Heartened and off-guard by this unexpected windfall of hospitality, Fleet Admiral Vladimir Grell gave orders to his captains to allow one-half their officers and one-third their enlisted men to go ashore at noon the next day, before the handsome offer was rescinded. The liberty parties totaled just under ten thousand men, most of whom were rounded up at gunpoint and re-

turned to their ships by armed patrols during the following ten days.

The day began sedately enough, with tight little
groups of sailors in freshly laundered whites fanning
out from the port area in search of the sailor's simple
pleasures. They quickly learned that pleasures in San
Diego were more abundant and available than they
could have dreamed, and best of all, they were free.
Taxis refused to accept payment, as did the restaurants,
which heaped their plates with seafood, and the bars
and lounges, which plied them with spiritous bever-
ages. By midafternoon, their anabasis had carried the
ten thousand from Chula Vista to Encinitas, from
Coronado to El Cajon. Considering their numbers, they
were relatively invisible during the course of the afternoon and early evening, for most had gravitated to the
myriad bars, where they were made welcome, and were
proceeding to drink their way through the available
stock of firewater. In this endeavor they were ably
assisted by the platoons of lissome women, and regi-
ments not so lissome, whom Lorry Vine had recruited
from up and down the coast to do what, after long
experience, came naturally.

Of liquor there was too much, of female companion-
ship too little—even Lorry Vine couldn't at such short
notice assemble more than a fraction of the host—or
rather, hostesses—required, and the disparity led to discussion between the haves and have-nots, in the best
Marxist dialectical tradition. By ten o'clock that fateful
day, 22 June, the wail of police and ambulance sirens
became continuous, as did the crash of shattering glass,
stentorian cursing in an assortment of Slavic and Altaic
languages, the crack of chair against skull, and, above
all the rest, the outraged howls of the damsels caught
in the cross fire. Such were the beginnings of that
muggy June night, and from that point onward the
fortunes of the great city of San Diego declined.

It was two days before order was restored, by the
combined police forces of neighboring cities of southern

California. (Admiral Grell wisely forbore to launch his
shore patrols into the maelstrom, fearing they would
be sucked into the melee in their turn.) Bloody, tattered survivors were flung into their whaleboats and
motor launches en route to the brigs aboard their
respective ships, which soon resembled so many floating
Black Holes of Calcutta. Some sailors had taken their
liberty literally, seeking it as far away as Des Moines,
Iowa, before being rounded up and brought back. The
city itself looked as if it had come through—only
barely—a typhoon. Mayor Archibold Grace was in
hiding, wondering bitterly whether the money he had
skimmed from Forte's bankroll before the descent of
the Slavs would be sufficient to put out a contract on
that eminent Texan's life.

Admiral Grell released to the press an excoriation of
the city of San Diego, which had with consummate
capitalist cunning provoked his blameless men into
riotous excesses, and hinted darkly that they had been
drugged, seduced, poisoned, debauched, and otherwise
abused by the scheming natives. With that, the Soviet
Seventeenth High Seas Fleet raised anchor and stood
out to sea.

The devastated and benumbed city tallied the cost of
its hospitality. With the results still incomplete, the
score stood at 2 murders, 76 rapes, 332 aggravated
assaults, 13 arsons, 20 kidnappings—mostly of teen-
aged girls—56 robberies with violence, uncounted
cases of public drunkenness and disorderly conduct,
and several thousand lesser misdemeanors such as child
abuse, micturating on and throwing bottles at pedes-
trians from hotel windows, driving stolen buses off
bridges, hijacking an airliner, pulling down statues in
public parks, defilement of churches and cemeteries,
and destruction, theft, burning, and looting of private
property valued at $33 million.

Gwillam Forte read the reports with both distress
and exhilaration. He grieved for the bereaved, and felt
a twinge of guilt for having been the author of their

misfortunes. On the other hand, viewed as realpolitik, a decisive victory had been won by making the fraudulent Washington Protocols politically unacceptable to all thinking Americans. Seen in this light, the costs had been negligible compared with the eventual, inevitable defeat and enslavement of the United States. It was thus with sanguine expectation that Forte awaited the outpouring of national indignation from the media, which would crystallize resistance among Americans against the Russian foe.

He waited in vain.

With the exception of his own newspaper and television chain and that of New Hampshire's J. D. Pascal, the media seemed to have taken its cue from TASS, blaming "rightist adventurers" and "cold-war mastodons" for inciting the impressionable young sailors of the Russian fleet to ungentlemanly behavior. Establishment editorialists attributed the tragedy of San Diego variously to youthful high spirits, the collision of cultures, tensions of shipboard life, and the innocent misunderstandings that must always arise at the interface of linguistic, social, and geographical disparities. None were so indelicate as to recall parallels of Soviet criminality and rapine in Berlin, Prague, Vienna, Warsaw, and Budapest in 1945 and thereafter.

By the end of the first week in July, except in California, where the Russians had been, and Texas, where they were headed, the San Diego 'events' had been obliterated from the American consciousness by the deluge of euphoric newspaper and television commentary on the benefits of prosperity that the Washington Protocols promised—just around the corner.

In Las Vegas, political pollsters were giving eight-to-one odds on a national consensus that would make the protocols law of the land by October, ushering in a new era of international relations and peaceful cooperation between the Russian and American blocs. At a press conference televised nationally, President Wynn stated that, as he had always done, he would respond to the will of his countrymen; when pressed, he admitted that, up to the present moment, that will was overwhelmingly in favor of the Washington Protocols.

He wasn't speaking for Texas.

In the State house in Austin, the legislature had gone into continuous executive session at noon on 24 June, when the true dimensions of the sack of San Diego became apparent. The lawmakers were of one mind concerning the imminent visit of the Soviet Seventeenth High Seas Fleet to Houston: they wanted it canceled. To allow the Russians to repeat their barbarities on the maidenhood and the business capital of the southwest was obviously unthinkable, especially in view of the refusal of the Russian high command to take any responsibility for the tragedy of San Diego—which practically guaranteed its repetition in Houston.

A resolution outlining the reasoning of the legislature, and respectfully requesting that the President of the United States change the venue of the Soviet fleet's visit to another site, was drafted, passed unanimously, endorsed by Governor Tom Traynor, and sent by hand of a confidential messenger to the White House.

The president read the missive with relief. Here was the first evidence of the existence of an organized, powerful, and vocal pressure group opposed to the Russian program of creeping conquest of America. A whole state, and a pivotal one, was on his side. California, too, had weighed in against the Russians. This antipathy could, if nurtured, be translated into active political resistance against the protocols. But even as President Wilson Wynn savored the thought, his political instincts told him Texan and Californian anger would not be enough for victory against the overwhelming influence on the electorate of the media, which had come down hard on the side of the Russian initiative. From this point of view, and incidentally that of the Californians and Texans, the situation would have to get worse—much worse—before it would get better.

The president took pen in hand, and using it like a coal scoop, shoveled salt into the open wound. The messenger who brought the Texans' courteous petition took back President Wynn's blistering response.

The president reminded the governor and legislature that when he, as president of the United States, had informed them of the Russian request that the Soviet Seventeenth High Seas Fleet pay a courtesy call at Houston, they had answered that Texas would be "honored and delighted to receive" the fleet with the "customary and generous hospitality for which Texas has been famed down through history." He declared that it was much too late in the day for the President of the United States to face the embarrassment of telling the Russians they would have to cancel their ten-day port call, disrupting their logistical arrangements and necessitating finding another port that could accommodate the fleet on short notice, an obvious impossibility. He observed that any disruption of plans now would imperil delicate negotiations between the two powers, and even jeopardize the signing of the Washington Protocols, which all thinking and patriotic Americans realized represented the only hope for a peaceful and secure future. He added that only small-minded and vicious men could doubt the friendship of the great Russian people and the benefits that would evolve upon closer cooperation with them. He warned that neither he nor other decent Americans would tolerate any break in the united front for peace by renegade troublemakers. He cautioned the Texans, saying that this matter transcended petty state interests, and indeed impinged upon foreign policy, reserved to the president and the Senate. He recalled the fate of Texas when, in 1864, it reaped the bitter harvest of sedition, and suggested that a short memory should not put Texas in a position to suffer the same tragedy once more.

*   *   *

The speaker of the Texas House of Representatives rose behind the lectern before the joint session of the legislature and ceremonially received the letter of the President of the United States from the courier. He slit the envelope and removed the message. The chamber was hushed as he scanned the single page and opened his mouth to begin reading. He closed it again, as his eyes swept the lines of text. His face flushed, then slowly paled.

He leaned over and whispered a few words to the clerk of the House, who got up and replaced the speaker at the lectern.

The speaker retired to the well of the House and took a seat. He remembered that the messenger who brought evil tidings to the king in olden times generally had his head cut off. He was afraid he wouldn't be so lucky.

8 JULY 1998

FOR SIX MONTHS—EVER SINCE HIS DISCUSSION WITH President Wynn and Nikolai Vasilievich Grimm— Gwillam Forte had heard the time's winged chariot hurrying near. In the past weeks, when it became apparent that no engineering miracle could be wrought that would give the *Texas* the blazing speed that must scare the Russians into sinking the ship in panic, the pressure had become unbearable. Forte was one of those who compulsively step on the lines on a sidewalk, though knowing it breaks his gait and slows his pace— and is stupid, to boot. So it was with the larger things in life, projects he had spawned, promises he had made:

they had, somehow or other, to be reconciled; until they were, each night he went to bed a miserable man.

He had promised Governor Traynor to make the U.S.S. *Texas* a spectacular symbol of a proud, progressive state. He broke that promise with another, one to President Wynn, to bait the Russians into sinking the *Texas*. The promises were irreconcilable.

But now the San Diego Outrage, as his headline writers called it, changed everything. American public opinion would now tilt aganst any dealing with Russia, reprieve the *Texas* to lead the Texas Millenary Celebrations, and save Forte from welshing on either of his promises. Anti-Russian feeling was at high pitch in the Statehouse, he knew, and it would spread like poison throughout America. By midweek, the President would cancel the fleet visits altogether, tear up the Washington Protocols draft, and thus buy time for the nation to put its defenses in order. With the Texas legislature still in secret session, he couldn't predict the exact sequence of events, but he was so confident of the final result that, when he slept that second night in July, for the first time in months he was not afflicted with nightmares.

The next morning, refreshed and filled with unaccustomed vigor, and the *Texas* on the back burner, he was ready to give full attention to urgent matters that had been piling up since that White House conference the last week of December.

His administrative assistant had thoughtfully arranged the problem files in his in-box in the order of priority, the toughest on top. When he saw the first, he almost wished himself back in SD-1 grappling with the problems of the *Texas*.

The folder was labeled "Stenco."

Stenco was the acronym for Satellite Technology and Extraterrestrial Nucleonics Company. Around the shop it was referred to as "Stinko," and there was no denying that it gave off a disagreeable odor.

Sunshine Industries had acquired Stenco when space technology had been full of promise and atomic fuels were the propellant of choice for maneuvering large structures in space during the building of agricolonies, powersats, and free-fall factories. But all such projects withered quickly in the shadow of the East-West armed-satellite confrontation in outer space. Stenco, always a bridesmaid, never a bride, stayed alive on hope and the expectation of lender banks that Gwillam Forte, with his riches, would eventually bail it out.

Forte had no such intention. He had never taken day-to-day charge of its activities or research—its projects were much too recondite for him to understand—and in the end, it was wise that he hadn't. For its company officers had begun to share his disenchantment despite—or perhaps because of—having acquired a majority interest in the company through the purchase of stock Forte was only too glad to sell. He had quietly reduced his holdings to their present level of 16 percent, sufficient to exercise control over the faltering company, but not enough to give him a bath if it went under.

When it went under. Persistent reports claimed the president of Stenco was, with the active collaboration of certain other officers, looting what cash remained in the till. Investigators from the Bureau of Internal Revenue, the state's Attorney's Office, and the Securities and Exchange Commission were sniffing around, holding perfumed handkerchiefs to their noses. It was only a matter of time until the chief thief grabbed his satchel and ran. Gwillam Forte could easily have replaced him. But executives who could turn Stenco around also knew that whoever occupied the executive hot seat when the sheriff came calling would spend a long time repenting it behind big doors that cast narrow shadows. A real hoodoo, Stenco.

It was after some minutes of idly shuffling through Stenco papers, his mind mostly elsewhere, that Gwillam Forte became aware that a voice at his elbow had been making sounds for what now seemed quite some time.

"Yes, Miss Barker?"

"It's a Mr. Opal, sir."

Gwillam Forte eyed his secretary's legs. They were long, slender, shapely, and, despite all their antiseptic excellences, extremely sexy. They must have won her the job; it couldn't have been her syntax.

"What's a Mr. Opal?" he asked.

Her jaw fell just enough to reveal a row of perfect teeth. He thought back. It may have been the teeth. And those lovely lips, which always seemed swollen with sleep.

"The man in my office," she stammered. "Izard T. Opal."

"Ah—that explains it. Push him in, preferably with a long stick."

She walked out, her hips swaying like ripe grain at harvest time. It could, Forte decided, have only been the hips. The reflection was brief, for this pleasant train of thought was abruptly derailed by the appearance of Dr. Izard T. Opal. A week's absence had not squared his rounded shoulders, or corrected his insolent stare, or straightened the vulpine curve of his lips. He was every bit as disagreeable to the eye as he had been the last time Forte saw him.

Forte rose and extended his hand with a smile. After all, the man was his guest. Perhaps he had come to make amends for his none-too-subtle blackmail a few days earlier.

"An unexpected pleasure, Dr. Opal," he said, batting exactly .500 in the truth department.

"Hi there, Will," Opal replied, causing the corners of Forte's smile to wilt.

Opal sat down without invitation, pulled a pack of cigarettes out of his pocket, and lit one. Gwillam Forte was a nonsmoker, and his antipathy was complete when Opal blew a plume of smoke in his direction. Forte decided that the man had come to put the bite on him again: his manner was that of a pimp making the rounds to collect the day's take.

"Care for coffee, Dr. Opal—or perhaps you'd prefer a drink?" He waved his hand at the rows of bottles and crystal behind sliding glass doors at the far end of the room.

Opal shook his head.

"I'm here on business."

"Business? I thought we concluded our business last week."

"That was last week's business. I'm here on this week's business."

"I see."

Opal examined the end of his cigarette. It seemed to annoy him.

"I guess you, with your scientists in white coats and big underground laboratories, think nobody else can do research—one of the little people like me, for instance."

Forte felt his choler rising. Those who identified themselves with the great faceless masses—the stock-in-trade of politicians and other charlatans—never failed to enrage him.

"What research have you been doing?" Forte enquired softly.

Opal puffed his cigarette and looked at Forte with a self-satisfied smirk.

"I knew you had something up your sleeve when you—" He tensed suddenly and looked about the room. Then he relaxed and with studied casualness took another drag on the cigarette. ". . . when you and I had that discussion."

"Personally, I'd put hot water pretty far down on the list of mortal sins," Forte observed.

"The government doesn't," Opal snapped.

"So you've reported the incident, after all?"

"Not yet."

"Why not?"

"You see, a few days ago I rented a helicopter and fitted it out with high-resolution infrared sensors. Then

I coupled it to the helicopter's own inertial navigation
system. I taped the output of both devices over a thirty-
square-kilometer search area around SD-1. I then ran
the tapes through the NRC computer and had a print-
out superimposed on a map of the channel area. What
do you think I found?"

"That a straight beats three-of-a-kind?" On the kneehole speed key he tapped out a message to his security
staff to have two men standing by outside his office.
He didn't have to specify that they be tough, mean,
and efficient: they all were.

"I found," Opal said, "that the thermal energy radi-
ated by the heat sinks you have registered with the
NRC for recirculation of nuclear reactor water in your
test units was close to zero. On the other hand, that
emanating from the *Texas* basin damn near busted the
readout."

"So? You knew that when you came calling on us
at SD-1 last week."

"Yes, but I hadn't checked the currents in the channel then. I did yesterday. For all practical purposes,
the channel is filled with dead water. And that changes
the whole picture."

"I don't see how."

"Come on, Will." Opal chuckled. "Of course you do.
I had naturally assumed that the reactor heat had been
carried far out into the channel by currents. But if the
currents don't exist, then the only explanation for temperature transfer of that magnitude is by *radiation,* not
convection. Heat radiation through water is a much
slower process than convection. That means that the
diversion of hot water has been going on—not days or
weeks, as you had led me to believe—but months."

"Pretty shrewd, Doctor."

"Just wait. . . . Early this morning I took a stroll
along the channel bank. I talked with some of the old-
timers there, asked about their catches lately. Surprising
thing, they told me—ever since January, fishing has im-

proved considerably in waters around the *Texas* basin.
They couldn't account for it. But *I* could: the heated
waters, particularly during winter and spring, had
caused a proliferation of macroscopic fauna and flora
on which fish live. I rented a boat and spent two hours
trolling along the channel. Didn't catch a thing, except
three little ones down near the *Texas*. Get the picture,
Will?"

"Draw it for me."

He did. . . .

According to Opal, creating a new cooling basin of
adequate dimensions for Sunshine Industries' nuclear-
reactor testing program would have meant the sacrifice
of a large land area adjacent to SD-1. Land in the area
was at a premium because of its proximity to the Houston Ship Channel. Rather than condemn valuable land,
Forte had drilled an underground conduit to the *Texas*
basin, where he thought it wouldn't be noticed. Except
of course, Dr. Opal admitted, by someone of extraordinary perspicacity. Somebody like Dr. Opal.

Forte breathed a silent sigh of relief. So the nasty
little man wasn't a threat to the *Texas* project after all.
National security was no longer at issue, since the
Washington Protocols were as good as dead, but those
four nuclear reactors aboard the *Texas* were something
the NRC had best not learn about.

Forte tapped out a message on the kneehole speed
key.

"I wish I had met you before you went to work for
the NRC," Forte said wistfully.

"Why?"

"Isn't it obvious? You're a fast thinker. Fast thinking
is what makes my business go. You don't think I built
Sunshine Industries all by myself, do you? No, indeed—
this empire was built by smart, resourceful, imaginative
men. About the only smart thing I did was recognize
them and hire them."

Dr. Izard T. Opal, who had come to the office with

the intention of talking about hard cash, was startled
into another train of thought.

"Well," he said, choosing his words with care, "I am
not, after all, *married* to the Nuclear Regulatory Commission. If ever the occasion arose that my special tal—"

The door opened, and an erect, distinguished gray-
haired man came in.

"Oh, I'm sorry, Mr. Forte," he apologized. "I didn't
realize you had company. Your appointment calender
was clear."

"Come on in, James," Forte said, introducing his
executive vice-president, James R. Rogette, to Opal.
"What's on your mind?"

"Oh, nothing that can't wait," he said, looking side-
wise at Opal.

"Go ahead and talk. We were just shooting the
breeze."

"It's—uh—rather sensitive."

"Dr. Opal is a man who can keep secrets—isn't that
right, Doctor?" Forte said conspiratorially.

"Right."

"Well . . . it's about Stenco."

"Stenco." Forte grimaced.

"Yes. We've got troubles."

"Stenco's *always* got troubles," Forte scoffed. "I
can't figure why. If you'd only hire and keep the right
executives, it'd run like a clock. Great future, Stenco—
space travel, nuclear development, broad-spectrum research."

"This is different. Jackson Freed has just resigned."

"Jack? I don't believe it!"

"Effective immediately. Cleaned out his desk and
took off. Pressure got to him. He said bleeding ulcers
aren't worth *ten* times what the president of the United
States makes, let alone three times."

"But—but—"

"Yes, I know. Who can replace him? Freed is a rare
type—sharp brain, understanding of nuclear engineering,

enough experience with government to handle bureaucracy, a young man with vigor and imagination, the kind of man who gets things done."

"And ruthless," Forte added. "Just what we needed to get rid of the deadwood. I guess we'll have to go with Alcott now. He's next in line."

Rogette laughed. "Alcott's a pussycat. You need a tiger."

"Then Bascom?"

"Good administrator, but no imagination. Can't risk it."

"van Cleve, then. He's got imagination."

"Yes, but he has to call a meeting to decide whether to scratch his itching ass. I'm telling you, Mr. Forte, the cupboard's bare."

Forte sighed heavily.

"Then get your outside-recruitment people cracking. Meanwhile, let me sleep on it. Maybe I can shift somebody from one of my operating divisions. I'll let you know when I've seen your list."

After Rogette left, there was a long silence as Forte stared out the window, apparently in deep thought.

A discreet cough roused him from his reverie.

"Oh, excuse me, Dr. Opal," he said, turning around in his chair.

"Maybe it won't be such a hard job as you think."

"What's that?" Forte asked absently. "Oh, you mean the hot-water problem? No, I suppose it won't. We'll work out something."

"No, no—the job."

"The Stenco presidency? You're a hundred-percent wrong. It's probably the toughest slot of any in my forty-odd companies. A real man-killer."

"I didn't mean the job itself," Opal said, his voice tightening. "I meant *filling* it."

On Forte's face, comprehension slowly dawned.

"Me," Opal said. "The man Rogette described is me, isn't it—young, smart, conversant with nuclear engineering, a man of action, experience with the government. Fits me like a glove."

"Well, now, Dr. Opal—"

"Izzie."

"Well, now, Izzie." Forte repressed a shudder. "What we're talking about is big league."

"Put me in, coach. I'm ready. Besides, I'm wasted in this job—getting people in hot water. Get it—*hot water?*"

Forte produced a little gallows laughter.

"I can do things," Opal said, his narrow-eyed expression conveying just the right amount of menace.

"That's true," Forte said nervously. He rubbed his finger along his lower lip. "But you don't know what you'd be letting yourself in for. It's a big job, a *responsible* job."

"I eat responsibility for breakfast."

"Risky, too. It's a man-eater, a real meat-grinder."

"A job's no bigger than the man who fills it," said Opal sententiously.

"Knowing you might get burned? You wouldn't be the first."

"It's all settled, then," said Opal briskly, before the old fool changed his mind.

"There's a contract to be signed, of course," Forte said. "In Sunshine Industries' companies, the buck stops at the president's desk. He's the one who gets the pay and the kudos if all goes swimmingly. By the same token, he's the one who drowns if things go wrong. I must warn you of that."

But Dr. Izard T. Opal wasn't listening.

Forty-five minutes later Opal signed the contract that made him new president and CEO of Satellite Technology and Extraterrestrial Nucleonics Company. Right up to the last minute, Forte several times seemed on the verge of second thoughts. Opal did not, therefore, read the contract with the deliberation he usually accorded such documents. His chief concern was the clause concerning the salary, which was beyond his wildest ambitions.

"Board approval is only a formality," Forte said, after congratulating Opal on his new job. "I'll have an extraordinary meeting convened tomorrow. You can take charge immediately afterward."

"You won't be sorry," Opal assured him.

"I hope not."

"In fact, Will, what you did today is the smartest thing you've done in years."

"I hope so."

4 JULY 1998

For days, the Statehouse in Austin had been in a state of siege. None but legislators—not even clerks or coffee runners—were allowed inside the guarded doors. And once in, no lawmaker had been allowed to leave, for fear of premature disclosure of the seditious deliberations taking place in the chamber.

Sedition? Some called it revolution, and wanted no part of it. But they were distinctly in the minority, and took care to be inconspicuous, for their fellow representatives and senators were breathing fire.

The morning of American Independence Day found the legislators queuing up before the six wash basins in the men's lounge to shave, or taking delivery of cardboard boxes of pastry and big insulated jugs of coffee passed through by the Rangers, or gossiping in the cloakroom while doing household chores. One distinguished member from the Panhandle, temporarily manning a broom handle, observed that today would be the day.

"Not necessarily," his companion said, a lady who had so far forgotten her station as to be picking cigarette butts from a brass receptacle. "They're still three days away." She smoothed the sand with her hand. "I heard this morning over the radio they're steaming slowly northward off Vera Cruz."

"I wasn't talking about Russia's Seventeenth Fleet. I'm talking about us. If we don't decide to act today, it'll be too late to act at all."

"But you're sure we'll act?" the lady needled. Her distinguished fellow sweeper had made a career of fence-sitting. It was rumored that even when the voting was secret, he sometimes cast a blank ballot.

"Little lady," he intoned, brandishing his broom like a scimitar, "I speak not for the others, but as for me—"

She never learned the as-for-him, for at that moment the quorum-call bell shrilled, and the members hurried to their places, for Cherokee Tom Traynor was scheduled to address the House. His orotund delivery was worth a hearing anytime, especially by aspiring politicians seeking an effective oratorical style to emulate. Adding to his appeal today was his total ignorance of the past days' deliberations by the House and Senate. Would he take the line of moderation, wherein lay political safety, or would he opt for one of the two riskier extreme positions—prostration before the Russians as demanded by President Wilson Wynn, or defiance?

Striding down the center aisle of the chamber, his grim face looking neither right nor left, Governor Traynor ascended the podium. He grasped the lectern in both meaty hands and glared the buzzing House into silence. Another minute passed as his eyes touched, and briefly held, those of every one of the lawmakers. He was calling the roll. He wanted to know who it was who today would decide the fate of Texas. He opened his mouth to speak.

"Texans!" he roared, raising the hair on the napes of a hundred necks.

For a long moment he said nothing else.

He let the legislators simmer in the juice of that holy word, which evoked visions of endless vistas of lush cattle range, the golden wheatlands of the Panhandle, the spuming oil rigs of East Texas, leggy Cowboys' pompon girls, fresh shrimp from the Gulf, *haute couture* from the Galleria, line-camp camaraderie, eagles silhouetted against the sun, and that indelible image of the immolation of the Good at the Alamo fighting the forces of Evil. The word hung in midair. His eyes were on far horizons, as if the word had floated away from his lips and had come to rest somewhere way out there, like a guiding star by which mankind fixed its course.

For that long, long moment there was silence, an eerie silence, as if he spoke to an empty chamber. Then someone broke the spell with a rebel yell, and suddenly the capitol exploded with the thunder of shouting and deafening, sustained tumult.

At that moment, Cherokee Tom Traynor could have run for God and won by acclamation. Wistfully, he reminded himself to use the device—which in fact had been no device at all, but merely a pause to give himself time to think of something appropriately solemn to match the gravity of the occasion—during his next campaign . . . if there ever would be one, after the Russians.

He raised his hand for silence. After a few moments he got it.

"Texans are not strangers to peril," he began, in quiet tone. "We have had famines, hurricanes, Indian massacres, outlawry, dust storms, floods, range wars, foreign invasions. Some we have won, some we have lost. But we have never run away from adversity, never shirked battle. We've fought for our freedom on many past occasions, and it looks like," he went on, his voice rising, "if you ladies and gentlemen concur, that—"

He was drowned out in a flood of acclaim.

The governor raised his hands.

". . . and it looks like we'll have to do it again. We won't run away, and we won't surrender, for we know that those who won't fight for their liberty don't deserve it. Besides, the odds are right: *Texas against everybody else in the world!*"

He waited for the laughter and cheering to subside. Then his tone became serious once more.

"Fighting for what's right has been the basic philosophy of Texas ever since this beloved land was first hacked out of the wilderness by men who valued their independence and self-respect more than they did their lives. We, their sons, must be worthy of those men.

"Is it possible for free and self-respecting men to submit to the indignities and foul ingratitude and blatant criminality that the Russian Seventeenth High Seas Fleet heaped upon the good people of San Diego, in the name of *friendship?* I say to you *no!* We will *not* submit. We will *not—*"

This time the cheers were louder, even more frenetic than before.

Cherokee Tom, a medicine man expert in taking the political pulse, recognized the fever signs of willing submission to messianism. This moment would be the pinnacle of his career. Never again would he command such support; if only he could freeze-dry it for the senatorial campaign in 2000 . . .

"All my life I've been a patriotic American," he went on. "But I was born in Texas, and have allegiance to this great state as well. God forbid that I should ever have to choose between the state and the nation. Certainly, that choice need not be made today, for when I say that I, Cherokee Tom Traynor, will fight and die for my State of Texas, I am also fighting to protect the best interests of the United States itself, which the Russians seek to destroy.

"We cannot defy our president. We cannot allow our land and our daughters to be ravished by the Russian serf. Then what *can* we do? We can do this: we can inform the President of the United States that we refuse to allow the Russians into Texan waters, and that if they come, we will fight. One part of the nation cannot be at peace while the other is at war, you'll say. True— and therefore we further say that the moment a Russian man-of-war enters Texas's territorial waters, it will be fired upon. And at that instant the Sovereign State of Texas will secede from, and declare its independence of, the Union.

"The choice devolves upon our president. Does he want Texas to remain in the Union? Then he must tell the Russians to refrain from sullying our shores. Does he wish to sue for a craven peace with the Russians without the encumbrance of a restive Texas? Then he will bid us farewell and Godspeed, taking no responsibility for our actions.

"Ladies and gentlemen, I recommend to your consideration a bill, a declaration of independence of the Sovereign State of Texas, to become effective the moment the Russian fleet invades our waters. This bill gives to us, *and* to the President of the United States, the widest scope for action for our mutual benefit. It also narrows the choices of Russia to two: war or peace."

No cheering punctuated the conclusion of his speech. When he stepped down from the dais, a reflective silence closed about the chamber. For the remainder of the morning that mood prevailed, as the legislators debated the issue.

At noon, with twelve members voting nay, and one abstaining, the two houses overwhelmingly approved the draft bill for the independence of Texas, conditional upon the outbreak of hostilities between the State of Texas and the Soviet Union. . . .

At nine o'clock that cloudless night, an hour after sunset, Governor Traynor went on television. His appearance had been announced at ten-minute intervals since early afternoon. It was estimated that fully 97 percent of the population of Texas would be watching.

His speech was dignified and brief, with none of his customary imagery and rhetorical flourishes. He spoke of the Russian menace. He gave a résumé of his remarks in the Statehouse that morning. He noted the resolution by both houses of the Texas legislature calling for immediate sucession from the United States of America and the promulgation of the Second Republic of Texas in the event of Russian incursion into Texas' waters. Then his voice became grave.

"It is for us, your representatives, to propose. It is for you, the people of Texas, to decide. At this moment, in geosynchronous orbit 38,000 kilometers above Texas, the lenses of TexComSat 23-LBJ are focused on us. In exactly five minutes"—he consulted his watch—"at 9:25 P.M., all power-generating equipment in the State of Texas, except for emergency facilities, will be cut. The state will be in total darkness.

"Those who favor Texas remaining in a union that submits to the Russian yoke—if any such there be—will step outside into the night and show a light. A match's flare, a flashlight, even the glow of a cigarette, will be picked up and registered by TexComSat 23-LBJ and relayed to Earth for instant tabulation. I say again: anyone who wishes to remain a citizen of a craven, misguided, gutless United States will step outside, and in his loneliness show his feeble beam."

He paused.

"At 9:35 P.M.," he resumed, "just fourteen minutes hence, all those in favor of a proud, independent Republic of Texas, ready to fight anybody and everybody who denies us the honor we will die to preserve, will step proudly out into the velvety blackness of the Texas night and light the lamp of freedom. . . ."

At nine-twenty-five, there were brief, isolated flashes of light from one end of Texas to the other. More ofen than not, they were followed by even briefer flashes as indignant Texans, their firearms at the ready for such expressions of disloyalty, zeroed in on the dissidents and let fly. As a test of loyalty toward the United States, it was a candle snuffed out in a high wind.

At nine-thirty-five, firehouse sirens wailed in every city in the state, and people poured out of houses and apartment buildings. From the Rio Grande to the Oklahoma Panhandle, from the borders of Louisiana to the sands of New Mexico fifteen hundred kilometers away, the state was ablaze with the light of impending battle in twenty million defiant ayes of Texas.

6 JULY 1998

PRESIDENT WILSON WYNN HAD LEFT INSTRUCTIONS TO be awakened the moment the Texas referendum results were in, and shortly after midnight he was.

The frown of his political counselor, Manuel Silva, told him all he needed to know. It was what he expected. A spellbinder like Cherokee Tom Traynor, the lessons of the Civil War forgotten in an appeal to state pride and states' rights, the colossal arrogance and stupidity of the Russians during and after the fleet visit to San Diego . . . The result could scarcely have been otherwise.

"How bad?"

"As bad as bad can be, Mr. President. The nays were about as numerous as Bible salesmen in Mecca."

"That's good."

Silva was taken aback.

"I beg your pardon, sir?"

"Sit down, Manny," the president said, motioning his

aide toward a chintz-covered chair. "I'll tell you a little
bedtime story . . . Once upon a time there was a Little
Red Riding Hood—no, that's not quite true. I'd better
begin again. Once upon a time there was a Big Red
Hood named Ivan, an ambitious but very careful man
who one day felt the breath of his fellow wolves on his
neck. As a ranking member of the Kremlin hierarchy,
he was naturally privy to their secrets. The most important of all was Project Lime Kiln, Russia's plan to
use the Washington Protocols to destroy our manufacturing capabilities while they themselves stockpiled
grain, whereupon they would present us with an ulti-
matum to surrender. The story has many twists and
turns, but that's the bare bones. And the barest of all
the bones is that we'd have no choice but to accept,
as our defenses would by then be in shambles. We—"

"But why wasn't I *told* of this, Mr. President?" Silva
asked indignantly.

"Manny, there's an old saying: He that tells a secret
is another's slave. But keeping you in the dark about
Lime Kiln was more than a matter of security. Your
job is to reflect the *sense of the nation,* without being
influenced by any inside information the electorate
doesn't possess. You're my sounding board. As your
heart beats, so does that of America. I feel your forehead and know whether John Citizen is running a fever.
Why do you think I never look at polls but have you
read them and tell me what, if anything, they *mean?*"

"Because what people say and what they think so
seldom correspond."

"That's it—and you're expert in deducing one from
the other. Now, then, what was the nation's mood
about the Washington Protocols yesterday, Manny?"

The small man with the dark eyes and six-hour
stubble shrugged. "Well, Mr. President, yesterday they
were for the protocols. Naturally enough, after the
media gush about the manifold advantages of lower
taxes thanks to decreased defense spending, the boon
for the corn-belt farmers, the boom for the inner city

and small industry—oh, the man-in-the-street's for it, no question."

"That's yesterday. And tomorrow?"

Silva shrugged. "About the same, I'd guess. People prefer the comfortable lie to the inconvenient truth. They *want* to believe the Russians have changed."

"What it amounts to," President Wynn concluded, sinking back in the pillows and regarding the ceiling, "is that unless I rescind the invitation for the Soviet Seventeenth Fleet to visit Houston, the State of Texas will secede—that's sure, because you can always count on *somebody* shooting off a gun in Texas."

"We could send federal troops to prevent it."

"Federal troops," Wynn said wryly. "In the current state of our defenses, they'd need six weeks to ford the Potomac . . . What happens if I accede to Texan pressure and rescind the fleet invitation, Manny?"

Silva drew a finger across his throat.

"Impeachment—probably no later than next Friday, considering the strength of the peace-at-any-price party. The only states you could count on to vote against your ouster are California, Texas, Arizona, New Mexico, Vermont, New Hampshire, and Wyoming. I've already made soundings. In which case Vice-President Blackborn would be in, and his first act would probably be to reinstate the invitation. Back to square one."

Wilson Wynn was silent. For five minutes he lay there, drumming his fingers on the night table. At last he turned to his political aide.

"Thanks for coming in, Manny. See you at the seven-thirty briefing."

"But—but, Mr. President, what have you decided? The staff is waiting outside. What shall I tell them?"

President Wynn rolled over on his side and snapped out the light.

"Answer to both questions: nothing."

The red hot-line telephone just sat there, silent. It had been silent when Wilson Wynn entered the Oval

Office at seven-fifty, following the overnight briefing at breakfast, and it had been silent ever since. It was now eleven-thirty, and just seeing it there made Wynn nervous. More than likely, Premier and Secretary-General of the Communist Party of the Soviet Union Vasily Vasilyevich Vavilov was sitting in *his* office in the Kremlin, looking at *his* red telephone, waiting for the proper psychological moment. Well, Wynn was good at waiting . . .

The telephone shrilled. Wilson Wynn reached for it automatically, caught himself, dropped his hand, and leaned back in his chair. He let it ring six times before he picked up the receiver and said a cheery "Hello, Vee! You caught me just as I was on my way out the door for lunch. Nice to hear from you."

"Hiya, Will—how's tricks?" Vasily Vasilyevich prided himself on his command of American slang, which went back, new words mixed indiscriminately with old, to the 40s.

"Not bad, if never worse," said Wynn mischievously, knowing that Triple Vee would instantly commit to memory the phrase translated literally from the Spanish, but never heard in English.

"Good deal . . . Not bad, if never worse, eh? Yet, from what I pick up at the hustings, your not bad could become very worse at any minute."

"Translation?"

"Governor Traynor's declaration of independence—on July fourth, speaking of interesting timing."

"Oh, *that*. You know how impulsive these Texas cowboys are—shoot first, ask questions after."

"So you think there *will* be shooting?" the Russian said darkly.

"I sure hope not—not by anybody."

"But you can't guarantee it."

"Who could? There must be eighty million unregistered guns in the United States—if you can believe *Trud*. And there's always some hothead—on one side or the other—wanting to make a name for himself as the fastest gun in the west."

"Then I take it that you, the president of the United States, are *not* recalling your official invitation for the Soviet Seventeenth High Seas Fleet to visit Houston, Texas, the day after tomorrow?"

"God—if you'll excuse the expression—no!" said the president. "Why should I?"

"Have you communicated this to the authorities in Texas?"

"I'm afraid such a question intrudes in the internal affairs of the United States, Vee," President Wynn noted stiffly. "But between us, I have not and will not. I alone, with the advice and consent of the Senate, have sole jurisdiction over our foreign policy. Texas has nothing to say about this visit. Nothing at all."

"And yet," Premier Vavilov persisted, "what if they . . . what if firing breaks out between our fleet and certain unruly elements?"

"It won't, if the Soviet Fleet doesn't enter Texas waters."

"But you just said—"

"—That it's welcome, as indeed it is. It is for *you* to decide as to the advisability of the visit."

Wilson Wynn could visualize Vavilov squirming and making silent appeal to the other members of the Presidium tuned in to the telephone conversation. The reply took some time in coming.

"We—I see no reason at this moment to instruct Admiral of the Fleet Grell *not* to visit Houston as planned and approved by your government." Vavilov chose his words with care.

"So there's no problem."

"There is if we're shot at. I demand you provide the protection any host guarantees for the safety of his guest."

"And how do I do that, Vee—station a soldier with his rifle at the head of every Texan?"

"Gee whiz, Will, you're making it tough on me."

"You can always skip Houston," President Wynn suggested.

Ho-ho! Vavilov thought. *Now* I have the picture. This is all an American plot to induce the Russian fleet to *avoid* Houston, thus making the Russians look like cowardly fools in the face of Texan bluff. He nodded knowingly to his comrades around the table. Their smiles told him they had seen through the American trick, too.

"Nooo, Will, I think we should stick to our arrangements. But I still hope shooting can be avoided."

"Me, too, Vee," the president said. "Especially since once fighting erupted, I would be in a very peculiar position."

"How so?"

"That Declaration of Texas Independence is conditional upon hostilities erupting. So long as they don't, I'm still president of the fifty United States. But the moment they do, Texas will become a foreign country, and I shall cease to exercise control over its foreign policy."

"Unless you send American troops to put down the rebellion."

"Never. I will never allow American soldiers to fire on their fellow citizens," Wynn declared firmly. "We've made that mistake once. Never again."

But you won't mind if *we* shoot a few of them, you cagey old fox, Vasily Vasilyevich Vavilov remarked to himself. That would solve a lot of problems for you, wouldn't it, Wilson Wynn? Your hands would stay clean. We'd administer a badly needed taste of discipline to the rumbustious Texans, which you'd much appreciate, since they never voted for you, anyhow. Your commitments to the fleet visits and the protocols would be intact, and your Eastern-establishment constituents would be delighted to see the Texans chastised. *Of course* you wouldn't shoot your fellow citizens,

Vavilov thought dourly. Why should you, when we're willing to do it for you?

"I believe we understand each other," Vavilov said.

"I hope so, Vee. But in the event I have not made myself clear, let me reiterate that the official invitation of the United States to the Soviet Seventeenth High Seas Fleet remains unaltered and in force. I trust it will be concluded to the complete satisfaction of all who love peace."

"Governor Traynor on one," President Wynn's personal secretary announced in midafternoon.

Wynn lifted the receiver and said smoothly, "Tom! How nice of you to call, and how opportune—I was just about to call to congratulate you on your speech at the Statehouse yesterday. A real stem-winder. If I could declaim like that, I'd have been elected president twenty years ago."

"Thank you, Mr. President. I just said what had to be said."

"I know. Public service can be brutal."

"Mr. President," Traynor said, clearing his throat, "I have something disagreeable to say. Disagreeable, but necessary if innocent lives are to be spared."

"Then by all means say it."

"I may have got carried away with my rhetoric— I'll admit that—but I've dealt the hand and we'll play it. Trouble is, we're short of chips."

"By which you mean, I suppose, that you lack the arms to launch a rebellion against the United States?"

"We lack arms to defend our homes and families, sir. The National Guard is standing by, awaiting orders. But there are tens of thousands of veterans and plain Texans armed only with deer rifles and Saturday-night specials. As their governor, I cannot let them commit suicide."

"Then let them stay at home. That would be a wise course, and a dignified one. It would—"

"Sorry to sound impatient, sir, but that's neither here nor there. My people need weapons. There are plenty in the federal arsenals at Nacogdoches, El Paso, and Amarillo."

"Hmmm, that would be a problem, Governor. You see, yesterday, to celebrate Independence Day, I gave all employees at federal arsenals in Texas a week's holiday. My secretary of Defense said they'd been working overtime and badly needed a rest, I seem to recall. Now, ordinarily the commanding officer of the arsenals would be available to tell you why it is legally impossible to release any matériel for the purposes you have in mind. But under the circumstances, I doubt that you'd find him or anybody else within miles of Nacogdoches, El Paso, or Amarillo. I'm really sorry, Tom. . . ."

Even now, at close to midnight, they kept coming. Texans were alive to the Russian threat; they had voted secession from the United States rather than submit to it; and they were coming to Houston to fight for it.

None came unarmed, but other preparations—provisions, accommodations, a supply of ready cash—had been ignored in the rush of the moment. The urge to kill their invader blotted out all other considerations. Sleep? They would have little time for that. Hunger? They hungered not for food but for Russian scalps. Money? What they wanted only courage, not cash, could buy.

From his office high in the *Herald* building, Gwillam Forte watched them come, and wished Karl Marx could be at his side. That bearded philosopher conceived of man as an economic animal, a puppet pulled this way and that by the strings of the profit motive. What would he have made of this ingathering, where men were ready to sacrifice fortune and life for that most impalpable of things—self-respect?

His secure-line telephone rang.

"That you, Will?" Governor Traynor boomed.

"It's me, Tom. I heard your sermon in stone, and I want—"

"My wants first, tonight."

"Shoot."

"Have you observed the traffic lately?"

"I have."

"Well, so far it's only cars. In about an hour you'll be seeing trucks coming down from Nacogdoches. Early tomorrow they'll be rolling in from El Paso and Amarillo as well. Thousands of trucks, full of arms and ammunition, from anti-tank guns to Peregrine missiles to .45-caliber pistol ammo. Thousands of tons of the stuff, and it's got to be put out of sight on arrival. If it isn't, it will be spotted by Russian spy satellites."

"Where did this stuff come from?"

"It's where it's going that matters now, Will. It's got to be undetectable by the Russians, yet accessible to the ship channel for our defenders when the Russians come."

"SD-1?"

"I was thinking of those huge tunnels you drilled under the channel. Open up the entrances, and the trucks could drive right in."

"Tell them to come right along."

"Thanks, Will—I already have."

6 JULY 1998: MORNING

AT DAWN, ALONG THE FIFTY-KILOMETER-LONG HOUS-
ton Ship Channel from Houston down to Galveston
Bay, factories and refineries, warehouses and wharves,
were astir with business. The business was war.

Behind the earthen bunds that surrounded oil tank
farms, men young and old were digging in and siting
artillery pieces. Atop the tangled scaffolding of cat-
crackers and fractional distillation columns snipers
stockpiled food, water, and cases of ammunition for
the long day ahead, already as hot and muggy as a
tropical swamp, when they would pick off individual
sailors on warships steaming up the channel. The roads
were jammed with vehicles bearing supplies and ammunition, some already daubed with red crosses to bear
away the inevitable casualties.

Here and there ingenious citizens were preparing a
welcome of a different sort for the Russians.

At a loading dock, a hundred men and women
formed an assembly line to make mines to be sown in
the path of the advancing Russian column of ships.
Oil drums were filled with dynamite, with just enough
air spaces to provide buoyancy, then sealed, painted
dirty brown—the color of the channel water—and festooned with contact fuses. The drums were linked together and towed downstream in a long line, with an
interval of a hundred meters between drums. One end
of the string was secured to a convenient dock, the
other to the opposite shore. When the first ship hóve
into view, the string would be loosed from its moorings.

The lead ship would run into it, and the drums would swing in toward its hull. Three or four would explode, sowing others along the path of the following ships. Wholesale devastation would ensue. . . .

Old salts gave the sweaty saboteurs the horselaugh: dynamite wouldn't so much as dent the Russian waterline armor plate, they claimed. The grim man in charge—a former captain in the U.S. Naval Reserve, newly commissioned at the same rank in the Texas Navy—told them to sheer off. He was well aware that it was all labor in vain, but the exploding barrels would make a hell of a racket, convey the illusion of fire power the Texas Navy didn't possess, and give his people something to keep their minds off the overwhelming superiority of their foe.

Another group of enterprising if misguided defenders had somewhere collected five solar mirrors ranging up to two meters in diameter and were installing them atop a grain elevator at water's edge. Their leader, who recalled the legend of Archimedes setting fire to the Greek fleet at Syracuse, proposed to make the blazing sun their ally. The concentrated rays of the sun were to be focused on the bridges of the oncoming ships, blinding helmsmen and navigating officers conning the ships and causing them to run up on the channel banks. There they would be game for the slum youth, who were already busily digging foxholes from which they intended to emerge, like pirates of old, boarding the enemy with grappling irons and bashing Russians with ball bats and bicycle chains.

Meanwhile, three dredges used to keep the channel clear were busily shifting the bottom and building shoals in the hope that deep-draught Russian vessels would run aground. Like a lot of other Texans that day, they were embracing fantasies and clutching at phantom hopes.

By four-thirty that July morning, with the sun lazily hugging the horizon, an estimated 600,000 men, women, and what the courts called children but their families proudly called men, had converged on the ship channel from all over Texas.

They were the amateurs.

The professionals—men who had served in the American armed forces, made more practical dispositions. The earliest-mobilized sited their artillery at advantageous points along the entrance to the channel, with overlapping fields of fire, reinforcing them with sandbags and even hastily poured concrete revetments. They organized provisioning parties, ammunition trains, first-aid stations, command posts, and observation stations, and were linked together by citizen-band radios from their automobiles. Enough ex-generals were on hand to staff twenty divisions, but Governor Traynor went over the heads of all of them to appoint a young, tough, energetic colonel to command.

By 0800 on 6 July, Colonel Walker had his day-old Texas Army in position facing the channel mouth, waiting for the enemy, as ready as it would ever be.

Fifteen miles out at sea, just over the horizon, the Soviet Seventeenth High Seas Fleet and its train of auxiliaries steamed slowly toward the Texas coast, just making steerageway. In the van, with destroyers on each beam and off the bow, was the flagship *Karl Marx,* a huge long ship whose main deck seemed to hug the surface of the sea. In the cabin of Admiral of the Soviet Union Vladimir Grell stood a handsome young man at rigid attention.

The young three-striper repeated his orders: "Sir, I am to take the point with the destroyer under my command, the *Borodin,* and proceed to the mouth of the Houston Ship Channel at normal cruising speed. One kilometer from the channel marker buoy I will break out holiday bunting and muster the men on the main deck for coming into port. I shall order speed reduced to ten knots. If any challenge comes by radio, blinker, voice, or other means, I shall ignore it. If any hostile fire comes from air, land, or sea, I shall ignore it, not returning fire. If no fire or hostile action prevents it, I shall proceed to the designated anchorage in the ship basin in downtown Houston. Sir, this is my understanding of the admiral's orders."

The admiral looked at him sadly and nodded. The destroyer *Borodin* was a stalking horse. The young man knew it, his crew knew it. It was their reward for being the best destroyer complement in the Seventeenth Fleet. None other could be depended upon not to fire back, possibly destroying the battle plan. Because they were the best, they had been chosen for the suicide mission—for reconnaissance of the Texan's dispositions and their repeated warnings for the Russians to keep their distance left no doubt that, within hours, they would all be dead. They were going to their deaths because he had ordered it, just as many Texans would die immediately after because the Kremlin had ordered it. The admiral wished there was another way.

"Good luck, Captain," the admiral said, saluting.

The young commander saluted, his jaw line firm, tears springing to his eyes. He knew how much the old man must be suffering.

The admiral suddenly stepped forward and clasped him in a hard embrace. "God bless you," he whispered, then turned away.

When he turned again, the young man was gone. He cursed himself for an old fool, but then, with sagging shoulders, excused himself on the grounds that this was the first such emotional display of which he had been guilty in his forty-four years in the Soviet Navy. And the young captain was, after all, his only son.

"Range?" said Major Motley, commanding the Channel Delta Sector.

"Eight hundred fifty meters and closing."

The major swore.

"All means have been used to raise them—you're *sure?*"

"Yes, sir," Captain Biddle replied. "We've been

guarding their radio frequencies for the past thirty-six hours, and have sent warnings in English and Russian at one-minute intervals since the first sighting to stay clear of our territorial waters or be fired upon. We've used international code, signal flags, loudspeakers on the pilot boat that was sent to intercept them—everything. Chief Charley Red Horse even tried Indian sign language."

"And they refuse to reply?"

"Yes, sir. They stand at attention on deck like dummies in a show window, and take no notice of us whatever."

"Are they bluffing?"

"That's a negative, sir."

"I suppose not."

"But I can tell you one thing, Major: if *I* were the admiral, I'd kill myself before I sent my son on a suicide mission like this."

"That's why you're a captain, not an admiral. Besides, he may have switched commanders on the *Borodin*."

He studied the advancing destroyer, a sleek white ship sliding through the water, as eerie in its silence as the Flying Dutchman. "Try raising it once more," Major Motley said.

Keys rattled and voices spoke urgently into microphones as the ritual warnings were repeated.

There was no reply.

"Range?"

"Two hundred twenty meters, sir. Point-blank."

"All guns on target?"

"Yes, sir."

"*Commence firing!* Blow the son-of-a-bitch out of the water!"

And within twenty seconds, they did.

6 JULY 1998: NOON

THE SEA LANES BETWEEN TAMPICO, VERA CRUZ, AND other Mexican oil ports and the European continent, which depended largely on Mexican oil products, were as crowded during the closing years of the twentieth century as the Straits of Hormuz had been a generation earlier. The million-ton tanker was now standard among world fleets, an immense brute that looked like a black iceberg looming over the relatively tiny ships of the few remaining navies. The 98,000-ton aircraft carrier U.S.S. *Truman,* for instance, was dwarfed when crossing the bows of the Russian tanker *Omsk* during fleet maneuvers in the Caribbean, and its flight deck was only two or three meters higher than the main deck of the *Omsk* when the tanker was fully loaded; in ballast, it towered over the *Truman* and every other man-of-war afloat.

Built in Soviet shipyards on the ultrasecret warm-water coast of Khuzistan, far from inhabited areas of the Iranian Soviet Socialist Republic, the construction of the *Omsk* and other such megatankers had aroused speculation among naval architects as to the reason for all the mystery. After all, it was just another tanker, wasn't it?

Not quite. As a tanker, its compartmentation was singularly ill-designed, and its full cargo of crude would scarcely have fueled the automobiles of Pocatello, Idaho, for a year. "Loading" operations in Mexico, however, were always handled by reliable Communist

Party members, who also fudged account books and
tank farm records to conceal the fact that no more than
a few thousand tons of crude were loaded at any port
of call. Yet the ship sank steadily in the water during
its loading, and nobody who didn't need to know ever
realized that the cargo was salt water. This it would
pump out in Europe—where onshore "oil" tanks registered as filling—only to take on later somewhat less sea
water for the return to Mexico in ballast. In common
with many Russian inventions, its purported function
was camouflage.

The *Omsk*'s real cargo was not crude at all, but very
refined. It had been designed by the best naval architects in the Soviet Union, and tested in computer simulations for every possibility, for to participate in live
maneuvers would have given away its vital secret to
enemy reconnaissance satellites. The crew was trained
and retrained to razor sharpness. During the Soviet
Seventeenth High Seas Fleet's courtesy calls at Seattle,
San Francisco, and San Diego, the *Omsk*'s sister ship
Pinsk had three times been "incapacitated with main-
shaft lubrication problems" just out of sight of land,
but never more than a hundred or so miles from the
fleet's anchorage. When the fleet sailed south to pass
through the Soviet Union's Panama Canal, the *Pinsk,* too
large to clear the locks, proceeded from its station off
San Diego to its usual destination, the oil terminus of
Callão, Peru. As the shadow of the Seventeenth Fleet,
it was replaced in the Gulf of Mexico by the *Omsk,*
which had been cruising on station just over the horizon from the fleet ever since.

At dawn on 6 July 1998, the *Omsk* received orders
to move toward the Texas coast at full speed, with all
hands at action stations.

When it received its orders from Admiral Grell, the
Omsk was eighty kilometers south of Galveston. The
day was hot and sunny. Not a cloud obscured the sky.
Perfect helicopter weather.

*   *   *

"Pilots! Man your planes!" ordered Captain Ugarov, air operations officer of the *Omsk*.

The main deck of the tanker at the moment of the command resembled that of any other megatanker at sea—a sailor in salt-streaked blue dungarees was on his way by motorcycle from his fo'c's'le quarters to the bridge aft, two of his mates were over the side on staging touching up the black paintwork, a lookout was aloft in the crow's-nest on the foremast. But otherwise the decks were devoid of humanity. Running fore and aft were the huge layers of pipe, neatly aligned like black spaghetti, that allowed crude to be pumped from one compartment to another to maintain the ship's trim. Aft, the multiple decks of the poop reared like a ten-story apartment building grafted onto the ship's fantail.

As the echoes of Captain Ugarov's order faded in the air, the *Omsk* began to undergo a metamorphosis, like an enormous black caterpillar giving birth to butterflies. The mass of the deck piping parted down the middle and rolled back smoothly to the port and starboard sides. Below was a grid of forty-eight round wells in the main deck, in mathematically precise ranks of twelve fore and aft, four athwartships. Sunlight flashed from the blades of forty-eight helicopters as they rose on their elevators into the light of day. A moment later the tiny craft lifted into the air, four by four, and bored through the hazy sky toward Galveston. The elevators sank out of sight only to deliver another brood of black gunships three minutes later. Wave on wave the *Omsk* disgorged, until from a distance they appeared as a swarm of monstrous mosquitoes homing on the fat flank of southern Texas.

"Course!" barked Captain Gregori Semenev, leader of Red Wing One, the first group of eight helicopters launched.

"Two hundred and seventy degrees true," the navigator replied.

"Distance to target?"

"Seventy-three kilometers, sir."

The pilot cranked the information into his autopilot and read off the estimated-time-over-target. At his present speed, his ETOT would be twenty-four minutes hence. "Very well," he said, leaning back in his armored seat and lighting the last cigarette he would have before finishing the run. He handed the packet over to his copilot.

"Visuals?"

"In a few minutes Galveston will come up off our port beam, sir. Won't see much of it at sixty meters altitude, of course. Then we cross Galveston Bay with Texas City off our portside, northwest of Galveston. Open water until our check-in position over Smith Point. According to the briefing, Texas air defense will have been alerted by then, and we can expect light to medium flak as we approach Baytown on the north side of Jacinto Bay, where Galveston narrows into the Houston Ship Channel maze."

"Pick it up," Semenev said to his copilot.

"Yes, sir," said the copilot. "Galveston Bay is pinched in by Baytown on the north and La Porte on the south. From there to downtown Houston, a distance of some forty kilometers, the channel dodges peninsulas and islands all the—"

"Good enough. References, Navigator—and don't use the map."

"Yes, sir." The navigator looked up from the chart table. "Hog Island first, then Spilman Island, then Black Duck peninsula to the right and Jennings Island to the left, around Alexander Island and Peggy Lake, skirting Crystal Lake peninsula to the starboard side, and the U.S.S. *Texas* basin. Then we make a ninety-degree turn to port, enter the narrower portion of the navigation channel, which snakes into the old city past La Porte and Galena Park. Near the—"

Captain Semenev yawned. "Okay. I guess between the three of us we'll find it somehow. And speaking of Peggy Lake, did you ever hear the one about

A lovely young dancer named Peggy,

Whose performances were always quite leggy,
Could spread her—"

"We're expected," said the copilot, nodding toward the puff of black smoke up ahead, over Smith Point.

A moment later an antiaircraft shell burst ahead of them, too far off-target to do any damage.

Captain Semenev unhurriedly reached to one side and pulled the red handle that armed the helicopter's machine guns and rockets. He pressed the mike button on the control column.

"All units: fifty-five-degree descent. Fan formation. Take evasive action."

In his earphones he heard the crackle of acknowledgment in quick succession from the seven other gunships in his wing. Meanwhile, his helicopter slid down through the sky until he was flat-hatting across the water at five meters. He inched the throttle forward. His air-speed now registered 311 kilometers per hour. Compensating for air pressure, temperature, and an eighteen-kph tailwind, they were clipping the waves at 340 kilometers per hour.

As they made landfall, the flak seemed to become a solid curtain. The Texans were shooting at them with everything they had, but without coordination or significant effect. Intelligence reports from agents among the defenders had assured the Soviet fleet commander that, while the Texans expected helicopter reconnaissance and would do their best to down the choppers, the defenders were certain that the main assault would come from the fleet's shipboard weapons as it attempted to shoot its way up the channel. Therefore, though tactical surprise had been denied the Soviets, they achieved strategic surprise, for relatively little Texan fire-power was deployed against low-flying aircraft. Even the Texans' dual-purpose "Chicago organs," firing 52-mm shells from eight barrels at a rate of 550 per minute, were aimed in flat trajectory, and were not brought to bear effectively until the first wave of Russian aircraft had already passed overhead.

Captain Semenev glanced down the line of helicopters to his port and starboard. The ten wings, eighty aircraft, were largely intact and almost perfectly aligned. Once the coastline was crossed, the formation would separate into two columns. The lead helicopter would speed up, while each one behind took up position in echelon. The two columns, starting at a point five kilometers from the banks of the channel on each side, were to come together like the blades of a shears, one at twenty meters altitude, the other at fifty meters. Instead of successive targets, the defenders would have only a single helicopter to shoot at before the whole flight passed over. The starboard flight would then crisscross below the port flight, and each wing would make a pass at the opposite channel bank before reforming and repeating the maneuver farther upstream. The tracks of the flights were like two sine waves canceling each other out, except that today it was the Texan enemy that was to be erased.

In the brief moments they overflew their confused adversaries on the ground, the Russians unleashed a furious barrage of Gatling-gun fire, rocket-propelled explosives, nerve gas, and napalm. The wake of each Russian gunship was a broad band of desolation. The answering fire was brief: before the antiaircraft batteries could swing around to follow an attacker disappearing over the channel, another would come in low from the oposite direction, its guns belching fire and streaming a deadly fog of poisonous gas. Like twin shuttles on a loom, the Russian columns stitched together the two sides of the channel in devastation as complete and terrifying in its magnitude as a thousand Stalingrads. For while the World War II Battle of Stalingrad claimed the lives of 175,000 Germans in ninety days, the Battle of the Black Channel, as it would become known to history, witnessed the slaughter of double that number in half as many minutes.

The Russians were not invulnerable. Despite heavy

armor on the underside of their aircraft, the sustained Texan barrage, which became more concentrated and effective as the battle raged nearer the city proper, brought Russian gunships smoking down in growing numbers. Those who survived the crash were hauled out of smashed cockpits by eager hands. Some died quickly.

Of the 498 Russian helicopters that participated in the Battle of the Black Channel that July sixth, fewer than three hundred returned to their cryptotanker. Though the surviving air crews didn't share in the general jubilation of the senior officers, who had viewed the battle as televised from airborne and satellite cameras, there was no question that the day had been a huge success for the Russians. Compared with World War II battles against the Germans, the costs in men and matériel had been trifling. More important was the Russian political victory.

So long as Russia's military and naval might had not been demonstrated, there would always remain some residual doubt as to its efficacy after so many years of disuse—at least in the minds of Americans. President Wynn's hands-off policy had given the Soviet Union a treasure that the signing of the Washington Protocols later in the year would merely formalize: proof of the futility of defying Russia's awesome power.

The icing on the cake was the extraordinary propaganda value of the battle. Within hours, Russian reports were being picked up by American newspapers and television from intercepts of Russian communications traffic to Moscow. Sent in the clear after suitable laundering to conceal the extent of Russian losses, the news was heard and seen in American homes even while the battle still raged. The contrast between American and Russian casualties was appalling: an estimated 450,000 to 500,000 Texans dead—mostly by gas—and uncountable wounded, as against a reported Russian loss of thirty-seven helicopters and

their crews, scarcely more than a hundred men in all—
an unprecedented kill ratio of five-thousand-to-one.
Russian reconnaissance planes had been scanning the
battlefield from low and high altitudes since the moment the last helicopter wheeled and headed for the
Omsk. The vision of hell their cameras relayed to
American television networks was etched forever in the
minds of those who saw it.

Close-ups showed mangled, incinerated bodies hud-
dled around their pathetic World War II weapons, no
match for the enemy's sophisticated machines of destruction. Buildings were splashed and spattered with
human remains, as if a city of slaughterhouses had
been simultaneously detonated. Here a child's arm lay
in the middle of the road, the leg half a block away,
the rest of the body God knew where. From the rubble
came whimpers of the half-dead, mangled, and blinded
in the darkness of fallen structures, struggling for breath
that would, when it came, bring the peace of the grave,
for the air was still layered with the haze of masonry
dust mixed with poison gas. The horror of the carnage
up close was compounded by the view of the battle-
ground from high altitudes. For a stretch of nearly
twenty kilometers, from Galveston Bay almost to the
San Jacinto Monument, where it makes its looping
swing to the west and south, the ship channel was a
huge, angry black scar. The channel waters between
the ravaged banks glistened with oil from ruptured
tanks. Charred flotsam—the bodies of the dead and
carcasses of ships that had been in the path of the
raiders—clogged the shallows of the wide waterway.
By midafternoon, not a living thing save for the in-
domitable Houston cockroach was stirring in an area of
some one hundred square kilometers.

The American people saw it all, and pondered its
implications.

The holocaust had been wrought by the helicopter

complement of a single Russian ship, which had, more-over, survived unscathed. One Russian ship. And it was a mere auxiliary to the main battle fleet, untouched, not having deigned to risk smudging its paintwork by engaging the ragtag Texans. In a sense, the Russians were merciful, for the tens of thousands of entrenched Texans around the channel bend, close in to the downtown district, had been spared. The Russians announced over helicopter-borne loudspeakers, however, that anyone showing further resistance would share his countrymen's fate.

The announcement, curiously, had the opposite effect.

Like lemmings in the grip of the irresistible magnetism of the sea, American men—and not a few women, too—were being drawn to Texas. Many were veterans of earlier wars. They switched off the television in quiet rage, and decided forthwith they had had enough. According to the television news, on the morrow the Russian Seventeenth High Seas Fleet, bunting aloft, would steam up the Houston Ship Channel and anchor in the densely populated downtown area. There the Texans, having been given a lesson in manners, would honor their visitors with a twenty-one gun salute, following which the Russians would parade en masse down Navigation Boulevard. Led by Admiral of the Fleet Grell, they would be met by the mayor of Houston and the governor of Texas and be given the Peace of the City and the Key to Houston. So, at least, did the Russians propose, and let it be known that eager compliance was expected.

The mass of quiet Texans, hitherto uninvolved, exploded in rage. If the Soviet Union believed Texans behaved like Russians, who, once given a taste of the knout, are as docile as sheep unto the tenth generation, they were much mistaken. By the thousands, grim-faced men and women, carrying anything that would fire, converged on the city during the night and found places in rooms and offices overlooking Navigation Boulevard.

By daybreak, whole buildings were crammed to the eaves with hunters determined to bag the limit during the open season on Russian bear.

6 JULY 1998: EVENING

IT WAS CENTRAL TO RUSSIAN STRATEGY TO TRUMPET the horrors of the attack on the Houston Ship Channel to the widest possible American audience, in the conviction that fear of a similar fate would cow the rest of the population into terrified submission. Thus the helicopters of the half-dozen local television stations, circling like carrion over the scenes of devastation, had not been molested in any way. Flying at altitudes above 1,000 feet, where they could get the big picture, the commercial copters interfered not at all with the combat operations of the low-flying Russian aircraft.

On a large screen in the bar of SD-1, Gwillam Forte's *Texas*-project division chiefs—Dr. Ed Curry, Dr. Herbert Chilton Fallows, Professor Hamilton Reed, and Emilio Salvatore—watched the slaughter grimly. They had imagined that the Russians would make a short, sharp response to the sinking of the *Borodin,* perhaps the shelling of Galveston by the Seventeenth Fleet, but had been unprepared for the unparalleled ferocity of the Russian attack.

"They're crazy," Ed Curry whispered when the last of the black helicopters wheeled against the sun and headed back to the *Omsk.*

Ham Reed nodded. "They read no history books but their own. If they did, they'd remember Pearl Harbor and how it took that humiliation to get America off its, ass and on its feet. Can they really believe we'll roll over and play dead after *this?*"

Herb Fallows laughed mirthlessly. "Why shouldn't they? What can we do about it? Our fleet's in Hamburg today, under a thousand Russian guns. All we've got here is the old *Texas*. What do you think they'll do now?" Fallows asked Reed, the mathematician who had spent a career at the Pentagon trying to second-guess the Russians.

"Today's made a hash of all my assumptions," Reed confessed. "From here on, it's all surmise. But my guess is that they'll now proceed precisely as planned, to demonstrate that *nothing* stands in the way of the Soviet steamroller. If we'd sunk half their fleet, they'd *still* come. It's essential to their strategy of giving the appearance of invincibility. Once that façade is cracked, the whole myth of Soviet superiority crumbles."

"You think they'll really come into Houston?" Salvatore asked.

"With bells on. They said they would. I believe them."

"In the face of *that?*" He pointed to the television screen, which now showed the superhighways leading into Houston, still choked with incoming traffic as if nothing had happened, although descriptions of the fighting and the Russian victory had filled every radio channel.

"Sure. The Russians think they can't lose against a disorderly mob of civilians, however numerous. And why shouldn't they think so, after today?"

The four men finished their drinks thoughtfully.

The bartender, a dignified, gray-haired man, had kept discreetly to one side but listened to every word of the scientists' desultory conversation. He now approached and filled the glasses.

"Pardon me for intruding into your discussions,

gentlemen, but am I correct in assuming that we would like to inflict the maximum possible damage on the Russian fleet?"

"You can say that again, Charles," Salvatore affirmed flatly.

"But if Professor Reed is correct in his assumption that the Seventeenth Fleet will steam into the inner-city basin as planned, surely there is an obvious way to do them grievous bodily harm."

"It isn't obvious to *us*," said Fallows, stung. "Being a bartender, you obviously know all about the *Texas* preparations—not to mention dendrochronology, genetic engineering, astrophysics, and plate tectonics—but we are—"

"Oh, I wasn't thinking of the *Texas* at all," Charles said equably, for like all professional barmen he was impervious to taunts.

"No?"

"I had in mind, rather, those under-channel tunnels. They have been crammed with ammunition and other explosives for the past two days and nights, and the trucks are still streaming in. It occurred to me that if, as the *Karl Marx* was passing along the channel above, the tunnels were detonated, why—"

The four men looked at one another, stunned. They smiled. A cry of delight went up, and a joyous clink of glasses.

"Of course—the tunnels! Talk about tunnel vision," Salvatore said, "just when we most needed it, it failed us. Pour yourself a drink, Charles—on second thought, take the bottle . . ."

Adjourned to a conference room, the four scientists fell to their calculations. Charles's idea, while basically sound, was susceptible to a single, exciting modification, and it took the four men until early evening to determine whether it was within the realm of technological feasibility.

"Well," Curry asked Reed, who was at the computer

terminal keyboard making final calculations, "will it fly?"

"There's your answer," Reed said after a moment, pointing to the VDU.

"Damn!" Curry slapped Reed on the back. "I never imagined it would really work. But if you and Chill haven't goofed somewhere, maybe—just maybe. . . ."

Reed sighed. "All this is paperwork, you know. We haven't had time to plan a single experiment. We've had to work from raw figures, like the approximate amount of explosives in the tunnels."

"Not quite approximate. We've got the exact figures from the loading sheets."

"Sure we have," Salvatore rejoined. "But we don't know how old each lot is—and explosives become notoriously unstable and enfeebled with age, you know—or whether some inspector at the factory was bribed to pass a substandard load of mortar shells, or—hell, the variables are endless."

"We've made allowances at both ends of the curve."

"Still, we're taking a big chance."

"But not, mind you, with anybody's life. Even if it doesn't work, not a single American life is jeopardized. If it does work, a lot of Russians will be pushing up daisies."

"Okay. But what about old Forte? What if he doesn't approve of what we're doing? His idea was to have the Ruskies sink the *Texas,* not vice versa."

"Tough. Times have changed. If he doesn't like it, we go ahead without him. But knowing him, I think he'll like it."

Dr. Fallows made a gesture of impatience. "We're wasting time. We've still got a lot of work to do. You, Emilio, recalibrate the Elbows so they'll fire concentrated rather than dispersed beams. Tomorrow, they've got to *kill.* See if you can beef up the magnetic defenses, too; though you may not have enough time for them all, at least strengthen those around the flag ridge relay center."

"It means going aboard and activating the auxiliary control system to test power and alignment."

"Then go aboard and activate it. Tonight, nobody is going to pay any attention to the *Texas*. Tomorrow, when the Russians come, we'll switch control to SD-1."

"Then there's the matter of filling the interstices between the ammunition boxes in the tunnels. I've got an idea about that."

He outlined it. Like most good ideas, it was simple in concept, but it did require a certain administrative talent to carry it out. Dr. Curry volunteered to supply it.

"The gasoline is no problem," he observed. "Dozens of tank farms within spitting distance, many of them intact. As for the aluminum soaps, I know offhand of three sources, all within ten miles."

"It's only nine hours to daybreak."

"If you stop jawing and get to work," Curry said, "it'll be enough."

6 JULY 1998: MIDNIGHT

DR. IZARD T. OPAL SAT ALONE AT THE BAR OF A DARK, dingy cocktail lounge on the fringes of Houston International Airport, north of the city, nursing the second of two stingers, which were his self-imposed ration for a twenty-four-hour period. He was feeling mellow, full to the brim with self-satisfaction.

In addition to the Russian attack, which would be remembered as one of history's great victories, there was the matter of his personal coup, which had vaulted him into the presidency of security-sensitive Stenco.

Uncle would be astonished at his success, no doubt, but
even more pleased and grateful, for was not Stenco a
veritable cornucopia of space secrets? He might be
promoted to KGB colonel, even brigadier general. So
carried away with the euphoria of his speculations was
Opal, that he knocked back the stinger and ordered a
third. Tonight he owned the world, and felt a little
reckless.

A heavy hand fell on his shoulder.

He turned and looked up into the face of Hobart
Caulkins.

"You're late," Opal complained.

"I'm half an hour late," Caulkins admitted. "You're
two *days* late. Where have you been, Little Bo-Peep?"

"Ah!" Opal said, savoring the moment, for Caulkins
had always shown contempt for his talents. "That is the
question."

"That is. Answer it, and make it snappy. I have
other people to see tonight."

Opal looked slowly around the bar. Two men in
battered ten-gallon hats were arguing about the Russian
attack at a jukebox over in one corner, a couple with
heads together occupied one of the booths, and a drunk
slumped at the far end of the bar. Otherwise, they were
alone.

"You're looking at the new president of Stenco,"
said Opal proudly.

"I'm looking at *what?*"

"Stenco—Satellite Technology and Extraterrestrial
Nucleonics Company. I'm the new president."

"Tell me what happened. Tell me fast, tell me
straight, and don't leave anything out, Opal." Caulkins
was obviously furious.

Taken aback, Opal hesitated, thought fast, and gave
a carefully edited version of the previous days' events.
He had, per Caulkins's orders, investigated the hot-
water emissions violations at SD-1, he said. The emissions were indeed a violation of the NRC regulations.
But it had been going on only for four days due to an

inadvertant valve blockage, which blockage he had confirmed by an inspection of maintenance reports. However, more detailed investigation at the *Texas* basin—*undertaken at his own initiative*—revealed that the discharge had been going on for some time, maybe months. He confronted Gwillam Forte with the evidence. The violation, though venial, Opal had cleverly parlayed into the job of president of Stenco; the threat to report the infraction to NRC had apparently been enough. They both knew that if Forte hadn't come across, he was in danger of losing his huge government contracts for submarine nuclear reactors.

Hobart Caulkins listened to the story impassively.

"So you see," Opal continued, "I am now on the inside, and can feed the Center every single scrap of classified information on the premises. What do you think of that?"

Caulkins regarded him coldly. "I think you're a stupid, greedy, lying little man, Izzy. I've had a man in Stenco for years. Now, then, I want to hear your story again. Just the parts you left out. Tell it straight, or I'll kill you here and now."

Dr. Opal, suddenly stone sober, told it straight, omitting no detail.

"You're a scientist, Izzy," Caulkins said thoughtfully when the other had finished. "What do those hot-water emissions tell you?"

Opal licked his lips. Maybe he could save himself if he told Caulkins something really useful.

"That nuclear reactors are aboard the U.S.S. *Texas,* of course."

"How do you figure that?"

"Cooling water temperature. The temperature of the cooling water that comes from the reactor jacket is known. I measured the temperature that comes from the *Texas* basin. The two are almost identical."

"They would be."

"Only if the water *came* from the *Texas,* you see. If it was merely discharged into the *Texas* basin, having come from SD-1 some nine kilometers distant, as Forte claimed it did, the water would have lost a significant amount of heat."

"Well, that makes sense, Izzy." Caulkins smiled for the first time since he came in. "So Forte has reactors aboard the *Texas*. Why?"

"Propulsion."

"Propulsion *where?*"

"Down the Houston Ship Channel, obviously. Into the Seventeenth High Seas Fleet. My guess is it's loaded with TNT to blow up the *Texas* itself along with as much of the fleet as possible."

"You know something, Izzy," Caulkins said gravely, "I think you're right. Why didn't you tell me?"

"I—I was going to."

"When?"

"Tonight. I was going to give you a full report."

"Uh-huh." Caulkins marveled at the ease with which Opal's greed had overpowered his political judgment and instinct for survival. Too bad, Opal.

Opal grinned weakly. "It's just that with all these things going on, I haven't had time to write it up yet."

"Well, don't you think you'd better?"

"Yeah. I'd better get on it."

He rose, and put a ten-dollar bill on the bar.

"I'll go with you," Caulkins said.

Outside it was dark, the clouds mixed with the black greasy smoke that still boiled up from the fires far to the south. Half a dozen cars were parked haphazardly by the side of the rundown building, whose isolation was its reason for having been chosen by Caulkins as a meeting place. A neon sign leaned forlornly into the night wind, casting a pool of dappled red light on the bare earth beneath. Hobe Caulkins inspected the surroundings. No one seemed to be around. He walked to one side of the little frame building, and in the shadows unzipped his trousers.

"That cheap beer gets to you," he said. "Join me?"

Dr. Izard T. Opal knew that if he didn't, Hobe Caulkins would laugh at him for being a snob; he had done it before. Opal didn't like that snide laugh. He went to stand alongside the other man.

Suddenly Caulkins's hand clamped around his throat. Opal tried to kick him in the crotch, but Caulkins blocked the kick with his thigh and kept on squeezing. Opal battered at his attacker with his fists, but his fists were too small, his arms too short, his muscles too soft to discommode the other man, who was, without haste, squeezing the life out of him.

Opal felt his eyes starting from their sockets, the ringing of a million bells in his ears, the blood rushing to his head but not getting there. He tried to bite, and bit his tongue half in two, although he didn't notice the pain. He tried to scratch, but his nails futilely clawed the air. He tried to scream, but could only manage a faint gurgle.

Trying became too much of an effort. He felt death stealthily edging closer. It was a more peaceful sensation than he had imagined it would be. He wondered why he was bothering to put up a fight at all. It wasn't dignified for a man in his position, a doctor of philosophy, the president of Stenco. He wanted to turn to greet it, but before he could do so, he found it was already there, grinning at him. . . .

Just before he died, a brilliant flash of light illuminated his fading vision. A glimpse of heaven?

It was the headlights of a police cruiser, which had turned off the access road into the lane leading to the bar-and-grill, and for a brief instant it trapped the two men in its beams. Caulkins wasn't sure he had been seen, so brief had been the stab of light. Nor was it likely that, if he *had* been seen, he had been observed, for his body partly obscured that of Dr. Opal.

He squeezed on, and didn't release the body until he was sure the other man was dead. Then he stepped away, started to go back the way he came, changed his mind and walked quietly around the back of the building where there was nothing but darkness.

A flashlight beam struck him squarely in the eyes.

"Hold it right there, bud," a deep voice said.

Caulkins stopped, smiled his best yokel smile, and held up his hand before his eyes.

The police officer marched him at the point of his revolver back the way he had come, grunted when he saw the body of Dr. Opal, and instructed Caulkins to spread-eagle on the hood of the patrol cruiser.

Hobe Caulkins complied.

With the revolver pressing against his prisoner's kidney, the policeman slowly but methodically fanned him for weapons. Finding none, he straightened.

He was a man built along Texan lines—big, beefy, and hard. He was half a head taller than Caulkins and outweighed him by fifty pounds. Looking down at the smaller man, the policeman holstered his pistol and reached for his handcuffs.

Caulkins held out his wrists and in the same forward movement plunged what seemed to be a ball-point pen into the other man's neck.

It went in too easily and too deep to be a ball-point pen.

Caulkins leaped lightly back to avoid the gush of blood as the policeman staggered back against the wall of the bar-and-grill and slid to the ground. Caulkins bent over him and examined the wound in the dim light. It was gushing blood, which confirmed to Caulkins that he had, as he had aimed to do, punctured the carotid artery, which would leave the policeman dead within two or three seconds.

He returned unhurriedly toward his car, unlocked it, and got in without another glance at the man he had just stabbed.

The flow of blood, copious though it was, was steady rather than pulsating. It came, not from the carotid artery, but from the superior vena cava. The policeman remained conscious just long enough to drag his re-

volver from its holster, raise it shakily, and fire a single
shot before the recoil knocked the weapon from his
hand. Ten seconds later he was dead.

Hobe Caulkins wasn't. But the bullet slammed
through the window frame of his car into his left shoulder. Unless he got medical attention, and fast, he knew
that he too would bleed to death.

7 JULY 1998: DAYBREAK

GWILLAM FORTE WAS ALOFT IN THE *Houston Herald*'s
television helicopter *Fubar* before dawn, winging south-
ward toward the mouth of the ship channel near
Galveston. The helicopter flew with navigation lights
blazing and transponder on, its pilot hoping that the
immunity that had spared it and other news-gathering
choppers the day before still prevailed. Apparently it
did, for the reconnaissance helicopters and jet aircraft
from the Russian carrier that flew by northward seemed
not to notice them.

The channel had been cleared of major obstructions
during the night by Russian minesweepers, but evidence
of the previous day's battle saturated the air, for from
the blackened banks on both sides, and the channel's
black, waxy, fetid water, came the stench of tens of
thousands of charred and decomposing bodies, streaming through *Fubar*'s air intakes.

According to the Russian announcement broadcast
on American television the evening before, the Red
fleet would proceed as scheduled, one day late, up the
channel to its reception in the inner city. The *Karl
Marx* would lead the column and drop anchor in the
Buffalo Bayou Basin. In its wake would come two

fixed-wing-aircraft carriers, three helicopter carriers, six missile cruisers, and eleven destroyers. The train of fleet tankers, mine-sweepers, amphibious support ships, communications ship, tenders, and the cryptotanker *Omsk* would remain in Galveston Bay; that they were defenseless against even the most modest conventional naval force was simply another indication of their contempt for the Texans they had defeated with such ease the day before.

Russian intelligence, as usual, had been excellent. The channel bottom was sounded by airborne depth finders to confirm the accuracy of the latest navigation chart. The survey showed that even megaton tankers could still maneuver without difficulty over the hulks of ships sunk the day before. Aerial reconnaissance had revealed no appreciable signs of life in the twin belts of desolation along the channel banks. Russian precautions even extended to sending an agent disguised as a Coast Guard commander to inspect that forlorn old relic, the *Texas*, to ensure that the Texans had not somehow contrived to put its rusty guns back into commission. At virtually point-black range, the ship's two twin-turreted fantail guns could maim the bigger ships and even sink destroyers in a single salvo. The agent found the ship completely deserted, and the guns' muzzles fouled with birds' nests. There would be no surprises here. . . .

The *Karl Marx* was just entering the channel. It proceeded slowly: speed would have conveyed an impression of nervousness the Russians didn't feel.

"Can you estimate the speed of the column?" Gwillam Forte asked of the pilot.

The pilot nodded. "I can do better than that." He flipped on a radio switch, exchanged some esoteric palaver with an unidentified contact, and reported that the fleet was making something over eight knots.

That would put the flagship opposite the *Texas* basin in about three hours, Forte calculated, and in Buffalo Bayou Basin in less than six, just before noon.

"SD-1," he instructed the pilot.

Ten minutes later the *Fubar* fluttered down like an autumn leaf atop the blast shielding that served as SD-1's heliport. Some miles to the north of the region of devastation, El Caballejo Ranch and the adjacent industrial areas had been untouched, but the ghost-town quiet of the streets and workshops testified that the workers who had once populated them had gone, never to return. Forte stepped wearily out of the helicopter, grim-faced and gray.

He rode the big elevator alone down the manway to SD-1. Here, a mile underground, the workers were few, hollow-eyed, and pale. They avoided his eyes, as if they shared some guilty secret. Forte walked through deserted passageways to the command center, where he had been told his department chiefs were assembled.

They were all there: the scientific department heads, the twenty-one veterans who had worked so hard and long on the *Texas,* and the two dozen technicians who had labored on the later stages of the Elbows installation, the computerized controls for the *Texas,* and the magnetic antibeam devices that were to protect the Elbows. Some were drinking coffee at the long mess table to one side of the large circular room, others stood in tight little groups second-guessing the previous day's events. A few men were checking the instruments and computer programs, already checked and rechecked during the past twelve hours.

Their greetings were subdued, but their expressions cool and determined. Whatever they had to tell him, he sensed, at least there was hope in it.

"Well, Ed," he said, leaning against the conference table, "what's the good word?"

"Better than it was yesterday at this time."

"I'm all ears."

"First of all, we've recalibrated the Elbows. Instead of emitting a diffused beam, the seventy-two weapons will generate a beam of the minimum possible spread. They're as lethal as we can make them."

"Good. What else?"

"We've devised a decoy. On the mainmast we've rigged an array of transmitters sending out UHF signals on thirty-five different channels."

"What does that do?" asked Forte.

"Not a damned thing—not for us, anyway. For the enemy, it sows confusion. He'll be trying to sort out the relation between the frequencies and the Elbows fire, which, because of the magnetic screening, he can't take out. Well, there isn't any relation, of course. So he concentrates his fire on the mainmast—now also heavily screened magnetically, I need not add—thinking it's some kind of fire-control apparatus. Meanwhile, our Elbows will be hammering away, their fire direction coming from this invulnerable, undetectable base down here in SD-1."

"Good. Anything else?"

They told him about the cross-channel tunnels. Openly skeptical at first, Forte was convinced by their calculations and fervent assurances that it might, after all, have a chance of working. Indeed, there was hardly any other.

"You really think exploding them will inflict major damage—like destroying half a dozen ships?" Forte said.

"More," Emilio Salvatore promised him. "Half a dozen destroyed outright, that many more disabled. If the *Texas* gets in among the survivors before their damage-control parties can take charge, we could even sink a couple more. But I've got to warn you, the whole proposition is untried. It's never been done before. We could fall on our faces, with not so much as a scratch to their paintwork."

"I guess we'll *have* to try it," Forte observed. "We can't let the Russians get away with what they did yesterday without *trying*. They probably think they've scared the American people into unanimous support of the Washington Protocols by their—"

"They nearly have," Ham Reed said dryly. "Despite

what you might think after witnessing the sight of thousands still streaming into Houston, the radio reported now that 88 percent of Americans polled by telephone last night, *after* the bombing, favor going through with it. Before the bombing, it was 79 percent."

"All the more reason to go ahead as planned. Who gets the hot seats?"

"We've drawn straws, Will," Ed Curry said. "Fred Bateson, T. D. Roebuck, Terry Jones, Ski Modeljewski, Gil Persoe, and Chill Fallows will be the gunners, and Ham Reed gets overall command by consensus, since he's the resident war-games wizard."

On a dais dominating the command center were six padded seats in two lines of three, back to back. A seventh faced them at right angles. Each of the six controlled twelve Elbows mounts, and each had responsibility for a sixty-degree field of fire, although Ham Reed, from his post, could override their commands. Together, the gunners covered the six sextants of the horizon depicted on the big wraparound television screen that girdled the room. The image televised from the ship's cameras was projected onto the circular screen. Each gunner was equipped with headgear linking his eyeballs' movements to the computer-driven fire control system. The gunner had only to fix his eyes on the target and press the firing pickle to activate his battery. Instantly the twelve Elbows would swing toward the target and loose their electron beams—eleven 6,000-MeV, 125-kiloampere bolts per second. The bolts could bore through three centimeters of armor plate per second at 1,950 meters. Repeated hits on the same spot could penetrate any known defensive armor, slice through the sturdiest steel beams, cut through mast and rigging as if it were so much soft cheese.

The battle would be fought from here. It would cost Russians lives—lots of them, but not a single American. The sparing of American lives was more than merely

humanitarian: Forte wanted to demonstrate to the
enemy that it could be made to suffer appalling losses,
at a ratio of—not five thousand to one, but five thousand to *zero*.

Gwillam Forte pronounced himself satisfied with the
preparations. They had now only to wait until the *Karl
Marx* and its sister ships ascended the ship channel.
Just beyond the bend, beneath the thick channel mud,
lay the two tunnel complexes. They were crammed to
their watertight doors with arms, ammunition, boxes of
TNT, RDX, and dynamite, the interstices filled with
gasoline and viscous aluminum soaps. Farther inland,
less than a mile distant, was the San Jacinto National
Monument, with its basin for the *Texas,* flagship of the
Texas Fleet. According to the dozens of surveillance
monitors aboard the *Texas,* all was quiet, not a soul
to be seen within range of its cameras.

But Gwillam Forte was restless. As the hour approached for the *Karl Marx* to appear on the television
monitors, as the super–battlecruiser turned southwest
toward the inner city, he could restrain his impatience
no longer.

"Where're you going?" Ed Curry asked as Forte
started out of the command center. "The big show's
about to start. Any minute now the *Karl Marx* will be
steaming onto the screen."

"Never much liked movies," he called back. "I want
to see the real thing. If you want me, radio the *Fubar*."

And he was gone. . . .

Ten minutes later, at fifteen hundred feet, Gwillam
Forte was witnessing the majestic procession of white
ships as they made their graceful turns, one after the
other, toward downtown Houston and Buffalo Bayou
Basin. Their formation was still single column, with a
destroyer between each capital ship. They were aligned
perfectly, like beads on a string, and the interval between ships seemed to have been measured off with the
same piece of string. As a demonstration of precision
seamanship, it was impressive but wasted, for the banks

of the channel—green here instead of black—were devoid of humanity.

Nearly a dozen helicopters were cruising the skies, some very close indeed to the Russian ships, transmitting their video record back to their home studios. The Russian sailors, now mustering at their coming-into-port stations on the weather deck, their anchor details already standing-by, waved cheerily to the choppers.

Two-thirds of the Russian ships had now turned toward the southwest, passing by the *Texas* basin, maintaining their stately eight knots.

Suddenly there was a cry from the cabin radio speaker on the SD-1 channel.

"Will—we've got visitors!"

"In SD-1?" This was a possibility he hadn't even considered. He damned himself for not having doubled the guard force at the entrance.

"No—aboard the *Texas*," Ed Curry's voice crackled.

"How many?"

"One. At least one's all we can see. He's prowling around the restricted area, and he's got a crowbar in one hand. He's trying to break in through the boatswain's locker."

"Isn't it welded shut?"

"Yes, but the paint locker isn't. He'll be there any minute."

"Can you get to him?"

"Not before he could do some damage. It's four minutes from here to the *Texas* tunnel, nine minutes by railway, three or so up through the— No, we'll never make it in time."

"Then I'll try."

Forte instructed the pilot to head for the *Texas*.

"How long will it take?" Forte asked anxiously.

"Minute and a half," the pilot replied.

"Make it snappy, and set me down on the dock as close to the gangway as you can manage."

"Aye, aye, sir."

"Any weapons aboard?"

"None. None at all."

"Jesus!" Forte couldn't see himself going up against a man with a crowbar empty-handed. He was too old for that.

"Nothing at *all?*"

"Well, there's a flare gun—a Very pistol—for emergencies."

"This is an emergency—gimme!"

The helicopter was settling onto the dock when Ed Curry's voice again crackled through the loudspeaker.

"Hey, Will!"

"What is it?" Forte paused with his hand on the door handle.

"We just got a glimpse of the guy close up. His left arm is in a sling—can't use it at all. And he's somebody we know."

"Well *who,* for the love of Pete?"

"Your old buddy Hobe Caulkins."

7 JULY 1998: 9:30 A.M.

ABOARD THE *Karl Marx* ADMIRAL GRELL PRESIDED AT the conference in the flag office, reviewing plans for the victory parade. He turned to Commander Blinovich, liaison officer of the *Omsk*'s aerial strike force. "How does your captain propose to neutralize resistance along Navigation Boulevard, Commander?" Intelligence had some hours earlier radioed a situation report, indicating the presence of more than 300,000 hostiles concentrated in that area of the city.

"Two hundred twenty gunships are standing by, awaiting your orders to take off, sir."

"Will the single strike by 220 gunships suffice?"

"According to our calculations—yes, sir."

"They'd better. We have to root out resistance in one strike. I won't permit any coming and going of aircraft. It would make our operation look like an aerial circus."

"I believe I can assure you on that point, Admiral. The first wave will drop high-explosive charges to destroy the structural integrity of the buildings where the guerrillas are concealed. The second will release napalm to set the buildings afire—Houston's housing is notoriously flimsy—and drive their defenders into the streets. The third wave will drop pellet-bombs to decimate those who remain. The final wave of sixty gunships will annihilate the surviving hostiles with Gatling-gun fire. We are confident of inflicting up to 98 percent casualties, most of them dead."

Grell's eyes drifted to the scene of desolation outside. Through the portholes of the cabin he could see little but blackened, smoking ruins of twisted metal and scorched earth. The devastation would not compensate for the loss of his son, but there was one small consolation in it: from this zone of destruction no resistance would again appear. As a naval man, he dealt in absolutes—war or peace, victory or defeat, life or death. There was no middle way. While one enemy remained alive, danger threatened. History offered abundant proof of that somber truth. Had a certain Corsican junior artillery officer been killed at the siege of Toulon in 1793 instead of emerging victorious, for example, Russia would have been spared the cataclysmic French invasion of 1812. From such examples Grell had forged a personal creed: diplomacy and debate, failing which, *annihilate!*

"I'd prefer 100 percent to 98. Cannot this be done?"

"Assuredly, sir. But it would take poison gas, and that would interdict the parade to follow."

"True." The admiral built a steeple of his fingers and prayed that Blinovich was right. One more good battering and the Texans would be completely demoralized, incapable of organized resistance, finished. Then the remainder of the port calls would be a succession of triumphs, with the momentum picking up right up to the moment the protocols were signed in Washington. "Very well, Blinovich," he said finally. "I depend on you. Now then, Kolkash, what are *your* plans?"

Rear Admiral Kolkash, the shaven-headed officer responsible for fleet amphibious operations, was in charge of the parade as well as of defensive actions by naval infantry in the event of opposition.

"The same as I outlined last night, sir."

"Some of the staff here weren't present."

"Yes, sir. We announced, gentlemen, that the parade would take place today on Navigation Boulevard, parallel to the channel on the southern side. This announcement was made to draw the Texas malcontents to this area, where, as you heard from Commodore Blinovich, they will be annihilated. The parade will actually take place on Campbell's Run, a new broad thoroughfare built five years ago on what used to be Clinton Road."

"Without advance notice," Grell noted, "the number of natives attending the parade will be much reduced."

"As will the risks, sir."

"Yes, there's that. What other steps have you taken to ensure security?"

"We'll have helicopter surveillance as well as armed troops lining the route," said Kolkash. "We'll give notice of the change of venue only after the parade parties disembark on shore. This will prevent unruly elements having time to assemble from other parts of the city to prepare against us."

"Very well."

One question remained: how many sections would participate in the parade? The Soviet Navy, like the

American, divides its crews into four sections. In times of danger, it is customary to have at least two sections on duty at all times, to keep the guns manned and the ship operating at peak efficiency. In peace time, usually only one section stands watch at any given moment, giving the crew four hours on duty followed by eight hours off.

Grell's innate caution told him to have only two sections parade. As a blue-water sailor, he didn't feel comfortable with land crowding him in on all sides, despite the absence of any armed force that could do his fleet injury. On the other hand, the intimidating presence and prestige of the Red fleet would be increased by 50 percent by parading three sections instead of two. In the discussion that followed, this was the course advocated by the fleet's political commissar, a man whose advice it was usually wise to take.

"Pass the word to execute the parade plans as detailed by Admiral Kolkash," Grell said to his chief of staff. "Three sections will participate."

This would leave his ships with only a quarter of their battle complement, but, as his political adviser noted, the danger was behind them.

Nine miles behind him, had he only known.

7 JULY 1998: 11:15 A.M.

GWILLAM FORTE FOUND HOBE CAULKINS ON THE NAVIgation bridge, trying to pry open the locked charttable drawer with a crowbar. To ascend the near-vertical ladder to the bridge with his left arm in cast and sling would have been impossible for the average man, but Forte remembered that Caulkins was a superb athlete, a reminder to keep his distance. He remained on the port wing outside the pilothouse, the Very pistol dangling at his side.

"Breaking and entering, Hobe? There seems to be no end to your talents."

Caulkins turned slowly, on his face a boyish grin.

"They seem to include getting taken in by you, Mr. Forte. Or maybe I should put that in the past tense." The grin dissolved. "What's the story on the nuclear reactors you've got aboard this old bucket? I want to know, and I don't have time to waste."

Obviously not. The Soviet Seventeenth High Seas Fleet would just have dropped anchor in Buffalo Bayou Basin nine miles to the southwest. The parade parties would be swarming over the sides into motor launches. In about a quarter of an hour the fireworks would begin, and Caulkins seemed to sense it. There was little he could do about it, so long as Forte kept him away from the flag bridge, the level above them on the foremast. On the flag bridge was the test console used to calibrate the electron-beam weapons, and through it ran the control circuitry. If Caulkins pried the lid off the console and wrecked the equipment— a lively possibility since the anonymous unit with its push-button combination lock would probably strike Caulkins as anachronistic—the Elbows would be inoperative. And without the Elbows, the *Texas* was just what Caulkins called it, a toothless old bucket.

"They're not nuclear reactors—they're nuclear *devices,* Hobe. They're going up any minute, and unless you get some yardage between this ship and yourself, you're going up with them—you and the Soviet Seventeenth High Seas Fleet."

"You're lying."

"Stick around and find out." Forte was mentally calculating. In fifteen minutes the balloon would go up. During that interval, Forte had to get clear himself, or meet an unpleasant fate. But if he could keep the newspaperman entertained a while longer, the operation would go off as planned.

Hobe Caulkins apparently wasn't going to wait. He pulled a .38-caliber hammerless pistol from his pocket. For all his athletic prowess, he wasn't a quick-draw artist, and Forte could have slammed the pilothouse door and made a getaway, had that been his purpose. Thinking of the vulnerability of the Elbows control unit, he stood his ground, hoping to buy a little more time.

"Talk, Forte. Talk fast. What's going on here?"

"All right, Hobe. There's a regiment of U.S. Marines hiding in the spud locker, with a—"

Caulkins fired. He had aimed at Forte's right knee-cap, but the pain of the bullet wound in his own shoulder, his exasperation, and above all the fact that he was not a very good shot anyway conspired to send the bullet into what would have been his right calf—if Forte had had a right calf. Instead it shattered the steel-and-plastic carapace protecting the electronic circuitry, springs, rods, and other gear that constituted his prosthesis.

He stumbled, and in muscular reaction discharged the Very pistol. The flare struck the binnacle in a shower of sparks, caromed off the overhead and the bulkhead behind Caulkins, and hit him a glancing blow on the backside before shooting past Forte out into space.

Caulkins's trousers were ablaze. He dropped the pistol and tried to beat out the flames with his one good hand.

Forte hobbled toward the ladder down to the main deck, hesitated, and dragged himself up the ladder to the flag bridge. There was still time for Caulkins to beat out the fire, climb to the flag bridge, and wreck the Elbows control panel. Caulkins had probably inspected each separate level in turn as he ascended the mast from the main deck. The flag bridge would be next.

Forte needed a weapon to replace the Very pistol, its sole cartridge expended. He tore open a gear locker. Nothing there but wads of oil waste, two unopened gallons of red lead, an oil can, some brushes stiff with dried paint, a broom with a shattered handle, a pair of overalls. He slammed the locker shut.

He ripped open the drawer of the flag bridge chart table. Empty.

From below, he heard the scraping of feet on the steel deck and the hollow ring of the ladder tread as Caulkins put his foot on the bottom rung. One thing was sure—Caulkins couldn't climb with one hand and hold the pistol at the same time. Maybe that shattered broom handle would be enough. He could use it like a spear as Caulkins's head came flush with the uppermost rung, to send him plunging to the deck below.

Forte limped back to the locker and grabbed the broomstick. His eye fell upon the oil can. With a malicious grin, he dropped the broomstick and picked up the oil can. It was full, and provided with a handy spout for those hard-to-reach places.

Forte dragged himself onto the starboard wing, cursing his maimed leg. Caulkins was halfway up the ladder, breathing hard. He was pantless, and the pistol was tucked into the arm sling, but he didn't look any less dangerous. Forte looked down and caught Caulkins's eye.

With deliberation, he raised the oil can and squirted a thin stream of oil down the ladder rail Caulkins *wasn't* clinging to. As Caulkins watched it, fascinated, the color drained from his face.

"You son-of-a-bitch!" he rasped.

"Ain't it the truth?" Gwillam Forte shifted his operations to the rail that Caulkins now gripped like death.

The oil streamed down. Caulkins strove mightily to retain his hold as the oil soaked his hand, but gradually he weakened, and he finally dropped to the deck eight feet below with a thud and a bellow of pain from the jolt to his injured shoulder.

"Write about *that* in your next column," Forte said. He tossed the oil can contemptuously down at Caulkins, barely missing his head.

Caulkins looked up, his eyes alive with triumph. He had him! The stupid old fool had thrown away his only defense. Caulkins would simply climb the ladder on the port side, and hammer the truth out of him before chucking him over the side.

He ran quickly to the other ladder, and had reached the top rung, one laborious step at a time, when he heard the *thump!* of Forte's feet on the navigation bridge below. The old man had foxed him again, sliding down the greased handrails, intent on a getaway. But it wouldn't do him any good. He was old and crippled. Caulkins was young and in splendid condition, despite a shattered left shoulder and third-degree burns to his backside. He lowered himself, a rung at a time, listening to the retreating feet, confident he would catch the old man before he could escape from the ship.

Forte had calculated as closely as he dared. He wanted to get clear of the ship and lure Caulkins after him before the big explosion. As he limped down the main deck toward the gangway, he heard Caulkins running aft on the opposite side of the ship. A few more steps and he would be clear, down the gangway onto the pier. Within seconds, Caulkins would follow, thirsting for blood.

As he hobbled toward the gangway, he glanced at his watch. There were still six minutes to go.

Too much. If he made it ashore now, Hobe Caulkins would be right behind him. Caulkins would have ample time to kill him, regain the ship and the flag bridge, and disable the Elbows console. He must, somehow, throw Caulkins off the scent.

If Caulkins started down the gangway and didn't see Forte on the pier, he would assume the old man had hidden himself among the bushes, or behind one of the refuse barrels, or in the men's room of the deserted snack bar.

Forte reversed his course. Forward of the gangway brow was the galley, its door open. He remembered the galley from the old days, when he was dispatched to fetch big pots of coffee for the watch. Careful not to drag his wounded foot, he scuttled through the doorway just as Hobe Caulkins shot across the ship from the port side and halted, looking down the gangway to the deserted pier.

Caulkins cocked his ear, listening for some sign of Forte's presence. Somewhere came the screech of metal—familiar, yet for the moment unidentifiable. It sounded as if it came from the ship—forward. He padded softly up the main deck. He stopped at the galley, went in, opened the lockers. He remembered now—it sounded like a locker opening. But all were empty. He shot another glance around the galley and ran out. He looked around him. There was no other place aboard Forte could have hidden so quickly. He *must* have managed to get ashore and hidden.

Like a sprinter leaving the starting blocks Caulkins was over the brow and down the gangway, his footsteps resounding on the wooden slats as he pounded onto the pier, an incongruous and somehow sinister figure in scorched underpants, with his left arm in plaster cast and sling, his right hand clutching a pistol. Had anybody been there to see him, he would have laughed, until he saw the look of murderous rage in Caulkins' eye.

Caulkins was some distance from the ship, searching the grounds in ever-widening circles, when the explosion came. It was as if an atomic bomb detonated, in a mammoth, long, slow-motion eruption that would envelop the world. The jolt knocked Caulkins off his feet. When he sat up and shook the dust out of his

ears, he was surprised to find the *Texas* still afloat at
its moorings. If the *Texas* hadn't exploded, what the
hell *had?*

Aboard ship, the shock wave popped open the doors
of the big galley ovens. From one of them tumbled
Gwillam Forte, who, curled into a ball, rolled halfway
to the door before coming to rest, unconscious.

7 JULY 1998: 11:22 A.M.

AFTER IT DEPOSITED GWILLAM FORTE ON THE *Texas*
pier, the argus-eyed *Fubar* lifted off and lumbered after
the Russian fleet. At two thousand feet, its panoramic,
fish-eye, and zoom lenses captured and transmitted in
a steady stream to the *Houston Herald*'s channel 16
the varied images of the Soviet Seventeenth High Seas
Fleet proceeding majestically up-channel to anchor. As
they reached their anchorage, the ships let go their
anchors and swung to a standstill like soldiers at drill.
Within seconds their motor launches and whaleboats
were swung over the side, loaded to the gunwales with
white-clad sailors ready to assemble ashore for the big
parade. The small boats made their short run, disgorged their cargoes and sped back for more.

Through a medium-magnification lens, the picture
on the number-3 monitor was a study in speed, meticu-
lous organization, and nautical splendor. Sky Crew
Chief Producer Ken Clover, in *Fubar*'s rear compartment, which served as the aerial studio, had to admit
it, even though his brother and a nephew had been incinerated the day before by these same precision-parad-
ing barbarians.

The Russian ships were dressed in holiday bunting running from the bow to foremast to mainmast to stern, twenty-three rainbows of brilliant colors resplendent in the morning sun. The colors complimented the long low lines of the men-of-war, all of them painted an arctic white, and the long still columns of men waiting at parade rest at the gangways to take their turn in the small boats scurrying to shore. Seen from above it was hard to associate these peaceful ships and their orderly crews with the massacre of the day before. Yesterday's horror was too vivid in Clover's mind ever to be washed away, yet the placid scene below was lapping at the edges of his recollection, and he had to keep jerking his mind back to the reality that these particular men in white were doctors of death, and America's mortal enemy. He wished that some miracle would happen, that the earth would open beneath them and—

The shock wave struck the helicopter and sent it reeling across the sky. Clover was flung into the monitors, badly bruising his head and shoulder. He slid to the floor groggily as the pilot wrestled the helicopter back on even keel. For a moment, he thought the Russians had lobbed an antiaircraft shell at the *Fubar,* then realized that a shock that severe would have been accompanied by enough shrapnel to riddle the cabin.

Clover got shakily to his feet and resumed his seat before the bank of small screens, this time buckling his seat harness. Whatever happened, he realized, would have been recorded on tape. He rewound the videotape and played it back.

Far down the channel, some ten miles away it seemed, the waterway had suddenly erupted with the force of a volcano blowing its top. In fact, the playback he viewed *looked* like a volcano. A gigantic discharge of fiery stones and rubble mixed with thousands of tons of channel mud and water, which vaporized in a cloud of superheated steam, seemed to have issued from the depths of the Earth right in midchannel. As the enormous mass of mud and earth hung in the sky, for a moment the channel bed ripped open by the explosion of thousands of tons of high explosive, packed in nine tunnels, was desert dry. During the space of several seconds, there was nothing but a huge, raw transverse ditch, dry and wide enough for Moses to have marched the children of Israel across from bank to bank, if they stepped smartly. Then with an earthshaking rumble, the parted waters, hurrying to fill the vacuity, met in tremendous collision. Another wall, this one of water, shot heavenward. The wall of water was taller than a redwood and stretched across the width of the channel.

As it collapsed, it generated two mighty tsunamis.

They weren't ordinary tsunamis, of the type that roll across the Pacific from undersea earthquakes and depopulate beaches and sometimes whole islands with thundering force. Not only were these two larger than had even been seen by man who lived to tell about it, they were sheathed in *fire,* for the combination of gasoline and aluminum soaps with which the tunnels had been charged formed jellied gasoline—napalm—which ignited with the blast of the detonating incendiary explosives.

The fiery waves fled from each other, one downstream toward the sea, the other inland toward the Soviet Seventeenth High Seas fleet riding placidly at anchor. The burning waves, some eighty-five meters high, swamped and seared everything in their paths.

Huge coal barges tied up at wharves were upended like cardboard boxes, their flaming cargo sown across a square mile, bursting like shrapnel and impaling whomever it hit with its fire-tipped, needlelike shards. Smaller craft rolled like dice and disappeared promptly from view, or else were tossed, bits of blazing firewood, hundreds of feet inland. One proud seventy-six foot yacht landed a mass of pulped steel and wood atop a distillation tower of a nearby refinery, a moment later exploding and ripping the tower apart. Those in small boats out in the channel heard the first premonitory thunder, and scrambled frantically for shore as they saw the wave bearing down upon them. But, at nearly a hundred miles an hour, the wave was too fast for the fleetest craft, and it engulfed all with democratic impartiality.

The wave that boiled downstream toward the sea found little to oppose its passage. The attack of the day before had killed almost every mortal being on the channel, leaving only charred specters floating dead in the water. Like a great cleansing hand, the wave scoured both banks, leaving behind a solid sheet of fire to burn them anew. So great was the force of the water that it uprooted buildings and flung them end over end into the depths of the channel. As it surged silently seaward, the wave and its fiery tongue gradually lost height and fury, for the channel steadily widened toward its estuary. Still lofty enough to inundate and set fire to low-lying Alexander Island and Jennings Island, by the time it reached Galveston Bay, its force had largely been spent, the napalm nearly all burned out. Ten miles down the coast the wave aged and withered, the flame in its eye grown dim; it was now scarcely a meter high, a threat only to children's sand castles along the beach.

Upstream, the situation was reversed. The channel progressively narrowed as it approached the Buffalo Bayou Basin. Instead of subsiding, pressure of the constricting banks caused the upstream wave to mount ever higher. Sluicing over the shallower portions of the banks, it swept people, cars, houses, trees—even the streets—into its fiery maw. It was as if some monstrous bulldozer with a white-hot blade had made a single untidy pass, leaving behind a scorched wasteland.

Three minutes and fifty-five seconds after the upstream wave reared into the air and rumbled off on its destructive course, it reached the Russian fleet at anchor.

Sonarmen registered the explosion—they would have

heard it clearly even without their earphones—and immediately signaled the bridge. Simultaneously, Russian radarmen reported the sudden appearance of an enormous unidentified flying object bearing down on the fleet. It had, they reported in panic, a wingspan that filled their scopes, yet was flying at an altitude of less than one hundred meters. Their commanding officers on the bridges of a dozen ships heard the report with incredulity, notwithstanding which they immediately sounded General Quarters and Recall of the parade parties.

All hands were running to their battle stations when the great red wave struck the last ship in line, the missile cruiser *Suslov*.

The *Suslov* had set bow anchors to port and starboard. The muddy bottom furnished small purchase to the anchor flukes; little was needed, for the flow of the channel this far upstream was so slow as to be scarcely perceptible. Still, when the wave smashed into the stern of the ship, pooping her, the leverage of anchors and chains held the bow just long enough for the wave to swing the stern broadside. Broadside it rose up to the crest of the wave with roller-coaster speed, hung there for a sickening instant with the flames climbing her sides, then cartwheeled into the trough as the wave passed. Trapped air brought her stern briefly to the surface half a minute later, before it dissipated in a burst of huge gurgling bubbles and the ship sank slowly out of sight in the midnight-dark waters.

From the moment the *Suslov* was seized by the wave until it capsized and disappeared from view, less than ten seconds elapsed. By then the crest of the wave was racing upstream, scattering the Red fleet like chaff.

The slender destroyers were easy victims of the wave's fury. One was caught broadside and thrown, like a stick to a dog, high up on the banks of the channel, streaks of fire licking at its hull. Minutes later, as the waters drained away, the few bruised and dazed survivors heard the clatter of feet on the decks above. Wounded, unable to fight, the crew waited terror-struck and helpless in their darkened compartments as the flashlight beams of vengeful Texans sought them out.

In *Fubar,* Ken Clover lived a nightmare. Though he knew what appeared on his screens was actually happening, he couldn't quite grasp it. As the wave struck the line of ships, they rode to the top one by one in slow motion, there to be enveloped by flames, which set off machine-gun ammunition like strings of Chinese fire crackers. But as the wave slid away from under them, their fates were various. Like the *Suslov,* some were flipped end over end and plunged straight to the bottom. Others balanced on stern or bow at the peak of the wave, then fell with sickening suddenness, their hulls striking the water with a bone-shattering jolt that sent a sheet of boiling waters and fire a thousand meters in all directions. Even the stoutest ships are not built to resist tsunamis, and all along the line hull plates were sprung and water flooded engine rooms while bilge pumps worked frantically against the rising tide. Only the biggest ships survived, and not all of them. Stunned but still afloat were the flagship, super–battle cruiser *Karl Marx,* the helicopter carriers *Beria* and *Yezhov,* the missile cruisers *Rykov* and *Litvinov,* and the aircraft carrier *Dzerzhinsky.*

Six ships, of a fleet which a moment before had been twenty-three.

All had been flung on their beam's ends. Their superstructures had been smashed out of shape by the crushing impact of the water. All of the helicopters and planes and most of the men aboard were at least temporarily out of action. Enveloped by flaming napalm, many of the crew on weather decks leapt in agony from their ships, to drown in the channel's muddy waters. Lifeboats were ablaze, the proud bunting was but a string of dangling cinders, and the smoke from countless fires rose in a pall around each of the six ships.

Leaks from ruptured plates sent dark channel waters
coursing through their lower decks, and emergency
power was switched on to run the pumps and lights at
top speed while damage control parties rigged collision
mats against the worst rips in the hull. Injured seamen
screamed in pain, but their grievously bruised and
shaken shipmates could spare no time for them. They
staggered to their emergency stations down smoke-
filled passageways, men drunk on the dark wine of disaster.

Once the wave receded in the distance, the channel
was silent except for the cries of the wounded and
dying, many of them on the channel banks. The water
itself swirled with eddies from the suction of sunken
ships, trapped communist bodies making a few point-
less revolutions on circular currents before sinking into
a darkness as black as a Siberian winter's night. Bubbles
belched up from the channel bottom as water invaded
the inner spaces of the sunken ships. Occasional secondary explosions occurred as hidden fires reached muni-
tions or overheated cryogenic accumulators. The entire
waterway was littered with smoking, floating human
remains, the wreckage of lifeboats, wooden ammunition
boxes, and the roofs of nearby houses carried away by
the wave. Atop one crouched a black cat, aloof and
uncaring. Coating the water and flotsam was a greasy
layer of oil from sunken ships, patches of which were
aflame, quickly to spread the width of the channel.

The fate of the thousands of sailors lined up for
parade on Campbell's Run was quick, nasty, and inevitable: those who weren't crushed by the wave drowned
in it, and those who didn't drown—along with those
who did—were promptly cremated by the blazing
napalm.

Ken Clover urged the pilot to lower levels. He
realized he risked the fire of antiaircraft crews crazed
and vengeful by the sudden catastrophe, but that day
God was his copilot. So busy were the Russians merely

trying to keep their ships afloat that none looked up, no more than a man clinging to a precipice notices the circling butterfly. He filmed it all, making pass after pass, from directly overhead to near water level, as order slowly returned to the ragged remains of the fleet. Fires on deck were extinguished, one by one. Soaked, sooty and disheveled sailors and officers appeared on deck, heaving dead bodies over the side along with other wreckage. But almost as soon as they appeared they took cover again, as sniper fire from the channel banks peppered their exposed decks. The Texans ashore poured in fire as if they would never have another chance. Indeed, they wouldn't, once the Russian gunners manned their proton guns.

Ken Clover felt he had been recording the carnage for hours. He glanced at the digital clock. He was shocked. Five and a half minutes had elapsed. Unbelievable, until he observed that the *Karl Marx* was still rolling gently from side to side, the oscillations set up by the wave not quite yet dampened.

He looked down at the monitors from which his eye had wandered and realized that he had missed something: the flashes of ten thousand Texan guns had abruptly ceased. The men who had been shooting from behind the concealment of uprooted trees and overturned automobiles suddenly stood up, looked downstream, and ran for their lives, up and away from the channel banks.

7 JULY 1998: 11:34 A.M.

GWILLAM FORTE STRUGGLED TO HIS KNEES. HE WAS too old for this, he told himself. Running up and down ladders, popping in and out of ovens, being chased by a would-be murderer with short pants and a long gun— that was young men's work. He shook his head to remove the last vestiges of muzziness, and wondered how long he had been unconscious.

Not long, for the *Texas* was still where it had been when the big explosion rent the skies. Down in SD-1 his scientists would now be watching the clock, their fingers hovering over the button. He wondered whether they had witnessed the chase on the closed-circuit television monitors that had first detected Hobe Caulkins. They must have, but they might not realize that, even though he had left the ship and was now out of camera range, Caulkins was still close enough to kill him.

Caulkins was facing away from the *Texas* now, looking upstream from his vantage point atop the concessionaire's stand about two hundred yards from the ship, which he had mounted to follow the wave's progress. In a minute or two, it would strike the first ships in line, too far away for Caulkins to see anything, but his busy mind would fill in the details. With Caulkins' attention thus engaged, Forte could steal off the ship and hide someplace where Caulkins had already searched.

Forte moved noiselessly toward the gangway. He had just reached the brow when a voice crackled over the ship's public address system:

"Thirty seconds, Will," came the voice of Ed Curry.

"Get clear! Countdown has begun. Thirty seconds . . . twenty-nine . . . twenty-eight . . ."

Hobe Caulkins's head snapped around, his eyes fastened on Gwillam Forte. In the next instant he had leapt lightly to the ground and was running across the parking lot toward the *Texas*.

Cut off, Forte could only retreat the way he had come. For a moment he considered leaping into the water to swim for it, but reflected that even Caulkins could hardly miss him at that range. Despite his battered leg and sixty-nine years, Forte moved fast, seeking a ladder that would even out the odds between himself and his pursuer.

"Twenty-one . . . twenty . . . nineteen—get the hell out of there, Will!—seventeen . . . *sixteen* . . ." Curry's voice was becoming frantic.

Forte reached the foremast and was scrambling up the signal bridge ladder. He reached the top just as Caulkins put his foot on the bottom rung. At least Caulkins wouldn't shoot before he found out what was going on. Forte limped over to the next ladder and went on climbing. By the time he reached the navigation bridge, Caulkins had closed to half a ladder length.

Forte seized the rails to the flag bridge ladder and nearly fell on his face when his hands slipped on the oily surface. He had forgotten all about the oil. He ran athwartships, wiping his hands on his trousers, and stumbled over the oil can he had thrown at Caulkins. He scooped it up and limped on.

"Four . . . *three* . . . *two* . . ."

Forte grabbed the top rung with his final reserve of strength and breath. He felt a hand seize his trouser leg. Holding tight, he kicked. The hand held fast.

"*One! Initiate!*" blared the loudspeaker.

From port and starboard, from bow, midships, and stern, came six staccato *cracks!* as explosive charges severed the hawsers tying the ship to the bollards on shore. Simultaneously, another explosion neatly cut the gangway in two, and it fell with a splash into the water.

The *Texas,* which had been prisoner in still water for half a century, was finally free.

So was Gwillam Forte. The sudden explosions had taken Caulkins—unlike Forte—completely unawares, and he relaxed his grip long enough for Forte to kick his leg loose and fling himself onto the flag bridge and out of sight. The frustrated Caulkins snapped off two shots at him, missing by a large margin. Then he began to mount the ladder.

Waiting until he was nearly halfway up, Forte stood up and looked down at his adversary.

"Your shooting's rusty, Hobe," he said mildly. "Maybe a little oil would help." Whereupon he liberally doused both rails with oil from the long-spouted can and watched grimly as Caulkins again fought the losing quest for the oily rails and slipped heavily back to the navigation bridge.

Forte dashed through the doorway into the flag bridge, dogged the door tight behind him, and shot the bolt. He was safe from Caulkins now, but it was the safety of a man who nails his coffin shut—from the inside.

He crossed the bridge quickly to the control panel. He slumped in the padded high chair and reached for the phone on the bulkhead.

"Ed."

"We see you, Will," said Ed Curry somberly. "We didn't know Caulkins was still—"

"Never mind that."

"No. Is there any way to get clear before the ship—"

Forte shook his head. He was safe from Caulkins in the flag bridge, but the ship and everything aboard it was doomed. If he opened the dogged-down door, he would be dead even sooner.

"No—no way."

"There *must* be," Curry insisted, knowing he lied.

"No." Forte felt suddenly drained. On this ship he had lost three-quarters of himself more than fifty years ago. Today he would lose what remained. He laughed bitterly. At least there wasn't much left to lose.

A jagged sound, like the ripping of a thousand sheets, tore through the ship. Looking forward through the bridge's portholes, he saw a sheet of fire carpet the weather deck. It blazed fiercely, but only for a moment. When the smoke cleared, the deck was a glaring white. An instant later, the crackle of high-voltage energy bathed the superstructure, rigging, and the hull itself with an aura akin to St. Elmo's fire. When it too vanished in a cloud of mist, the ship was no longer a dingy gray, but a uniform, aching white.

And then the *Texas* began to move.

It moved without sound, as softly as a zephyr across a millpond. But it moved fast—faster than ever before in its eighty-four years. Powerful jets of water from nozzles below the water line made a witches' cauldron of turbulence at the bow, and a rising white spume foamed about the stern as it parted the waters and the ship backed down into the channel. With the acceleration of an outboard racer, the *Texas* shot out into midstream. There the force of the port-bow and starboard-quarter thrusters slewed the battleship around in a quarter turn, her bow now headed upstream toward the Russian ships, still wallowing in the backwash of the wave nine miles away.

No escape now. For anybody.

"What's the combination on this doodad, Ed?"

Ed Curry read it off.

Forte's fingers groped for the buttons on the underside of the steel cover, punched them in the proper sequence on the second try, and dropped the cover into its slot. The console was alive and blinking, like some monster emerging from its cave, indicating the readiness of its weapons systems, performance of its power units, and quite a few other things that Gwillam Forte didn't pretend to understand. From a recess, he drew out the helmet, already plugged in, and buckled the strap under his chin. He climbed into the padded chair and fastened the harness around his shoulders. From this elevation his eyes could sweep a front of more than two hundred degrees; the solid bulkhead to the rear kept him from seeing what was behind, but that he already knew: Hobe Caulkins with a pistol in his hand and a lust for Forte's life in his heart—Unless Caulkins had been fried by the *Texas*'s new paint job.

Forte was as ready as he would ever be. Maybe, with a lot of luck, he might just manage to . . . Then he cursed himself for a fool, and switched off the dream machine. He thrust his feet into the metal stirrups beneath the console to brace himself against the thrust of the ship that would come momentarily.

He waited.

The great battleship began moving again, almost imperceptibly at first, then with increasing speed. He was pushed back into the padding of his chair by the acceleration as the *Texas* took off upstream, her stern settling into the water like that of a racing boat. Through the portholes, the hard hot wind whipped his shirt open in a shower of buttons. He felt alive, more alive than in years.

The digital speed indicator on the panel showed they were approaching critical speed. The *Texas,* with three nuclear power plants providing steam pressure for its water jets, had a revised flank speed of seventy-one knots, but his scientists had calculated 63.7 knots to be the critical speed at this moment. If they had calculated wrong, the *Texas* would be at the bottom of the channel in—he checked the estimated-time-to-run clock on the console—twenty-six seconds.

Suddenly the ship began to shake, like a rag doll in a dog's mouth, then a split second later a stupendous explosion sounded as the second of the channel tunnel complexes blew. The noise and vibration were even greater than the first, and the tsunamis produced by the explosion would be correspondingly greater. Again, channel waters would rush from both sides to fill the emptiness, carrying everything along with them, including the *Texas*. It was essential that the *Texas* be pulled as close to the brink of the enormous ditch as possible, in order to catch the tsunami as it was being created. But the slightest miscalculation and it would plunge over the precipice and be crushed under millions of tons of water.

Five seconds after the blast, the *Texas*'s movement relative to the shoreline slowed, then stopped. The ship began to move backward. The engines strained, but the backward pull was inexorable. Now they were racing astern at nearly fifty knots. Ships aren't built to back down at anything like such a speed, and it began to shudder and vibrate, threatening to throw Forte from his perch. Water was building up beneath the stern, lifting it ever higher.

But just as Forte feared it would be shaken apart, the ship slowed, stopped, and then again shot forward on its water jets. It steadied on sixty-eight knots precisely, and at that moment, suddenly the land on either side of the channel seemed to fall away before his eyes. The ship was borne higher and higher, until he could clearly see downtown Houston, with the banks of both shores now far beneath him. It felt like the *Fubar* when it hit a powerful thermal updraft. Yet the vertical ascent was inconsequential compared with the forward velocity that now slammed him back in his seat. It was as if he had been shot out of a cannon. The thirty-eight-degree bow-down tilt of the ship's deck had him clinging to the arms of his chair for dear life. If tragedy is going to strike, he thought grimly, now is the moment.

If the ship's forward propulsion, the speed and the height of the wave, the ship's alignment with the wave crest, its displacement—if all these and other factors so carefully computed and coordinated weren't absolutely on the mark, catastrophe was about to overtake them. If the ship's forward momentum, for example, was a fraction too great, it would slide down the wall of water into the trough, and the following wave would spin it around like a top, capsizing and sending it to the bottom. If the ship lagged, the wave crest would ride under it and it would tumble into the *following* trough, breaking up like kindling under the enormous impact.

Neither of these unpleasant things happened. They had mounted the curl of the wave like an expert surf-boarder, and the jet-propulsion engines automatically throttled back, keeping them balanced precariously on top of the world.

Forte's muscles uncoiled.

From the towering wave, he could now see the pin-points of Russian ships in the distance. In a matter of minutes the *Texas* would descend upon them. The first tsunami, judging by the evidence that came to his eyes, had apparently done its work well, for he could discern only a handful of survivors.

The gap between the *Texas* and the enemy shrank. Very soon the range would be optimum for the Elbows, and still the enemy guns were silent. Could it be that previous tsunami had destroyed their offensive capability utterly? If not, he would, he thought grimly, as the wave carried him onward. He glanced down. A display told him that the nearest enemy ship, identified by the comparator as the aircraft carrier *Dzerzhinsky,* was only 2,800 meters away, and coming up fast.

His hand closed on the pickle.

But before he could fire, the first salvo of Russian missiles from ships down the line struck the tsunami that bore the *Texas.* He counted six as they streaked toward the ship. Miraculously, all missed, drilling straight through the wave on both sides of the ship and exploding far behind with a tremendous din.

But already it was too late for the *Dzerzhinsky.*

The carrier loomed so close Forte felt he could have hit it with a flung stone. Through the high-magnification lenses built into the helmet he could see the crew, some frozen to the spot, others running frantically away from the oncoming wave.

He pressed the firing pickle. A chorus of shrieks enveloped the ship, like a million bows across a million rusty saws, as the Elbows unleashed an electron barrage on the hapless carrier. Forte's target was the enemy bridge, the brain and nerve center of the ship. Keeping his eyes focused on that point of maximum vulnerability, he poured it on. The fire of the thirty-six Elbows on the port side he could bring to bear on the enemy aircraft carrier in moments reduced the bridge to scrap metal. She was a ship whose captain would never give another order, whose crew would never obey one. The ship was dead.

But Gwillam Forte was alive, the fear that had clutched his stomach like a cold hand had disappeared, and his spirit was soaring near the realms of exaltation.

7 JULY 1998: 11:39 A.M.

FROM THE EMINENCE OF HIS FLAG BRIDGE, ADMIRAL Grell watched the second wave sweeping toward them from afar. Unlike his staff officers, who goggled at it in open-mouthed disbelief, he had half expected it. A wave of such magnitude as the first could not be natural. Had it been produced by an earthquake, the only logical explanation in the absence of a mushroom cloud, then why had the buildings ashore been totally unaffected? And they hadn't swayed by so much as a millimeter. True, a tsunami from some submarine convulsion in the Gulf of Mexico breaking on the shores of Galveston Bay could conceivably have sent a giant wave racing inland. But not to this particular stretch of channel, which dog-legged beyond the *Texas* basin. A wave from the gulf would have dissipated its force on the shore directly ahead. And then there was the flaming napalm. *That* was no natural phenomenon. The wave was man-made, and what man created once he could create again. In fact, he would: was not America the land of the assembly line?

These thoughts had passed in rapid review even as he battled a ship that bucked like a brahman bull. The diabolical mind behind the near-total destruction of the Soviet Seventeenth Fleet would send another wave, and another, until his fleet was wiped out. Grell didn't pause to speculate on the source of that gigantic wave, but concentrated on the problem at hand: how to counter its appalling power.

In the brief interval before another wave crashed down upon them he must align the ships so that their bows were struck head-on by the wave. So deployed, they could survive any number of tsunamis. Had not six of them done so? They would slice the wave cleanly, pitch bow-up, then bow-down, in a matter of seconds, but they wouldn't roll on their beam's ends and capsize.

He gave the order on TBS—talk-between-ships—to get up steam, up anchor, and come to a heading downstream exactly parallel to both banks. All ships acknowledged except the *Dzerzhinsky,* whose communication equipment had apparently been knocked out.

"All missile batteries load!" was his next command. "Elevation four degrees, deflection zero degrees. All batteries report readiness and stand by to fire."

One by one the batteries called in. Less than 10 percent were in operation. They might suffice, Admiral Grell thought, removing his drenched cap and wiping his sweating forehead with the back of his hand.

On the Russian ships, bruised and shaken officers were shouting orders to the damage-control parties, switching emergency power to cryogenic proton-gun accumulators, clearing passageways, juggling the depleted gun crews to man the missile batteries. A dozen things had to be done at once if the remaining ships of the once-glorious High Seas Fleet were to be saved.

Admiral Grell left them to it. To him, what mattered was the next wave. Putting dripping binoculars to his eyes, he peered down the channel.

Grell was tough and courageous, but the sight that greeted his eyes turned his knees to mush. The wave was coming! And poised below the lip of the wave like a surfboard was a vessel right out of a sailor's fantasy. The ship's lines and arrangement of guns told him instantly that it was the U.S.S. *Texas,* but a *Texas* transformed. For one thing, the old gray lady he had passed less than an hour before was now a gleaming white, from water line to foretop. All the painters in Texas couldn't have done the job so fast, and yet . . . More astounding, how did the *Texas* mount that rampaging wave, manage to maintain its balance just below the lip without being overwhelmed? Admiral Grell was so unnerved that he automatically crossed himself.

"Did you raise the *Dzerzhinsky?*" he demanded of his young staff lieutenant.

"No, sir. We're still trying."

"Don't bother. In thirty seconds the wave will be upon us. . . . *Forward missile units: stand by!*"

"All missile units ready, sir."

Grell watched in fascination as the American ship roared down upon the hapless *Dzerzhinsky,* blasting away with its Elbows. The Russian ship did not return the fire, and as the *Texas* shot past the battered hulk, the rearing wave engulfed the Russian aircraft carrier, flung it on its beam, and passed on. The *Dzerzhinsky* rolled slowly over, belly up, like a dead whale.

By then the *Texas* was well upstream, its carousels pouring a deadly fire into the next ship in line, the helicopter carrier *Yezhov.* But the wave was now at last within range.

"Forward missile batteries: *fire!*" Admiral Grell bellowed.

A blinding flash rippled outward in flat trajectory from the forward missile tubes of the remaining ships.

In less than a second, a missile from the *Yezhov* blasted through the wave to one side of the *Texas*. Two from the *Rykov*, a thousand meters upstream, struck an instant later—and went through. From the other ships three other missiles pierced the wave's wide front at the base and its very lip, barely missing the *Texas* mainmast.

And still the *Texas* came on.

"Aft batteries: *fire!*" Grell shouted.

This time there were only three missiles, and they missed the *Texas* by an even greater margin. But their fuses were correctly set. All three missiles exploded on impact with the advancing wave.

The tsunami collapsed.

It didn't collapse all at once, or along the full breadth of the channel. That segment descending upon the Russian fleet was dispersed in a roiling cauldron of steaming water, whirling the Russian ships like macaroni in a cookpot.

The *Beria* broached, capsized, and sank.

In the magazines of the *Litvinov*, a missile was jarred loose from its hoist. It exploded. A chain of detonations erupted within the ship, and it was blown apart in a cloud of smoke and flames.

Only three Soviet ships—the helicopter carrier *Yezhov*, the missile cruiser *Rykov*, and the flagship *Karl Marx*—remained afloat.

The three survivors regained steerageway. As one, they turned broadside to the *Texas*, which had come careening down on their port sides only to be smothered beneath a mountain of water from the collapsing wave, which completely obliterated it.

For nearly a minute, nothing could be seen where the American battleship had been save a curtain of water that kept coming down like a mighty cloudburst, flailing the channel surface into a cloud of impenetrable froth. But as the seconds ticked by, the faint outlines of the *Texas* appeared.

A single lifeless body hung in the foremast rigging. The ship's main deck was completely submerged, and the wreck appeared to be sinking. The stack was battered and its boats were swept away.

Then, shaking itself like a wet dog, it porpoised from the bow, with water cascading from its white decks, now a litter of snarled cables, mangled steel stanchions, and fittings flattened from the immense mass of water that had nearly sunk her.

Grell regarded the enemy ship with eyes of ice.

"All batteries—*fire at will!*" he commanded.

7 JULY 1998: 11:41 A.M.

RUNNING DOWN UPON THE SURVIVING SHIPS OF THE devastated High Seas Fleet in the comforting embrace of the gigantic wave, the exaltation Forte experienced was headier than sex, sweeter than love: it was the exaltation of victory.

The keels of capsized ships, the bobbing bodies of their crews, the hordes of Texans converging on the carnage in the hope that some Russians remained alive to nourish their vengence, and especially the disarray of the remaining men-of-war were evidence that the battle was won and that he and the *Texas* were triumphant. No matter that the combined fire power of the enemy ships would now be concentrated against them, or that they could not possibly survive the assault— they had struck a blow from which Russian prestige could never recover. The Washington Protocols, which would have ensnared the United States in Russia's diplomatic web, was a dead letter, as dead as Admiral

Grell and Gwillam Forte and the U.S.S. *Texas* soon would be.

For a moment, while the *Texas*'s Elbows had raked the *Dzerzhinsky* without drawing answering fire, Forte experienced a wild rush of hope: perhaps by some miracle the Russian fleet's guns had all been stilled and he would yet sink them every one. That hope drowned under the collapsing wave, which buried Forte and his flying fortress in a cataract of foam and spray.

Sputtering, half-blinded, and bruised by the force of the water, Forte was saved from being flung against the bulkhead and crushed only by his shoulder harness. The bridge was knee-deep in water that had poured through the open portholes during the inundation. It sloshed about the chair as the ship wallowed in the trough, where it had almost disappeared for good. The ship itself was out of control. It careened crazily from the opposing forces of gravity dragging its saturated hull down, buoyancy pulling it back up, jet thrusters propelling it around in a tight circle. Forte was riding a bucking bronco with a burr under its saddle.

"Why the hell are we circling?" Forte demanded through his mike. The radio circuits, at least, had survived, for Ed Curry's voice came crackling back.

"We're checking, Will. Stand by."

"The ship's spinning like a top."

"I know—something's gone haywire. Hold on."

"What the hell do you think I'm doing?" Forte growled, his left hand white-knuckled from his grip on the chair arms.

"Port-side stern thruster valves are inoperative—jammed shut," Curry reported after a moment. "The starboard thrusters are on full power, spinning the ship."

"Well, shut 'em down!"

"Can't. We've tried," Curry said unhappily. "They're jammed open. The impact must have knocked the control jet out of line or displaced the splitter."

"Well, do *something*! If the ship can't maneuver

before the Russians get steam up and close in, I'm a sitting duck."

"We're doing the best we can. But—"

But already through the spray and mist that still separated the *Texas* from its enemies, the Russian proton guns had found the target and were hammering away at the ancient ship.

The Russian weapons had high-capacity but old-fashioned cryogenic storage rings, which could deliver pulses with energy outputs of up to 175 kilojoules. Pulses at that level were as destructive as medium-size lightning bolts. But the ships' generators had been put on stand-by when they anchored. For the moment, the PGs scarcely pitted the armor plate of the old battleship. For the moment, the *Texas* was safe.

Still, power would build fast, and Forte knew that salvation lay either in flight or in sinking his three enemies before they could bring their combined power to bear. Fight or flight . . .

Flight was impossible—the jammed stern thrusters ruled out that possibility.

The crackle of proton streams striking the superstructure was a symphony of riveting guns as the power of the Russian weapons slowly built up. Hot metallic chips rained down on the flag bridge overhead, and the air was filled with the stench of burning paint. Somewhere nearby a stanchion was severed from its base, and tumbled to the deck with an ear-splitting clang. Another tremendous thud on the flag bridge as part of the mast fell indicated that the decoy transmission from the foretop was working, that the Russians were concentrating their fire on what they mistakenly considered the *Texas*'s nerve center. Sooner or later, though, despite the protection of its magnetic deflectors, it would be pounded into melted rubble.

Meanwhile, his own guns were exacting a toll from the enemy. As his ship swept around in circles, Forte blasted each enemy in succession. But with sinking heart he realized that the Russian fire power was increasing faster than he could destroy it, even though he zeroed in on the enemy's PG mounts rather than the ships themselves. At this rate, they would sink the *Texas* before he could put a single one of them out of action.

One more—that was all he asked. Just let him sink *one*.

And he would, if only his guns had more *power*. If only the damned ship would come to rest, rather than waste its . . .

Power.

"Ed!" he cried, "switch the power—"

"No can do," Curry interrupted. "The valves are stuck, and we—"

"Stick the valves! Switch the power from steam to electrical generation. Shift it from the propulsion units to the Elbows accumulators. Can you do it?"

"Why—why I guess—of *course* we can do it."

"How soon?"

"A few seconds." He turned away from the mike in SD–1 to issue a stream of orders. He came back on. "Listen, Will—there's one thing: those accumulators can store only so much juice without blowing up. Once the switch is made, you've got to keep those Elbows firing."

"Don't worry about that."

"Because if you stop for a second, the accumulators will overload, and you'll blow up the *Texas*."

"Got it—now give me the power, boy!"

"It's going on-line now."

The number-two reactor, generating power for the Elbows, was joined by the other three, as Ed Curry's technicians switched them one by one on-line.

The effect was, well—electrifying. The ship slowed, as the water jets and stern thrusters shut down, and the destructive force of the Elbows leapt to unprecedented, untested levels. Before, the electron beam had drilled holes in the enemy superstructures, cut through splinter shields surrounding enemy PG mounts, and creased

the armor-plated command centers. Now the beam
sliced through armor plate like a knife through water.
Up to this moment, Forte's battle plan had been the
methodical attrition of the enemy's fire power, since
there was relatively little of it. With the tremendous
power now at his fingertip, he could go after the ships
themselves.

The shorter the distance the electron beams had to
travel, the less energy was dissipated boring holes
through the atmospheric oxygen and nitrogen molecules. That meant that the *Yezhov,* the closest of the
enemy ships, was most vulnerable. By the same token,
its PG weapons were inflicting the most damage on
the *Texas.*

Forte focused his eyes on the *Yezhov*'s bridge, the
command center. A blaze of white light obliterated it,
and the vaporization of the boiling metal cast its own
yellow incandescence over the ship. Its support cut
away, the *Yezhov*'s foremast collapsed, toppling like
a giant of the forest onto the forecastle. The Russian
ship's proton weapons fell silent.

Forte's gaze fell to the *Yezhov*'s water line. Instantly a hole appeared in the hull of the ship, and
channel water heated to the boil by the beam-heated
hull surged into the ship. Forte's eyes moved fifty yards
aft, and another hole appeared in the water-line armor.
From within the ship came a brilliant flash as the
Elbows beam penetrated the after magazine, igniting
the missiles stored there in a chain of explosions that
tore off the whole portside of the helicopter carrier,
spewing fragments of its hundred aircraft broadcast
down the channel. Belching fire to the last, the *Yezhov*
settled on its side, the oily channel waters closing in
over it like a pall.

The vastly increased fire power of the *Texas* was as
yet unmatched by that of the two remaining Russian
ships, but the gap was beginning to close. Furthermore,
while the *Texas* lay dead in the water, the speed and
maneuverability of the missile carrier *Rykov* and the

superbattleship *Karl Marx* were rapidly increasing. Worse yet for Forte, to achieve maximum performance from their PG weapons, Admiral Grell had ordered his ships to steer straight for the *Texas* where they could fire at point-blank range, reducing the advantage of the *Texas*'s beefed-up electron guns.

The *Rykov* was now off the *Texas*'s port bow, a floating shambles that somehow kept coming despite the fire Forte was pouring into it. Its masts had been sheared off, its boats were cinders in their cradles, its stack and armored sides perforated with a thousand holes. Still, it didn't sink. He had knocked out at least 80 percent of its guns, but those PGs still operating blinked back at him with ever brighter eyes. Their aim, too, had been diverted from the foretop decoy to the bridge and superstructure. So far, magnetic deflection had turned aside the streams of protons directed toward the flag bridge, but the Russian crews were hammering away at the base of the mast now. Any minute it could begin to buckle; if the mast fell, Forte would fall with it.

Suddenly a bluish beam struck the rim of one of the portholes, and the hot twist of metal it had blasted away ricocheted off the control panel and buried itself in his shoulder harness. Instinctively he dropped the firing pickle and clawed the chip out with his right hand. The stink of burning plastic assailed his nostrils. He looked down: his prosthetic right hand was smoldering.

Warning lights flashed all over the control panel. The capacitors were overloading. *Where was the damned pickle?* Unless he discharged the Elbows—and quickly—the *Texas* would blow.

Forte groped for the pickle in the swirling smoke that was beginning to drift into the bridge from the ship, afire now in a dozen places. He finally found it dangling from the module jack, and pressed it frantically as his eyes found the *Rykov* bearing down on his ship.

The clangor of falling metal, the screech of the Elbows and the PGs, the whistle of severed rigging flailing the air like scimitars, were deafening. And the *Rykov* was looming larger every second. Nothing Forte had hit it with so far had stopped it. It was no more than four hundred yards away now, coming in on a collision course at some twenty knots, as fast as a man can run. At that speed, it would shear off the *Texas*'s bow and sink her like a stone.

Forte had been shooting at the PG batteries. Now, with sudden inspiration, he shifted his eyes to the prow of the missile cruiser. The Russian jack staff disappeared in a puff of smoke, along with the Red fleet jack that had proudly streamed there an instant before. The tremendous heat of the concentrated Elbows fire began to melt the steel stem. Liquid metal ran down the side plates where they met to form the bow. Loosened plates flaked off, like chips of old paint, from both sides. As the electron beams descended to water level, the two sides of the bow, with nothing to join them together, peeled back as though cleaved with a meat ax. The ship was transformed by the Elbows into a huge funnel, scooping up the unrushing water and pouring it into the bowels of the ship. It stopped as if it had run into a wall.

It was less than the length of a football field distant now. In an instant thousands of tons of water had been swallowed by the gaping bow. The weight of the water on the forward part of the ship tilted the bow below the surface. The ship's stern rose into the air, its screws spinning futilely. As though sliding down a greased ramp, the *Rykov* plunged toward bottom and was seen no more.

Forte wiped his sweating neck. He was numb with fatigue and strain. His left hand was wrapped around the firing pickle with a deathlike grip, and the bolts of man-made lightning streaked from the *Texas* in an unceasing stream, churning up the water even after the *Rykov* vanished.

Any moment now the *Karl Marx* would appear through that veil of mist and steam, Forte was certain, determined to ram and sink the *Texas*. Where its PG weapons had failed, its superior bulk would prevail. With its 76,000 tons hurtling along at more than twenty-five knots, it would run the *Texas* down like a truck squashing a jack rabbit.

But when the *Rykov* came to a sudden stop, the *Karl Marx,* only five hundred meters astern, had to swing wide to avoid ramming the doomed ship. As it emerged beyond the curtain of mist churned by the *Texas*'s batteries, for the first time it was exposed to the undivided fury of the old battlewagon, which heretofore had given the Russian flagship only intermittent attention.

Observing the enemy from less than half a kilometer away as he came abreast, Grell was astounded that so concentrated and deadly a fire could come from such a battered hulk. The *Texas* no longer had the appearance of a man-of-war, but of a barge-load of scrap metal, chewed up and spit out by the dogs of war. He wondered how the old ship stayed afloat, holed as it was in a million places from foretop to water line. Small fires had broken out the length and breadth of the ship, sending up clouds of smoke that blackened the immaculate paintwork. The mainmast had crumpled. The fourteen-inch guns, sheared off from three of the five turrets, were jagged stumps. Sheet metal, rigging, antennas, splinter shield, boat cranes, large sections of the bridge, aircraft catapault—all were piled amidships in an indiscriminate smoking mass. The foretop dangled drunkenly from one of the three tripod masts still intact. And yet the ship's electron-weapon fire continued unabated.

Grell's practiced eye noted anomalies in the picture of devastation. Certain areas of the *Texas* seemed relatively unaffected by the Russian fire. The navigation bridge was shot to pieces, yet the flag bridge above it was intact. And there were islands of seeming indestructability at regular intervals along the weather deck, and from these islands came the deadly fire that had destroyed his ships. A sailor's combative instincts ordered him to close in and engage the enemy, but an admiral's experience countermanded the order, and he instructed the quartermaster to come up on the helm and head down-channel at full speed.

As increasing distance attenuated the *Texas*'s fire, Admiral Grell pondered the significance of his observations. Foremost, it was apparent that the *Texas* had fire power superior to his own. In a battle of broadsides, the *Karl Marx* would be bested, despite the ruined condition of his adversary. That the *Texas* was still afloat, its weapons delivering a withering barrage, indicated that its batteries were somehow protected, which his own were not. Apparently, too, the *Texas*'s propulsion system had been knocked out. Its superiority in fire power was offset by its lack of mobility. In fact, now that the *Karl Marx* was some three kilometers beyond the American ship, well beyond the range of its particle weapons, nothing opposed its escape down the channel to the safety of the Gulf and open sea— nothing but Admiral Vladimir Grell's pride, and his anger and frustration at having been humiliated by this museum piece of a battleship and American cunning.

He wouldn't flee. He would fight. But on his own terms, and to win.

"Damage report," he said to his first lieutenant.

The first lieutenant began reciting what promised to be a lengthy bill of particulars. Admiral Grell cut him off.

"Just the condition of our missile launchers."

"Five are back in operation, sir. Another can be repaired within four hours. The others—"

"Crews?"

"Shifted to the PG mounts, sir. After the second salvo, the admiral so ordered."

True. Time had been short, and so was crew. Loading missiles into the launchers was a complicated process. With only remnants of the ship's company having survived the onslaught of the first tsunami, he had been obliged to divert the missile loading crews to the PGs. But now . . .

"All missile crews to their posts," he commanded. "Load all launchers and report readiness."

Admiral Grell raised his binoculars. The *Texas*, still firing steadily—why was he wasting his power?—in the direction of the Russian flagship, had not moved. Its stern was toward him and the ship seemed, as it had from the first, completely deserted.

But even as he watched, the *Texas* very slowly rotated ninety degrees and again came to rest, its starboard side, the least damaged, now facing him downstream. As it turned, it seemed to Grell that the particle weapons' fire power diminished markedly, and picked up again when the ship was again dead in the water. He conveyed his observation to the flag secretary, who agreed.

"Check with Fire Control Plot."

"Aye, aye, sir," said the flag secretary.

Moments later he confirmed that instrument readings showed a sharp drop in the strength of the enemy weapons during the *Texas*'s turn to starboard.

Grell nodded. This was consistent with the theory that was forming in his mind that, while the ship had power, and power to spare, its propulsion machinery was inoperative. Had it not been so, the *Texas* would certainly have pursued the out-gunned *Karl Marx*. Whoever was conning the American ship had done the next best thing to pursuit: turned its intact weapons broadside to the *Karl Marx*. The move was intelligent but futile: deprived of mobility, nothing in the world could save the *Texas* now . . .

On the flag bridge of the *Texas*, Gwillam Forte saw the *Karl Marx* steam out of range of his Elbows. Was the Russian ship seeking safe haven in the Gulf of Mexico? Forte doubted it. Admiral of the Fleet Vladi-

mir Grell had been the architect of the new Soviet
Navy, and until today he had never fought a major
naval engagement at sea. But he was known to be
proud and tough, and if he ran, it was from tactical
considerations, not fear. A man like Grell would fear
very little—not the death that would now await him for
allowing the High Seas Fleet to be destroyed by a
decrepit old American museum piece, not death at the
hands of the enemy. He would fear disgrace and the
laughter of history for running from battle. No, Grell
would be back.

"Ed?"

"My God!" cried Ed Curry. "We thought you
were—"

"Not yet. Ed, can you turn the ship broadside?"

"Sure. We'll just bleed a little power from the Elbows and—say, are you all right?"

"Yes," sighed Forte. "I'm all right."

"Then get out while there's still time. You've *won,*
Will."

"Not yet."

"Drop over the side and swim to shore. You can
do it, Will."

"Grell will be back."

"We'll fight him from *here.* The fire-control link is
intact. Sacrificing yourself will gain nothing."

Forte wavered. His eyes were fixed blearily on the
shadowy Russian flagship some miles down the channel.
His hand still gripped the firing pickle, and the streams
of electronic fire issued from the mouths of the Elbows
mounts without cessation, to be dissipated in space long
before it could reach the enemy ship. He felt a tremendous languor taking possession of him. He supposed this was the "peace" those with but moments
to live experienced at the end. Perhaps it *was* peace,
if peace meant the absence of thought, or desire, or
pain. He felt as though he were floating free of the
Earth and looking back at himself, imprisoned in that

familiar quarter-limbed body, which nevertheless seemed not to belong to him at all, he—

He blinked. The Russian flagship had ceased to shrink. It was growing again. The *Karl Marx* was coming back.

"Will, get *out* of there!" Ed Curry said with quiet intensity.

"Later, Ed. Right now . . ."

There was a glint of sunlight in the sky. The glints quickly resolved into trails of fire as the *Karl Marx*'s salvo of five missiles plunged toward the *Texas*. Instinctively Forte focused his gaze on the line of projectiles, the stream of particles from his Elbows lancing through the sky to meet them.

One exploded, then another, and a third, in rapid succession. But the fourth streaked down toward the *Texas*, passed across the old battleship's bow, and exploded with terrific impact in the water just beyond, a moment before the fifth missile struck the *Texas* squarely on the fantail.

The twin concussions knocked Forte out. His head fell forward on his chest, and the coupled Elbows, following the inclination of his eyes, bombarded the oily, flotsam-filled water between the *Texas* and the advancing Russian flagship. A cloud of steam rose between them, obscuring one from the other.

The Russian ship, its launchers reloaded, its missiles aimed by radar, sent its second salvo winging toward the *Texas* before Gwillam Forte, only slowly coming around, was aware of what was happening. He lifted his head and eyes only in time to see the five silvery fingers of fate coming directly at him.

This time, instinct didn't preserve him. One missile detonated before it reached its target, but the other four struck in deadly unison, two on the superstructure, the other two at the water line.

Within seconds, the *Texas* followed Gwillam Forte into the watery corridors of death. Battered beyond recognition, with columns of smoke rising high into the sky from a dozen raging fires, its watertight integrity breached, plates sprung and superstructure flattened and twisted or blown clear away, the old ship settled in the black channel waters and sank out of sight.

The victorious *Karl Marx,* now but a kilometer away, ceased fire and slowed to avoid ramming the sinking remains of its adversary.

The *Texas* seemed quite dead—dead and buried, in fact, but in the watery darkness the ship's heart still beat.

The old ship's power plant had been encased in ferroconcrete as a shield against radiation if the hull were breached and the reactor-room bulkheads fractured. The reactor rooms were separated from the rest of the ship by watertight doors. These doors had held throughout the battle. Only when the enemy's missiles slammed into the hull, twisting the frames, did they buckle. Water began to trickle in across the combing.

At the bottom of the ship channel, the dark waters invaded the reactor spaces. There the nuclear engines were pulsating, still producing power at such a tremendous rate that the high-energy-density capacitors became oversaturated. When the water at last penetrated to the reactors themselves, the result was cataclysmic.

The sunken hulk detonated with the force of an atomic bomb.

A column of water shot up from the bottom of the channel. Two hundred meters across, it flung the *Karl Marx,* at that moment passing overhead, into the Texas sky like a Ping-Pong ball lifted aloft on the jet of a garden hose. The shock wave knocked buildings flat halfway across Houston, and pieces of the *Karl Marx* were hurled miles across the Texas countryside. . . .

The Battle of the Black Channel, second day, had lasted sixteen minutes, and ended with the extinction of all combatants.

For the rest of the day and the following night, an unearthy silence hung over the city. The song of night birds was stilled, the blast having exterminated them along with townspeople for miles around. Here and there, a candle proclaimed the survival of some hardy soul, but the candles burned without a flicker of movement, like altar candles burned for the dead.

7 JULY 2002

THE MEMORIAL SERVICE ON THE BANKS OF THE HOUSton Ship Channel was brief, as brief as the occasion it commemorated, the Battle of the Black Channel and the historic defeat of the Russian fleet by the Texas Navy.

Cherokee Tom Traynor's address to the huge but subdued crowd was the shortest of all that day, but longest remembered.

"Ladies and gentlemen," he said, "Leonidas and his three hundred Greek soldiers sacrificed themselves to delay the advance of the Persian army of 180,000 strong at the Pass of Thermopylae, thus giving Athens and Sparta time to regroup, defeat the Persian invaders, and save Greek civilization for the world. That feat of arms has been justly enshrined for twenty-five centuries as the epitome of martial valor. If this is so, then how long will Captain Gwillam Forte of the Texas Navy be remembered, a triple-amputee of advanced years, who, alone in an ancient battleship, gallantly battled twenty-three modern warships, crewed by twenty thousand highly trained Russian sailors, and left not a single ship afloat or a single enemy alive on the field of battle?

"I shall tell you how long, ladies and gentlemen— *forever!*"

Later, with bowed head, listening to the benediction, his thoughts drifted off into the world of might-have-been. Had it not been for Forte and the *Texas,* would the Russians even now be launching their invasion of North America? Would the entire Earth be wrapped in a great radioactive cloud, its hapless inhabitants gasping out their last poisoned breaths in bomb shelters, tombs for the imminent dead? Would a single witness to the Russian will-o'-the-wisp of world domination survive to record this final stupidity of man, a creature who could conquer everything but himself?

But these speculations were philosophical, and being philosophical, futile. More rewarding were thoughts of things as they were, here and now, and considering them broadly, he could find little reason to complain.

The scorched banks of the ship channel had been plowed up, landscaped, and replanted. Now they were a verdant park linking Houston to the sea, trees and grass, young lovers and frolicking children keeping green the memory of Gwillam Forte and his fellow martyrs on that fateful day four years ago. Economically, his people had made a rapid recovery and were on the verge—if one were so naïve as to believe economists—of an unprecedented boom. With the closure of the borders to unrestricted immigration, a social and economic equilibrium among the diverse population was finally a beckoning possibility.

His personal destiny, while as blessed as that of his people, wasn't what he had anticipated seven years earlier, when he had roped in Gwillam Forte to assist his grand strategy for gaining the U.S. Senate and later the White House. He had never got to the Senate. Neither, to be sure, had Ernesto Gallego, although it had been Traynor's inspiration to rid himself of his rival by sending him to New York in the prestigious but empty post of ambassador to the United Nations. Nor, of course, would Cherokee Tom ever sit in the Oval Office in Washington.

No, being president of the Republic of Texas wasn't the same as being President of the United States. Certainly not.

It was better.

ABOUT THE AUTHOR

For 30 years Daniel da Cruz has lived and worked—as a diplomat, teacher, businessman, and journalist—in Europe, Asia, and Africa.

He spent six World War II years as a U.S. Marine volunteer, serving ashore, afloat (in 1941 aboard the Texas), and aloft in the three war theaters. A *magna cum laude* graduate of Georgetown University's School of Foreign Service, da Cruz has been variously a census enumerator, magazine editor and editorial consultant, judo master—he holds a second degree Black Belt of the Kodokan Judo Institute, Tokyo—taxi driver, farmer, public relations officers for an oil company, salesman, foreign correspondent, publishers' representative, vice-president of a New York advertising agency, slaughterhouse skinner, captain of a Texas security organization, American Embassy press attaché in Baghdad, and copper miner. He is currently Adjunct Professor of Anthropology at Miami University.

da Cruz has published eleven books, among them an American history text, a monograph on Amerindian linguistics, and three suspense novels for Ballantine Books, the most recent of which, *The Captive City,* was awarded a special "Edgar." He has written one other science-fiction novel, *The Grotto of the Formigans,* also published by Ballantine/Del Rey (1980).

From DEL REY, the brightest science-fiction stars in the galaxy...